More Advance Praise for *Oakdale Dinner Club*:

"The food in this novel had me salivating. The writing is excellent, witty, and spare. I recommend *The Oakdale Dinner Club* to anyone looking for a fun, lighthearted, yet quirkily introspective read."

— Robin Spano, author of the
Clare Vengel Undercover novels

Praise for *The Restoration of Emily*:

"A very funny, sometimes suspenseful novel for grown-ups … Moritsugu writes with dash and irony."

— *Quill & Quire*

"A fun, light, and adept piece of writing."

— *Globe and Mail*

"Funny, wise and sharp, this is a character all of us can see a little bit of ourselves in."

— *Chatelaine*

Praise for *The Glenwood Treasure*:

"*The Glenwood Treasure* has suggestions of the late Timothy Findley and more than a hint of the old Nancy Drew mysteries. But, given the strength of this book, it seems more fitting to drop the comparisons and allow Moritsugu her own place on the literary landscape."

— *Globe and Mail*

"Kim Moritsugu is a witty social observer and the book deftly blends a comedy of manners into the mystery."

— *Toronto Star*

"A cozy read … Moritsugu is a good writer with an appealing central character that will awaken the inner girl in all of us."

— *National Post*

The
Oakdale
Dinner Club

Kim Moritsugu

DUNDURN
TORONTO

Editor: Shannon Whibbs
Copy-editor: Cheryl Hawley
Design: Jennifer Scott
Printer: Webcom

Library and Archives Canada Cataloguing in Publication

Moritsugu, Kim, author
The Oakdale dinner club / Kim Moritsugu.

Issued in print and electronic formats.
ISBN 978-1-4597-0955-3 (pbk.).--ISBN 978-1-4597-0957-7 (pdf).--ISBN 978-1-4597-0956-0 (epub)

I. Title.

PS8576.O72O36 2014   C813'.54   C2013-906068-5   C2013-906069-3

1   2   3   4   5   18   17   16   15   14

We acknowledge the support of the **Canada Council for the Arts** and the **Ontario Arts Council** for our publishing program. We also acknowledge the financial support of the **Government of Canada** through the **Canada Book Fund** and **Livres Canada Books**, and the **Government of Ontario** through the **Ontario Book Publishing Tax Credit** and the **Ontario Media Development Corporation**.

Care has been taken to trace the ownership of copyright material used in this book. The author and the publisher welcome any information enabling them to rectify any references or credits in subsequent editions.

J. Kirk Howard, President

Visit us at
Dundurn.com | @dundurnpress | Facebook.com/dundurnpress |
Pinterest.com/Dundurnpress

Dundurn	Gazelle Book Services Limited	Dundurn
3 Church Street, Suite 500	White Cross Mills	2250 Military Road
Toronto, Ontario, Canada	High Town, Lancaster, England	Tonawanda, NY
M5E 1M2	LA1 4XS	U.S.A. 14150

The
Oakdale
Dinner Club

1

August 2010

On the last day of summer, Mary Ann Gray sat in a lounge chair by the side of the Oakdale Country Club pool, watched the children splash and dive, half listened to the self-important jerk on her left expound to his neighbour about the current state of the financial markets, and decided to have an extramarital affair.

It was time. She was thinner and blonder than she'd ever been since high school, a state she intended to maintain, no matter how painful the process. Not that she'd transformed herself into a babe, or anything close to it. All that the stress-induced starvation, exercising, and beautifying of recent months had accomplished was to move her physical attractiveness quotient up a few notches, from *not bad* to *oh yeah, her*.

No amount of non-surgical work could convert Mary Ann into model-perfect neighbourhood mom Hallie Smith, who reclined on the opposite pool deck, flanked by her two young daughters. Through her sunglasses, Mary Ann checked out Hallie's clean profile and taut bikini body — was she actually posing on that lounge chair? — and tried to imagine looking like her. What would it be like to have guys flirt with you all the time, to be the first asked to dance, to get superior service from car mechanics? What would it be like to be married to the winsome Sam Orenstein?

Mary Ann's best friend, Alice Maeda, emerged from the women's locker room with her four-year-old daughter, Lavinia, in tow. Mary Ann waved them over. "No problem getting in at the front desk?"

"It was tense at first, when they looked at me, pointed to the 'Whites Only' sign on the wall, and shook their heads."

Lavinia said, "What does *whites only* mean?"

Mary Ann reached for Lavinia's small hand and held it. "The club has a rule that people can only wear white clothes when they play tennis. And your mom was making a joke about it. A not-very-funny joke."

Alice grinned, and brought her index finger and thumb together in the universal sign for smallness. "Not even a little bit funny?"

"They didn't really give you a hard time, did they? I'll go roll someone's head if they did."

"They were fine. They didn't even make me recite the pledge of allegiance this time."

"Stop it." Mary Ann removed a towel from the lounge chair beside her. "And here: I saved you a seat."

"I want to go swimming," Lavinia said.

"Sit on your towel and let the sun make you hot first," Alice said, "while Mommy talks to Mary Ann. Take your Barbies." She pulled two naked Barbie dolls sporting morning-after hair from her tote bag and handed them to Lavinia.

Mary Ann offered Alice a tube of sunscreen. "How's your weekend been?"

Alice made a so-so motion with her hand. "Long. I can't wait for school to start tomorrow."

"Yours, or Lavinia's?"

"Both. The idea of lecturing to freshmen appeals at this

time of year. Until I meet them."

Lavinia dropped the dolls on the ground and stood up beside Alice's chair. "*Now* can we go swimming?"

"Okay. Let's put on your water wings."

Mary Ann waved them off and opened the book in her lap, a dense, award-winning novel she'd been trying to get through for months. She'd read two paragraphs when a burst of conversation nearby made her glance up, at Chad, the head lifeguard, he of the worked-out body, the pierced ear, and the wide shoulders.

"Now there's a guy who has no trouble getting laid," muttered the jerk on her left.

Mary Ann gave the back of the jerk's head a dirty look and watched Chad scale the side of the lifeguard chair and say something to the girl lifeguard on duty. A humorous remark, apparently, because the girl laughed, said, "You're crazy, Chad," and squirted him with water from her bottle.

Chad climbed down and strutted on to the next lifeguard station, his carriage that of a half-naked buff guy who believes every female eye in the vicinity is on him, and every female mind over the age of thirteen is fantasizing about licking his washboard abs.

Mary Ann didn't want to lick Chad's stomach. At twenty-one, he was a college student and much too young for her. She might be willing to commit adultery, but she drew the line at cradle robbing. Besides, she knew Chad's mother; the family lived on the street behind hers. A small stretch of their backyard fences touched.

She checked on her kids' whereabouts, spotted Griffin lined up to jump off the diving board and Kayla bouncing up and down in the shallow end. She closed the novel, pulled a food magazine out of her bag, flipped past pictures of hand-painted serving dishes, skipped the wine column and a feature on decadent desserts, and stopped to study a photo story about a Californian couple having a staged dinner party on the grounds of their vineyard estate.

Alice appeared at her side. "I sicced Lavinia onto Kayla and her friend."

"Good move. That's what older girls are for."

Alice sat down. "I saw Griffin. Where's Josh?"

"At home, refining his jump shot and pondering which act of teenage rebellion to try next."

Alice pointed to the open magazine. "And what's for dinner tonight?"

"At my house? Hot dogs and hamburgers. But listen, I've had an idea. What do you think about starting a dinner club?"

"Depends what it is."

"Like a book club. We assemble a group of people who can cook, set up a schedule, rotate houses, meet once a month. Everyone brings food, we dress up nice, have adult conversations, feast on elaborate culinary creations we wouldn't dream of wasting on our families."

"When did you come up with this?"

"Just now."

"I don't know. I don't own matching dishes."

"So we skip your house."

"Why?"

"Why skip your house?"

"Why do this, period?"

"It's new, it's different."

"It sounds like a lot of work."

"To break up the monotony of our humdrum lives — that's another reason."

"You think I have a humdrum life?"

"To break up the monotony of mine, then."

Alice waved at Lavinia. "No, you're right. My life's hum-drum too. Count me in. Who else would join?"

"I'd have to invite my school mom friends Lisa and Amy. And I'd include the guys from my office. Plus a few others."

"It's starting to sound like a freshman mixer, one of the reasons I left the country for college."

"I always hated those. There I'd be, brimming with poten-tial, and all the boys would be gathered around my class's version of Hallie Smith."

"Who's she?"

"Sam Orenstein's wife. The hot-for-her-age specimen in the orange bikini on the opposite deck."

They contemplated the figure of Hallie Smith for a moment, and Alice said, "What about your mom? She should be invited."

"I guess."

"Think of her baking."

"You're right."

"How many is that now?"

"Nine or ten."

"Double that if people bring dates."

"We wouldn't allow dates."

"I'm getting that freshman mixer feeling again. You're not by any chance trying to set me up, are you?"

"Far from it. We'll confine the guest list to people who are interested in food."

The girl lifeguard stood up in her chair, blew her whistle, and announced a fifteen-minute adult swim period. The chil-dren evacuated the pool and rushed over. Kayla and her friend each held one of Lavinia's hands. Griffin hugged his thin arms to his chest. "Mom," he said, "did you bring a deck of cards?"

When Griffin was settled on the pool deck playing soli-taire, and the girls had laid out their towels in a circle and set to work untangling the hair of Lavinia's Barbies, Mary Ann glanced over at the jerk to her left, also known as her husband, Bob. He was deep in conversation with the man beside him. She moved her chair a few inches closer to Alice's and half-mouthed, half-whispered, "So I've decided to have an affair."

Alice raised her eyebrows. "You have? With whom?"

"The whom part presents a problem. I can't quite decide."

Alice leaned back in her chair. "Now I get it: this dinner club is not about setting me up at all. It's about setting *you* up."

"Gee, Alice," Mary Ann said, "if I didn't know better, I'd think you'd read my mind."

2

October 1986

Alice was doodling a line of Greek key symbols in her notebook and trying not to fall asleep during class at Five Oaks High when the wall phone rang.

Her world history teacher answered it, listened a few seconds, looked straight at her, hung up, and said, "Alice Maeda, you're wanted in the principal's office."

Alice packed up her books and walked out, glad for the unexpected Get Out of Jail Free card, but a little worried about why she'd been summoned. She'd been involved in a minor incident during the first week of school, a month before, when she'd walked into English class carrying a lit cigarette. She'd forgotten where she was, forgotten smoking wasn't allowed inside the school. Or maybe she was *trying* to forget where she was.

Her English teacher, a crewcut-sporting reactionary, had commanded her, in a super-authoritarian tone, to put out the cigarette IMMEDIATELY, and Alice had got her back up and said no, why should she? Blah blah blah, she received a two-day suspension for non-compliance with school rules. To make matters worse, one of the more politically minded students wrote a fiery piece for the student newspaper that charged the school with violating Alice's civil rights and featured the headline "Student Defies Authorities" over a picture of Alice, a cigarette hanging from her mouth, flipping the bird to the photographer. Not the best way to start off her senior year.

She heard footsteps behind her, turned around, and saw Mary Ann MacAllister walking down the otherwise empty hallway. Mary Ann was in Alice's math class, but they didn't travel in the same social circles and rarely interacted outside an occasional "Can I borrow your protractor?" type of exchange. Why was Mary Ann walking the halls in the middle of the morning, when everyone else was trapped in class? It was unlikely that she was in any trouble: she was a model student, captain of the girls' basketball team, secretary of the student council, first chair of the flute section in the school band. One of those.

Alice pulled open the last door in their path and held it. Mary Ann ran to catch up.

"Were you called to the office, too?" Alice said.

"Yeah, I was."

"Good. That makes it less likely I'm being hauled in for another stupid rules infraction."

In the office, their math teacher Ms. Alexander was waiting for them with Mr. Dunston, the vice-principal. When the girls were seated and the door closed, Ms. Alexander said, in a tight voice, "I have good news and bad news." No smile. "The good news is that you two are the only students at Five Oaks who placed in the top one hundred in the state math competition test you wrote a few weeks ago."

Alice looked at Mary Ann. This had to be a mistake. Alice was decent at math, and Mary Ann was maybe better than decent, but neither were math geniuses, not as far as Alice knew.

"Aren't you wondering what the bad news is?"

Here it came.

"The bad news —" Ms. Alexander's voice cracked a little "— is that you two were also the only students who handed in identical answer sheets."

What?

The interrogation began. Had they cheated? HAD THEY? They had better confess right now if so, come clean. The results were pretty damning. Did they know what the mathematical probability of getting an identical result was? DID THEY?

Both girls denied collusion. Alice curtly, Mary Ann on the verge of tears.

"What's your explanation, then?" Ms. Alexander said. "How could this have happened?"

Mary Ann said, "Great minds think alike?" and earned them another ten minutes of haranguing.

"What about you, Alice?" Mr. Dunston said when Miss Alexander paused for breath. "What do you have to say for yourself?"

"I say this is a ridiculous accusation. Mary Ann and I aren't even friends — we've spoken to each other maybe five times in our whole lives. How could we have cheated?"

In the end, they were let go, told that without any concrete evidence of wrongdoing, the school had no choice but to accept the test results. But, they were warned, they would be watched closely for the remainder of the year. And they were strongly advised to avoid each other, especially in math class, and certainly during tests. Did they understand?

Mary Ann bowed her head and said yes, meekly. Alice looked at the wall calendar behind Mr. Dunston, counted the months until she'd be free of this sorry excuse for a school, and said, "Yeah. I understand."

Alice spent some time at the school library that afternoon, researching her international options for college, planning her escape. She was finishing off a cigarette in the parking lot just before the late bus was due to leave when Mary Ann came out of a side door and climbed aboard.

Alice chucked away the butt, got on the bus, sat down across the aisle from Mary Ann, and said, "Since when do you take the bus home?"

"Sometimes I do, sometimes I don't," Mary Ann said, and looked away, like she was hiding something.

That was when Alice recalled that Mary Ann had a boy-friend she'd been with for a year or more, a jock named Mike Reynolds. Alice had seen them drive to and from school together in Mike's Camaro, she thought. Maybe they'd broken up, and that's why Mary Ann was reduced to taking the bus.

Mary Ann said, "No offence, but we probably shouldn't sit next to each other. We're not supposed to be seen together, remember?"

Alice made an impatient gesture, and her bracelets jangled. "To hell with that. This whole thing's a big joke, if you ask me."

"A joke? Ms. Alexander seemed to take it pretty seriously. I'm glad she already wrote my letter of reference for college. Oh no. What if she tries to retract it?"

"She won't. And her suspicions make no sense, anyway. How were we supposed to accomplish this alleged cheating, when we weren't seated near each other during the test?"

"It *is* strange that our answers were exactly the same."

"Not that strange. I don't buy that mathematical probability shit. We're the exception, that's all." Alice was used to being the exception, having grown up the half-Asian, half-Caucasian daughter of two classical musicians — a violinist and a cellist — who had settled in suburban white-bread Oakdale. "By the way, that was a good line about great minds thinking alike."

"I only said that because I figured they'd freak out if they knew what I was really thinking."

"Which was what?"

Mary Ann hesitated. "Promise me you won't laugh. Promise? Okay. Don't laugh." She took a deep breath. "Did you ever think you might be telepathic?"

Alice laughed — a short, derisive bark. "No."

"Never? Not even for a second?"

Another no.

"Well, I did. I went through a period when I really thought I could communicate with my mind. I tried sending my thoughts out to everyone I knew."

"Okay. That definitely qualifies as weird. Are you weird?"

"I shouldn't have told you."

"When was this?"

"In my sophomore year, when my family moved to Oakdale from Michigan. I was the new kid in town, all the cliques were already formed at Five Oaks, and I badly needed secret powers to help me get in with the popular crowd."

"Except you didn't have any."

"I guess not. I couldn't get through to anyone."

"And now that you've made it into the inner circle at Five Oaks without any powers, you think we might have communicated telepathically on the day of the test? Without our knowing?"

"It's possible, isn't it?"

Not in Alice's opinion, it wasn't.

The bus turned down Forest Lane, and drove past Jake Stewart's house. Jake Stewart was a cocky, good-looking jock who played football and hockey, and was considered a school stud. Alice might have had a tiny crush on him when she was like, eleven, but she had no time anymore for him and his crowd, a crowd that included Mary Ann's boyfriend — ex-boyfriend? — Mike. And Mary Ann herself.

Mary Ann said, "You know, Mike turned out to be an ass-hole, but Jake's not that bad a guy."

Alice's ears felt hot all of a sudden. Was the heat on in the bus? "What?"

"We just went by Jake Stewart's house, and I'm saying he's not a total shit. Despite that stupid Jake the Snake nickname."

"Yeah? Don't forget I've known him since kindergarten."

"So?"

"So I know he's so vain he spends half an hour blow-drying his hair every morning, and uses Sun-In to lighten it."

"Come on."

Alice shrugged. "Maybe I'm just biased against pretty boys like him."

"You prefer ugly?"

"No. I prefer someone who's not so full of himself, who's capable of a little yearning."

Someone like Stephen, the British university student Alice had met and dallied with the summer just past, when she'd worked at an archeological dig in England. She kept a photograph of him at home, pasted into her journal, a picture she'd taken of him standing outside, leaning against a stone wall and squinting in the sunlight, looking Stephen-ish, with his scraggly hair, scrawny body, deep blue eyes, and crooked smile. She said, "You know what else pisses me off about this math test situation?"

"Oh god. How am I going to tell my mother they think we cheated?"

"Simple. Don't tell her. But what bugs me is the flawed logic in the accusation. We had no motive to cheat. The math competition doesn't count for anything."

Mary Ann gripped the handle of the seat in front of her. "There. We did it again."

"Did what?"

"Communicated telepathically. One minute we were talking about some skinny long-haired boyfriend of yours with a crooked smile, and the next we were back to the math test. Both at the same time."

How did Mary Ann know what Stephen looked like? "What did you say?"

"Both at the same time."

"Before that. About a boyfriend."

"Skinny guy with long brown hair and blue eyes? Leans against walls? Into yearning, I have a feeling?"

Alice felt her worldview tilt, and like maybe there'd just been a small earthquake. "That was Stephen. Someone I met in England last summer. But how did you —?"

"Don't you see? We're reading each other's minds!"

"No. We can't be."

"Get off the bus with me. Come to my house for dinner. We'll experiment, see if I'm right or wrong."

"This is crazy."

Mary Ann stood up in the bus aisle. "What's the harm in trying?"

"*You're* crazy."

"Maybe. Maybe not. Come on. This is my stop."

It wasn't like Alice had anything better to do.

Inside Mary Ann's plushly furnished house, Alice was introduced to Asta, the dog, and in the kitchen, to Mary Ann's mother, Sarah, a well-groomed blonde who was wearing a white chef's apron over what Alice thought might be golf clothes.

Mary Ann said, "Alice is a friend from school. She's staying for dinner, if that's okay."

"We're delighted to have you, Alice," Sarah said. "Do you want to call home? Let your mom know you're staying for dinner?"

"Thanks, but my parents are out of town, so no one's expecting me."

A line crossed Sarah's forehead. "All right, then."

Mary Ann said, "We're going to work on some math homework upstairs in my room. What time will dinner be ready?"

"In about half an hour. It'll just be the three of us. Your brother's at football practice, and your father won't be home till late. Would you girls like something to snack on? I baked Stilton shortbread today, for no real reason."

Mary Ann thanked her, took several pieces of shortbread from the offered plate, wrapped them in a napkin, and led Alice upstairs to her pink-and-white bedroom. She locked the door behind them, sat down on the floor, gestured to Alice to sit facing her, and spread out the napkin containing the cookies. "How about we start with something simple? I'll think about an object, and you see if you can read my thought. Here I go."

Alice had little faith in this experiment working, but her first bite of the shortbread tasted amazing. "This is so good. Does your mother bake often?"

"Yeah. Suzy Homemaker, that's her. With baking, especially. Are you ready to try mind-reading or not?"

"Ready."

"Where are your parents, anyway? Are they really away?"

"Yeah. In Boston. Just for a few days. Their quartet is performing."

"And you don't mind being alone in the house?"

"No, I like it. I can do whatever I want, whenever I want." Though, to be fair, she did what she wanted most of the time when her parents were home. They'd encouraged her to look after herself from an early age, in keeping with their benign-neglect model of parenting. And housekeeping, and cooking.

Mary Ann shuddered. "I'd be awake all night, hearing weird noises. But let's start. I'm thinking of an animal."

"Your dog, Asta."

Mary Ann jumped up. "See? It worked!"

"That wasn't telepathy. It was too obvious. Try something else."

"How about a number between one and ten?"

"I might guess it by chance."

Mary Ann walked over to her bookshelf, pulled down a dictionary. "Okay, then. I'm going to open this dictionary at random and pick a word, any word." She closed her eyes, stabbed the page with her finger, looked down. "Got it. I will now send the mystery word to you. See if you can receive it. Transmission beginning."

Alice stifled a laugh and said, "The lines are open."

Mary Ann scrunched up her face and seemed to be concentrating very hard. The least Alice could do was open her mind. She closed her eyes too, and tried to let her consciousness drift. She thought of Mary Ann's mother, alone in the kitchen, chopping onions, wiping tears from her eyes; saw Miss Alexander sitting at her desk, her head in her hands; swooped by Jake Stewart throwing a football with Mary Ann's Mike in front of Five Oaks; and came upon some bananas, arranged on an old-fashioned hat, displayed in an old-fashioned hat shop window.

"Well?" Mary Ann said.

Alice opened her eyes. "Sorry, I didn't get anything."

"Nothing at all?"

"Unless your word is banana."

"Banana?"

"I didn't think so."

"Banana in what context?"

"This sounds so stupid, but a banana on a hat. One of those nineteen-forties deals, with a pineapple?"

"Oh my god! That was it!"

"It was?"

"Sort of. My word was milliner. I was trying to send you a picture of a hat shop. One of the hats had fruit on it."

"Bloody hell. I need a cigarette. Can I smoke in here?"

"No. Now go. It's your turn. Send me a thought."

"Okay." Alice picked up the dictionary, opened it, pointed blindly to a spot on the page, peeked down at the word, which was *robot*, and shut the book. "Here it comes."

Alice visualized the robot from *Star Wars*. C-three-something. Had he been silver or gold? Gold, she thought. But how tall? She couldn't remember. She wiped that image from her mind's blackboard and sketched in the old robot maid from the *Jetsons* cartoon show. What was her name? Dolly? Dotty? Rosie! Rosie the robot with her apron and her duster.

Mary Ann said, "All I can see is my mother cleaning the house. Not it, right?"

"Fuck me. You're close. But it's not your mother. I'll try to send it out stronger." Alice animated her picture, added some background scenery, and brightened the colours — she made Rosie motor around in circles and dust the furniture of the future.

Mary Ann said, "Does your word have anything to do with the *Jetsons*?"

Could this really be happening? "The word was robot!"

"IT WAS?"

"Don't shout. What does this mean?"

"That we cheated on the math test?"

Alice reached in her bag for her cigarettes and lighter, Mary Ann shook her head no, and Alice put them back. "We didn't cheat," Alice said. "Not consciously, anyway."

"We must have exchanged the test answers without knowing it." Mary Ann had a big smile on her face. "This is so cool!"

Alice's head hurt from suspending so much disbelief. "You know what's crazy about this? I mean, aside from every single aspect of it?"

"What?"

"That this thought-transference ability — or whatever the fuck it is — if we really have it, only works between you and me. Because you said you tried it on people before, right? And it never worked?"

"I tried it on my brother, my parents, on Asta. On kids in my class." Mary Ann pinched her lower lip with her thumb and forefinger. "Maybe the reason it didn't work on any of them is because you and I were destined to be telepathic partners. Or something."

"Even a semi-scientific explanation isn't plausible, how likely is it that we both carry a chromosomal abnormality that results in telepathic ability, for instance?"

"I know, we're mutants! Like the X-Men."

Alice gave Mary Ann a withering look. "You're right. That has to be it." She got up and began to pace. "Here's another puzzle: what good is telepathic ability, really? What could we do with it?"

"Cheat on more tests?"

"And what else? If we *are* telepathic, and only with each other, I'm not sure I know how we could use this thing to our advantage. Do you? You who once badly wanted to read minds?"

"Come on, there has to be a bunch of applications for telepathy."

"Like what?"

"Like that we could talk to each other without using a phone."

"Sort of like we're doing right now, face to face."

"Or we could talk to each other without speaking. If we were bored in math class, we could carry on a private conversation in our heads, and no one would know what we were saying."

"Which would be like passing each other written notes. Except without the writing. Or the notes."

Mary Ann tsked. "Stop being so negative. Let's develop this thing and see where it takes us."

At that point, Mary Ann's mom called up the stairs that dinner was ready, and Alice said, "Let's not tell your mom about this. Or anyone."

"Of course not. It'll be our secret."

Over the next few weeks, Mary Ann and Alice spent all their spare time in telepathy training. They started out sending each other words and pictures in close quarters, and when they'd mastered that they tried it from different rooms, then from opposite ends of the school — Alice making Mary Ann laugh out loud during chemistry when she sent over a montage of her geography class sleeping through a video on "Mexico, Our Neighbours to the South."

Soon, they could communicate house-to-house, and could engage in telepathic conversations while talking out loud to someone else. The only problem was Mary Ann's occasional loss of control.

"So there I am in the library after school," Alice said one night on the phone, "studying away, and suddenly, wham, I get you, full blast, in my head, raving and cursing about how you're going to rip the head off number fourteen. Did you play basketball today, by any chance?"

"You should have seen this bitch from St. Theresa's. She played so dirty. She hacked me non-stop, and the ref didn't call any of her fouls. To top it off, the whole time she's taunting me. I wanted to punch her out."

"You've got to exert control, Mary Ann."

"Over my temper?"

"No, over your thoughts."

"Shit. I forgot to put up the wall again."

"Any time we enter into a situation with the potential for strong emotion."

"You're better at it than I am, though."

"That's because my telepathic power isn't as strong as yours. You seem to have higher wattage than me."

"Okay, from now on, I'll try. I promise."

"Good, because when you go out with that guy you met at the game, I don't want to live through the date with you."

"Davey? How'd you know about him?"

"How do you think?"

"I gave him my phone number. Did you know that?"

"What's he like?"

"Cute. A junior. He complimented me on my jump shots."

"Sounds like the perfect candidate for a fling to help you get over Mike."

"If he calls me," Mary Ann said, "should I ask him if he has a friend, so we can double?"

"Please, no. I don't date high school boys."

"More for me, then."

Mary Ann's first time out with Davey Zimmerman was at a big house party in Oakdale — the host's parents were away, and there were kegs. She and Davey talked for a bit, drank a lot of beer, and made out for hours on a basement family-room sofa, until the cops showed up and closed the party down.

Mary Ann had trouble walking in straight lines on the way home afterwards (all the more reason to lean on Davey's shoulder). When they finally got back to her house around two a.m., she kissed him goodnight on the curb, staggered up the walk, and let herself in.

She groaned when she took her shoes off. She moaned when she dropped her coat on the floor, and the coat-floor combination looked so tempting that she lay down on it, just for a second. And started at the sound of her mother's voice, very quiet, coming from the darkened living room. "Mary Ann? Are you all right?"

"You scared me," Mary Ann said. "What are you doing in there?"

"I couldn't sleep." Her mother got up and came over, stood beside her, looking down. "How was your evening?"

Mary Ann closed her eyes. "Good. Great."

"You didn't do anything you'll regret tomorrow, I hope?"

"No. Did you?"

Her mother didn't answer.

Mary Ann said, "How come you're up so late?"

"Your father and I had a few words." She reached out a hand. "Come, sweetheart, don't lie on the floor. Come in here on the sofa, at least."

Mary Ann let her mother help her up, guide her into the living room, and settle her on a sofa. The darkness was comforting. The cushions were soft.

"Is he nice, this new boy?" her mother said.

As if Mary Ann would tell her mother she was almost definitely in love again. "He's okay."

A minute or two of silence passed. Mary Ann considered getting up and going to bed, but she was too tired to move. "What did you and Dad fight about, anyway?"

"The usual."

"What usual?"

"Me going crazy being stuck at home."

"What are you talking about?"

"Go ahead and mock me. I've signed up to take a real-estate course."

"Why would I mock you for that?"

"Your father seems to find it a comical concept."

"So you'll sell houses? Have your name on lawn signs?"

"Eventually."

"Why does Dad care what you do during the day, anyway?"

"He doesn't want to help out around the house any more than he does now."

"But he doesn't do anything now."

Mary Ann's mother piled up a few cushions at the end of her own sofa, and lay down. "He'd like to keep it that way."

Mary Ann said, "I think maybe I'll never get married."

Her mother snorted. "You, who hasn't been without a boyfriend for more than two months since seventh grade?"

Mary Ann sat up. "Okay, I'm going to bed."

"There's such a thing as self-sufficiency, you know."

"Goodnight," Mary Ann said, and waited until she was halfway upstairs to stick out her tongue at the wall.

Alice called Mary Ann the next day. "How was your date with Davey?"

"It was good. I like him."

"Well, good work on getting that wall up. I didn't hear a peep from you the whole evening."

"Thank you. I laid the bricks extra thick."

"They looked very sturdy. But you can take them down now."

"I thought I had."

"I tried reaching you this morning and I couldn't get through. I'll try again."

Mary Ann sent a wrecking ball hurtling toward a wall she didn't think was there, and when the dust settled, she saw Ms. Alexander, in living colour, standing in the math room, writing an equation on the blackboard. "You've got it wrong," she said. "With those pants, she wears the plain black belt, not the braided brown one."

"So I *can* still reach you."

"Hey, what about the math mid-term next week? Are we going to use our mind skills to do well on it without Alexander catching on, or what?"

On the day of the exam, Ms. Alexander made Mary Ann and Alice sit in opposite corners of the classroom — Mary Ann in the front row by the window and Alice tucked in the back corner against the wall. They would have exchanged a mental laugh about this, if Mary Ann's mind hadn't been fully occupied staging a detailed reenactment, in stop-motion and with frequent replays, of the night before, when she'd deflowered Davey, her first (and only) virgin.

His parents had been away in Bermuda, his older brother out for the evening. They'd locked his bedroom door, put some makeout music on his stereo, and gone at it.

Davey had been so loving, so grateful, so willing to try everything. "Show me," he kept saying. "Show me what to do." So she had.

With a night like that to remember, who could care about some stupid test?

Alice was waiting for Mary Ann in the hallway when she came out of the classroom, waiting to grab her arm and walk off with her, away from Ms. Alexander's death-ray glare of disapproval that they were on speaking terms. "What happened back there?" Alice said, through gritted teeth. "I thought we were going to consult about the test answers, but I couldn't get through to you at all. There was no wall, just a big, blank void. And without your help, I'll be lucky if I got more than seventy percent."

"Oh, shit, sorry. I forgot. I guess last night took more out of me than I thought."

Alice pulled her into a corner of the hallway. "So can you read me now?"

"What?"

"I said, can you read me now? I'm sending you a thought picture."

Mary Ann closed her eyes and opened her mind, but all she could see or hear were her own Davey-centric thoughts.

"I'm not getting anything at all. But I'm pretty tired." She yawned. "Let's try again later, okay? After I've gone home and taken a nap?"

Davey was coming down the hall toward them, smiling and holding out his arms for a hug, making Mary Ann's heart swell with loved-up joy. "See ya, Alice," she'd said, and dived into his embrace, little knowing that their mind-reading days were over and done.

3

September 2010

The previous spring, Mary Ann had been driven to seek a job. After a ten-year stint as a stay-at-home mom, she wanted to regain a measure of independence, and make a little money. She also wanted to distract herself from Bob's cheating ways and the implosion of her marriage. And from feeling unwanted and unloved.

She lucked into a part-time job doing project management — her former, pre-kid, field of work — for Drew Wacyk, a thirty-year-old computer consultant with a storefront office in Oakdale.

She was mega-nervous about the job at first. Nervous about the tables-turned aspect of working for Drew, who'd worked for *her* when he was in college. The plaid-shirted young man who'd taught computer skills to kids in the After Four program she'd coordinated had morphed into a plaid-shirted hunky guy with eyes the colour of pecans — how would she deal with that? She was nervous that Phoebe, the junior college student doing an internship as Drew's admin assistant, might nurse an automatic hatred for everyone over the age of forty, or show contempt at Mary Ann's failure to grasp the many new concepts in office procedures that had developed during her absence from the work force. And she worried about dealing with Tom Gagliardi, the New York developer who was restoring the old train station and changing the face of Oakdale, and who had hired Drew to do some systems work for him. Mary Ann found Tom completely intimidating, what with his beautifully tailored clothes, his leonine head of hair, and his ornate manner of speech.

Six months into the job, she'd become accustomed to and fond of them all, and she thought — hoped — they liked her too. So she felt relaxed and comfortable on the Friday afternoon that she happened to be in the office reception area when Tom was on his way out. Drew and Phoebe were there too, the three of them gathered like they were olden days servants at an English country house, bidding the lord of the manor a safe journey.

Tom said, "My drive back to the city will be long, but a reward awaits at journey's end. I'm meeting a friend in the East Village at a Japanese noodle shop that he says is the equal of a spot where he once had a transformative gastronomic experience in Shinjuku." He waited a beat. "Do you know Shinjuku?"

All three shook their heads.

"My apologies for assuming you did. It's a colorful district in Tokyo that harbors at least one estimable noodle shop."

The usual stunned pause followed Tom's words, then Mary Ann said, "Happy eating," because someone had to speak before Tom could leave and Mary Ann could stand at the window and watch him walk to his car. All six-foot-four of him in his linen suit.

Drew spoke from over her shoulder. "Do you think he was born that way? Spouting big words, and gliding instead of walking?"

Mary Ann said, "He seems to come from another era."

"Maybe he's a vampire," Phoebe said.

"But women go for his approach, don't they?" Drew said. "That hand-kissing routine?"

"He's never kissed my hand," Mary Ann said. Wistfully.

Phoebe said, "He doesn't do anything for me. Even if he weren't way old, he's too intense. I like guys who are laidback, and Tom doesn't seem like he'd be much fun."

"I'm fun," Drew said.

Mary Ann and Phoebe both laughed.

"What? I am."

Phoebe said, "When was the last time you had a pillow fight with your girlfriend?"

"Never. I hate pillow fights."

"What a surprise."

"I don't like horseplay, either," Mary Ann said. "I had a boyfriend in high school who thought throwing people in swimming pools was a riot. I don't know what I ever saw in him."

"Hey, Mary Ann," Phoebe said. "If you like serious guys, why don't you have an affair with Tom, find out what he's really like? Drew — fifty bucks says he wears silk dressing gowns and sleeps in an antique four-poster bed. Or a coffin."

Mary Ann blushed. "What a suggestion!"

Drew wagged a finger at Phoebe. "Mary Ann's married, you know. And so is Tom."

"I was just joking," Phoebe said. "What's with you two?"

"So this spooky thing happened at work on Friday," Mary Ann said to Alice.

They were in Mary Ann's kitchen after a Sunday night dinner. The kids and Bob had dispersed to their playrooms, leaving the women to tidy up and converse in low voices.

Alice spooned leftover broccoli into a plastic container. "Spooky like you saw a ghost, or spooky like blood started to drip down the walls?"

"Neither. Phoebe made a joke about me having an affair with Tom, and I felt like she'd caught me in the act. When I haven't done anything yet."

Alice loaded some cutlery into the dishwasher. "What happened to your dinner club idea?"

"It's still festering in my mind."

"Maybe you should leave it there. A dinner club seems like a lot of work to organize and execute, with no guarantee of achieving your objective."

Mary Ann said, "But I have to do something soon. I haven't had sex in seven months."

"It's been seven months already since you found out about Bob's affair?"

"What do you mean *already*? Seven months is a long time."

"For you, maybe."

"Why? How long has it been for you?"

"Never mind. How did we get on to this topic, anyway?"

"I was talking about Phoebe, and how I freaked out when I thought she might be reading my mind."

"She must have made a lucky guess. Have you been acting transparent? Breathing heavily at the sight of Tom and Drew, swooning in their presence, wearing your heart on your sleeve?"

"Probably. It's been so long since I've been attracted to anyone, I haven't got the faintest idea how to act, how to arrange my face."

"You could work on developing a frown as your default facial expression. Whenever your mind wanders, slap on a frown, and repel the world. It's a technique that's worked wonders for me."

Mary Ann closed the dishwasher door, pressed the *on* button. "Don't you sometimes wish we had the telepathy back, though?"

"Not really. How long did it even last? Six weeks? Two months? Sometimes I wonder if we imagined the whole thing."

"Alice! How can you say that?"

"How can you not?"

"Because I know we were really reading each other's minds. In detail."

Alice sat on a stool at the counter. "Even if we really were telepathic, who knows why, for a strange, short time, it's over now. There's no point dwelling in the past."

"I never did understand why it stopped working."

"I had a theory that it was caused by a unique and short-lived configuration of the stars, moon, planets, and our menstrual cycles, and it only lasted until the universe shifted."

"Our menstrual cycles?"

"The tides may have been involved, too. And sun spots, possibly."

Mary Ann took out mugs and spoons. "Go ahead, make fun."

"I'm sorry. It's just that the only logical explanation I can think of for what happened is that we went temporarily insane. Or suffered from a case of dual simultaneous hysteria."

Mary Ann poured them both coffee. "I guess these days if we want to experience anything extraordinary, we have to make it happen, instead of waiting for the universe and our periods to coincide."

"Speak for yourself. I'm barely surviving in the state of ordinary."

"Hand me that notepad beside the phone. Let's get this dinner club going, change things up."

"Aren't you tired right now? I'm tired."

Mary Ann pulled up a chair, wrote away for a minute, pushed the pad over to Alice's side of the counter. "How's this?"

She had written:

The Oakdale Dinner Club

Founding members:

Mary Ann

Alice

Amy

Lisa

Mom

Phoebe

Drew

Tom

Sam Orenstein

Danielle Pringle

Alice said, "Who's Danielle Pringle?"

"Her son is in Kayla's class, and one time for a class lunch at school she brought an incredible salad made of blue potatoes and yellow cherry tomatoes and white beets. She's a foodie if I ever saw one."

"I see you've got your three affair candidates listed, your own personal *Dating Game* lined up. Forgive me for raising a technicality, but are they not all currently attached to someone else?"

"Yes, but I'm not trying to wreck any homes. I'm just looking for a fling. And besides, I recall hearing about a married man or two in your past, Alice."

"If I was ever involved with a married man, a) I shouldn't have told you about him, and b) I was in my twenties, and wild and uncaring."

"I skipped the wild and uncaring stage when I was young, so it only seems fair that I get to have one now."

Alice yawned. "At least these dinner club evenings won't be dull. If the conversation flags, I can always watch you acting like a degenerate."

* * *

Mary Ann's workdays at Drew's office started at ten o'clock. Giving her time in the morning after the kids were packed off to school to clean up the breakfast dishes, deal with her personal business, and start on her invitations, which she'd decided to do by phone — so much more gracious than sending a group email.

She kept the dinner club papers stored in a file folder in her desk drawer marked *Menus*, a folder guaranteed to hold no interest for Bob. Though Mary Ann had nothing to hide — Bob knew about the dinner club. She'd told him about it that morning before he left for work, and he'd grunted in acknowledgement when she spoke, grunted again when she'd told him the first meeting would be at their house, and that he would probably want to absent himself that evening, an evening when Josh happened to have an away basketball game, in Valleyview. How about if Bob took Josh to the game? Okay? Okay.

Her first calls were to her friends Amy and Lisa, a pair of bubbly moms who could be counted on to volunteer at school events, lived for their daily five p.m. glasses of wine, and whose roles in the dinner club would be to fill the room, and make Mary Ann's quest for a lover less obvious. They were both out when she called — probably doing errands, power-walking together, or having their hair done. She left them each a detailed message.

Next to call was her mother. Mary Ann would have preferred Sarah not witness her attempts at flirtation, but with Alice living in the second-floor apartment above Sarah, it would be too awkward not to ask her. And her desserts *were* very good.

Sarah said, "What an enchanting idea, Mary Ann. I'd love to come. But are you sure having an old woman around won't put a damper on your party?"

"Sixty-eight isn't old, Mom."

"Some days I feel like it is."

"And you know people on the list, so you'll feel comfortable, I'm sure."

"I must say, I like the no-spouse idea," Sarah said. "Women are so much easier to talk to when their husbands aren't around."

"Think about what you'd like to bring — I'd recommend something in the dessert line — and let me know."

"I will. And thank you again."

Mary Ann said goodbye, looked at the clock, and pulled Kayla's class list off her bulletin board. She had time before leaving for work for one more call.

After dropping her two boys off at school, Danielle Pringle drove back to the farm, poured a fresh cup of coffee into her travel mug, and took it outside, carrying it around during her morning inspection. She discussed the day ahead with her two farmhands — the pumpkins were coming along nicely, the radish bed needed weeding, the latest batch of mache was ready to pick.

She stopped by the kennels on her way back to the house, and found her husband Benny inside, kneeling next to his breeder, Daisy, who had given birth to six puppies a few days before. "See that?" he said. "See how the smallest one fights to get to her teat? Alex calls him Hero."

"I thought we weren't going to let the kids name the puppies."

"I know, but Alex identifies with the runt. You know what he asked me this morning? If dogs can get food allergies, too."

"The poor sweetie."

Benny stood up. "Maybe we should let him keep Hero."

"Maybe. What time is your first appointment today?"

"Nine-thirty. A cat needing shots. I should go open up the office."

"I should go to mine."

They walked out together and Benny said, "What's for lunch today?"

Danielle bit her lip and poured the dregs of her coffee on the ground. She hated when Benny asked her that question, or any question that implied the kitchen or the food that came out of it was her sole responsibility, though, to be honest, she'd cooked her own goose on that score.

She'd developed a measure of culinary prowess as a skewed act of defiance against her mother, Adele Beauchamp, a respected food writer and fine-dining snob whose specialty was enthusing about prepared food without ever cooking any herself. And now it sometimes seemed that looking after the food Danielle's family ate was all she did.

Every day, after her sons Ethan and Alex came home from school, she dirtied pots and pans and dishes and washed and dirtied them again. She loaded the dishwasher and unloaded it, peeled and sliced onions, washed and dried lettuce. Her own beautiful, buttery lettuces that looked so special on her table at the Greenmarket looked like a chore at home, in her kitchen, where she hacked off the ends, separated the leaves, picked out bugs and globs of dirt, and submerged them in cold water before placing them in the spinner.

If someone took all the lettuce leaves she'd washed and placed them end to end, they would reach China. Add on the onionskins she'd thrown on her compost heap, and the trail of vegetable matter would circle the planet.

So sue her if she resorted to an occasional passive-aggressive tactic when Benny asked her, every single day, what there was for lunch.

"I don't know," she said. "What are you having?"

"Are there any leftovers?"

"Maybe. You should check."

"I'll look later." Benny turned to his veterinary office, on the left, and Danielle headed right, toward a ringing phone in her office. She ran in, picked it up, and said, "Pringles," in her chirpy customer service voice.

"Danielle, is that you? It's Mary Ann Gray here — Kayla's mom. From Ethan's class?"

"Oh hi," Danielle said. "How are you?" And what could Mary Ann Gray possibly want from her?

"Fine, thanks, and I know this sounds out of the blue, but I'm calling to invite you to a join a dinner club I'm starting. Let me explain."

Danielle listened, and thought about the first time she'd met Mary Ann, at a volunteer potluck luncheon held at the school, in Ethan's kindergarten year. Midway through the proceedings, Mary Ann had crossed the room in her pale blue silk dress and singled Danielle out from the other mothers and nannies. "Someone told me you brought that beautiful salad," she said. "I don't think we've met."

Danielle introduced herself, thanked Mary Ann for the compliment, and hid her embarrassment over screwing up with her food contribution. Other mothers had supplied mini-pitas stuffed with egg salad, or a cheese tray containing the standard wedges of Brie, cheddar, and Swiss, but Danielle, foiled by her pretentious food upbringing, had brought a platter of her own baby white beets, blue fingerling potatoes, and filet beans, steamed, dressed in a herb vinaigrette, and topped with halved yellow cherry tomatoes and a chiffonade of mint and basil.

Mary Ann said, "And it doesn't just look good, it tastes delicious, too. Do you do parties? I'm kidding. But I'd love to serve this at my next luncheon."

Danielle said, "It wasn't very difficult to prepare."

"But where'd you get it all? At the farmer's market? Oh shoot, Amy is giving me the signal. It's time to present the teacher gift. Excuse me."

Danielle had listened to Mary Ann give a pretty speech of thanks to the teacher, admired the artfully wrapped gift — all shiny paper and organza ribbon — and wondered if there'd be any salad left over to take home for Benny's dinner.

"We'd rotate houses every month," Mary Ann said now, "and best of all: we wouldn't invite spouses. Just cooks. Let me tell you who else is coming."

Danielle let Mary Ann run down the unfamiliar names on her list, but she already knew her answer: no, thanks. Danielle would never fit in with Mary Ann's crowd from the rich part of Oakdale, she couldn't stand the thought of any extra cooking, she didn't own any clothes to suit the occasion, and she could just imagine Benny's pout if she told him he could fix his own dinner for once, because she was going out for the evening, alone.

Mary Ann said, "What do you think? A good meal, some entertaining people, adult conversation. Does this sound at all appealing?"

"It does, and it's so nice of you to ask me, but I'm afraid I'm not up to any extra food prep right now. Some days just the effort of putting dinner on the table for my family is more than I can manage."

"Tell me about it. I've recently rejoined the workforce, and it's convenience food all the way for my kids. But it's more fun to cook for a party than for your family, don't you think? More appreciated. And if you're coming out for the evening, don't make dinner at home. Get your babysitter to order in pizza."

Not a babysitter — Benny. And not pizza — Alex couldn't eat it, with his gluten allergy. But maybe Benny could take the boys out to the hamburger joint in Booth, where Ethan would be happy, and Alex could order meat patties without a bun and a large quantity of fries.

"Think of it as an escape," Mary Ann said.

Strange how the right choice of words could make such a difference. Like when Danielle's mother, Adele, in a restaurant review, described the ordinary mashed potatoes at some new bistro in Manhattan as "joy-inducing mouthfuls of butter-laced nostalgia," and the crowds followed.

Danielle said, "An escape does sound tempting. September 25th, you said?"

"At my place. Number 12 Green Street. See you then."

When Mary Ann got to the office at ten, Phoebe said, "I just made fresh coffee. And Tom called and said to tell you and Drew he's dropping in at eleven, with elevenses. Whatever that means."

"It means he's bringing food," Mary Ann said, and headed upstairs to her desk in the supply room.

By the time Tom came in, Mary Ann had put in a solid hour of work, had invited Drew and Phoebe to the dinner club as if she were equally interested in them both, and had secured their promises to come. So she was feeling confident about asking Tom when he arrived bearing samples from an artisanal baker who wanted to occupy a storefront in the development. He laid out small, irregularly shaped nut-studded chocolate chunk cookies on a blue paper napkin, arranged fresh apricot mini-tarts alongside, and requested that Drew, Phoebe, and Mary Ann try them and give him their opinions.

Drew spoke first. "They both taste good to me, but I've been known to eat Twinkies, so I'm not the right audience."

Phoebe said, "Both of these things seem high fat. Are they?"

41

Mary Ann swallowed a bite of tart. "The tart pastry's made with butter, and the fruit tastes sweet, intense, and unsullied by thickener."

"Ah," Tom said. "I sense the presence of a discerning palate. What do you make of the cookie?"

"It contains chocolate with a high cocoa content, if I'm not mistaken, the sea salt flaked on top is a nice touch, and the pecans and almonds make a good textural combination. I'd buy these from a bakery, for sure. The tarts, too. I'd serve them to my dinner club."

Drew said to Tom, "Mary Ann's starting up a dinner club here in town."

"It's a wonderful concept," Tom said, "if done properly. Each participant contributing a signature dish, everyone able to savour a variety of tastes."

Mary Ann saw her opening. "We'd love to have you, Tom."

"I'm sorry, I didn't mean to imply —"

"No, I wanted to invite you. First meeting is in two weeks, at my house. On September 25th."

"That's a most gracious invitation, and I thank you for it, but I couldn't intrude among strangers —"

"There'll be more familiar faces than strange ones. You know Alice Maeda, and we three will be there, plus a few others. And think how nifty a piece about the dinner club will look on the community page of the development-project website."

Drew said, "Don't worry, Tom — I'm bringing wine, not food. And Mary Ann's going to tell me which wines to buy, so I don't screw up."

"I think I'll bring ceviche," Phoebe said. "From my mother's recipe."

"I don't mean to pressure you, Tom," Mary Ann said. "If you think your culinary taste is too refined for Oakdale, well, I'm insulted, but I understand."

"It's not that," Tom said. "Naturally I would expect anyone who lives in the architecturally beautiful houses of Oakdale to have impeccable taste in all aspects of their lives."

"So we'll see you on the twenty-fifth, then? At seven o'clock. I live at 12 Green Street."

"It's difficult to refuse you."

"Oh, and Tom," Mary Ann said, "come solo. This isn't a couples event."

4

September 2010

Kate Maguire walked by the Whole Foods on Columbus on her way home from work and hesitated by the entrance. Had she promised Tom she'd pick up anything? As usual, he had called her that afternoon, this time on his way home from Oakdale, to discuss dinner. Yesterday he'd seared tuna with a hazelnut crust. The day before, he'd reminded her of a date they'd made to meet friends at a new nose-to-tail restaurant in Tribeca. What was his plan for tonight's meal? She struggled to extract the insignificant detail from her day's accumulation of information, but got sidetracked estimating how many hours she'd have to spend that evening reviewing the documents in her bag, and headed on home.

When she unlocked the apartment door, she smelled sautéed onions and peppers and remembered — Tom was making paella. She changed into comfortable clothes, joined him in the kitchen, accepted the glass of red wine he offered her, and set about assembling a green salad while he chopped the chorizo aggressively, as if he were competing on a cooking show. "How was your day?" he said.

"Busy. I brought work home that I have to start on right after dinner. How was yours?"

She half listened to his reply, finished making the salad,

decided which file to work on first, and almost missed hearing about an invitation to join a dinner club.

He said, "It was rather awkward. I stopped in at the office of Drew Wacyk, the computer consultant, to talk about the new bakery tenant, and I was invited to attend a dinner club in Oakdale. A dinner club convened by Mary Ann Gray."

"Who's that?"

"She's an influential local woman who works part-time for Drew."

"You didn't accept, did you?"

"I couldn't extricate myself."

Kate whisked the oil into the salad dressing. "Tell her you checked with me and I have another engagement that night."

"As a matter of fact, the invitation was for me alone. And I ought to go for goodwill purposes, don't you think? To build some local support for the development?"

"Lunch with the chamber of commerce is one thing. Since when is dinner at a suburban matron's house necessary to maintain good relations with a community?"

"This project isn't like the others, Kate. Oakdale is different."

Kate turned her back on Tom to set the table, and rolled her eyes at the ceiling. "Go ahead and have dinner with the ladies. What do I care? It just seems a bit beyond the call of duty." She laid out two place settings, each with a fork, a knife, a napkin, and a water glass, and stepped back to see if she'd forgotten anything. What kind of table would this Oakdale woman set for her dinner club? She'd use fussy antique gold-rimmed china that couldn't go in the dishwasher, probably. And a heavy white brocade tablecloth that cost a fortune to have hand-laundered and pressed, with matching napkins set in sterling silver napkin rings polished by the help. "What's the woman's name again?" she said.

Tom was intent on the paella. "What woman?"

"The organizer of the dinner club. Martha Stewart, was it?"

Tom picked up some salt between his fingers from a small open dish on the counter, and sprinkled it over the pan from on high. "Her name is Mary Ann Gray. And dinner's ready. Shall we?"

Kate had her college friend Hallie to thank for the introduction to Oakdale.

Kate and Hallie had become friends as undergrads at Cornell, back in the day, despite their differences — Kate was a dark-haired, serious, straight shooter from New York, and Hallie was an ambitious blonde looker from Fort Lauderdale. Assigned as dorm roommates in their freshmen year, they'd bonded over their shared preference to stand on the sidelines of any social gathering they attended and make sardonic comments to each other rather than join in. That and their shared drive to succeed, career-wise.

They'd gone their separate ways after graduation — Kate to NYU for law school, Hallie to Wharton for an MBA. But they'd kept in touch enough over the decades since that Hallie had called Kate to give her the news when she and her husband Sam decided, four years before the paella night, to move to the New York area.

On the phone, Hallie said that Sam had sold his Philadelphia-based food-manufacturing business for good money, and was trying to write a mystery novel, which was another way of saying, in her opinion, that he was having a midlife crisis. Either way, his new form of self-employment had left Hallie free to seek and snag a director of finance position at a magazine publisher with a head office in Manhattan.

"So we're moving to Oakdale," she said. "Near you."

"Oakdale? Where's that?" The phone was tucked under Kate's ear. One eye was scrolling her email, and the other was on her desk clock, her mental calculator computing the dollar value of the billable minutes this phone call was taking up.

"It's a suburb. Or maybe a small town. It's a pretty community upstate, full of mature trees and old houses, and it's only an hour and a half from the city. It's New York's best-kept secret, the real estate agent told me. And it's not marked on most maps."

Kate gave Hallie her full attention. Tom would love this story. "A modern day Shangri-La, is that what we're talking about?"

"More like a budding Scarsdale. There's a country club, some good public schools, peace and quiet for Sam and the girls, and I get to commute into Manhattan every day."

"It sounds wonderful." And to Kate, boring.

"You can see it for yourself when you come out and visit us. I'm calling to invite you to dinner at our new house. In six weeks. On August 15."

Kate flipped the pages of her datebook. "Looks like we're free. Why then?"

"We move in August 1. It'll give me time to get the house set up. Write down the date. And tell me: Is Tom still a food nut?"

"He sure is. Only yesterday he was talking about the relative merits of duck fat over peanut oil for making frites."

"You guys still eat French fries? I don't think a fried potato has passed my lips for ten years."

"I'm a firm believer in clinging to at least some of the extravagances of youth."

"Christ, you sounded just like Tom there. Do you two look alike now, too?"

"How'd you guess? I've grown six inches in the last few years. Must be all the French fries."

When Kate told Tom that night about Hallie's news, he said, "What do you mean, it's not marked on the map?"

"It isn't. I looked up the address online, and there's no Oakdale listed. The area seems to be part of a larger entity called Pembroke-Booth."

"Perhaps Hallie has stumbled onto the lost city of Atlantis."

"Or the lost town of Genoa City."

Tom looked puzzled, as Kate had known he might be. She had a bad habit of puncturing his high-culture pretensions with pop culture references she knew he wouldn't get.

"Genoa in Italy?" he said.

"No, the town in Wisconsin where *The Young and the Restless* is set. *The Young and the Restless* being a daytime soap."

"Ah, I see. And I agree. Something suffocating and parochial is far more likely. I'm curious, nevertheless, to see this Oakdale. The prospect almost makes me look forward to dinner with Hallie and Sam."

"They're not so bad."

"She never liked me."

"Because you never liked her, and her irresistibility is an important part of her identity."

Tom said, "Maybe we should go out a few hours early when we go for dinner, do some exploring. Mature trees, she said? And old houses? Did she say how old?"

First the highway, then a lesser road. A few miles down, a sign: WELCOME TO PEMBROKE-BOOTH. Followed by the usual fast-food outlets, a mini-mall containing a supermarket and a Sears, a couple of gas stations. Further on, a large school. "Oh, look," Kate said. "Five Oaks High School. Home of the Huskies. Talk about wasting a perfectly good Sunday afternoon driving out to nowhere. It's the next turnoff, I think. Oakdale Drive."

They turned, drove by a few miles of farmland, and entered a leafy residential neighbourhood. Tom slowed down the car and they cruised along winding roads named after trees and flowers. The brick and stone houses they passed were mainly of well-kept nineteenth-century origin, Tom informed Kate, in a mix of styles — he had studied art and architectural history in college and liked to show off his knowledge.

He pointed out an Arts and Crafts era house studded with protruding Klinker brick on one street, and a row of 1880s Second Empire cottages with mansard roofs on the next. There were newer builds too, the odd one stuck in between two older specimens, infill on what had once been sprawling lawns. And at least one mid-century subdivision made up of blocks of generic ranch houses. When they'd driven through it, Tom said, "Let's go back to the old part. It's much more interesting."

None of the houses in the older section of Oakdale were mansions, but they were all distinguished, in their way. They all had something to say.

"Who lives here?" Tom said, as they drove down a quiet street. "What kind of people?"

"Who do you think? Privileged white people."

"Like us?"

"No, nothing like us. Golf-playing, scotch-swilling, country-clubbing bankers and brokers."

"How are we different?"

"We live in the city. We read books. We go to the theatre. We care about things." She rolled up her window. "Okay, we've seen Oakdale. What are we going to do till six o'clock?"

They turned out onto a Main Street that was not major at all — it was neither long nor wide. They trawled by some boarded-up old houses and a tired-looking row of stores. A hand-lettered sign in the window of a hairdressing salon read: LADIES' WASH AND SET — $30.

Tom pulled to a stop at the end of the road, in front of a large, two-storey, multi-roofed building constructed of yellow brick decorated with intricate patterns of red brick insets. The roofs were crested with wrought-iron fencing, and a clock tower — bare of clock — rose fifty feet above their heads. An ugly rectangular lightbox sign bearing the words STATION BAKERY hung over the doorway.

"Now there's an edifice," Tom said. They gazed at it a minute. "Why *station*, I wonder?"

"Probably because the bus to Albany stops here."

"Let's take a closer look."

They parked the car, crossed the quiet street, opened the door to the bakery, and stepped into a nondescript space that could have passed for any of the three doughnut shops they'd seen out on the state road.

A teenage girl with hair bleached an unbecoming platinum shade sat behind the counter, staring at nothing. An annoying strain of rock music seeped out of the wall speakers at low volume. The only other customer was a woman who sat in a back corner reading the Sunday *Times*. Beside her a baby slept in a stroller.

The teenager stood up. "Hi. Can I get you some coffee?"

"No, thank you," Tom said. "We came in here hoping to glean some information about the history of Oakdale, and of this building in particular. Am I right to suppose it is late-nineteenth-century in origin?"

The girl's expression was blank. "What?"

Kate nudged Tom quiet. "We'd love some coffee," she said. "Two. And we'll have a maple doughnut to share, please."

The girl assembled their order while Tom prowled around the room. He checked corners, ran his hands across the wall surfaces, stared at the plate glass windows.

When it was time to pay, Kate said, "This building looks so old from the outside, and so new from the inside. It's a little confusing. How old is it?"

"Old. Especially the upstairs part."

The other customer came up to the counter, held out her mug to the teenager, said, "Another tea, please, Courtney, if you don't mind."

Courtney filled the woman's mug with hot water from a spout, handed her a paper-wrapped tea bag, and said to Kate, "There's a fridge up in the storeroom that's so old the freezer fills up with ice every couple of months."

"You don't say?" Kate smiled politely. "Thank you." She chose the table farthest away from the counter and she and Tom sat down.

"Excuse me," the tea drinker said, and walked over to them, mug in hand. She was in her mid-to-late thirties, Kate thought, had long, dark hair and good cheekbones, and was part Asian, possibly.

"I heard you asking about the building," she said. "I know a bit about it. I grew up in Oakdale, and I'm a kind of history buff. My name's Alice. Alice Maeda."

Tom jumped up, tried to pull out a chair for Alice, and would have if the seats hadn't been attached to the table. "Won't you join us? Provided your young charge can be left unattended." He glanced back at the stroller.

Alice looked, too. "That's okay. Lavinia's asleep."

"Lavinia?" Tom said. "An unusual choice of name."

"It's Roman."

"I'm aware of its provenance. What surprises me is to find it here, in this place, attached to an infant."

Alice grinned. "You have quite a way with the language." She turned to Kate. "Do you talk like him, too?"

"No," Kate said. "I'm normal. And we'd love to hear more about the building. This is our first time in Oakdale, and we're curious."

"This used to be a train station," Alice said. "Circa 1875. A pretty fancy one, I imagine." She gestured to the painted drywall surrounding them. "Difficult as it may be to visualize, the bones of the old building remain beneath this dreadful interior, forever obscured."

There was a short silence during which Kate and Tom searched in vain for any sign of the bones, then Alice said, "Did I start lecturing there? Sorry. It's a bad habit of mine. I'm a teacher."

Kate said, "Where do you teach?"

"I've been teaching in England for the last twenty years, but I start at NYU this fall."

"Not in architecture, by any chance?" That was Tom.

"No. Freshman Ancient History, heavy on the Greek and Roman."

"May we ask what happened to the railroad line hereabouts?"

"It disappeared sometime in the nineteen forties, after the lines were consolidated and service to Oakdale was discontinued. Though you can still find some old railway ties around, tucked away in people's yards." Alice looked back at the stroller. "It's not like Lavinia to sleep this long. I'll go check on her."

She stepped away, and Kate said to Tom, "I take it back. Coming here today is more interesting than it would have been to sit at home."

Alice wheeled the stroller over beside them and sat down again. "She's still breathing."

Tom said, "So this building is a relic of Oakdale's former glory?"

"The only relic remaining. You should see the photographs in the county archives of what Main Street used to look like, in its heyday. There was a big town hall and a fancy hotel

— the locals used to dress up and promenade down the street on Sunday afternoons."

"Until the decline."

"Since then, Oakdale's become not much more than a bedroom community for New York City."

Tom said, "The building would be glorious, restored."

"It would, but the local historical society can't afford it," Alice said. "Neither can the county. I've checked."

Tom walked to the glass door, looked out at the street. "There are ways, of course."

"Tom," Kate said.

Alice looked at her. "What does he mean?"

"Tom develops real estate."

"Is that why you're here?"

"No. Friends of ours from Philadelphia have moved into the neighbourhood. We came out to visit them."

"And how would building condos help restore the station?"

Tom turned around. "Not condos. Or only a few. In the existing houses on Main Street, the untenanted ones. We could save the façades, spruce them up, gut the insides, turn them into townhouses for young professionals who yearn for the simpler life and are willing to work from home, or commute. We could install a few small businesses along there too, and fix up the retail strip. A proper coffee shop would be a good addition, a bank branch, a business supply store with mailboxes and photocopying. The small grocery we passed could be converted into a gourmet fresh market. And there should be a real bakery." He gave the untouched doughnut a dirty look. "A bakery that sells goods made from scratch, not from a food-service mix.

"We could divert a portion of the profits from the sale of the condos and the retail spaces to restore this building completely, right down to the tile floor. We'd get rid of that false ceiling and open up the space — it must have been twenty feet high originally. We'd find antique train station benches and fixtures, and bring in plasterers to rebuild the walls and recreate hand-carved mouldings. We'd install a new clock in the tower. And when the building was brought back to its former grandeur, we'd find a use for it. It wouldn't be an empty museum, but a living thing. A bookstore, perhaps. Is there a bookstore hereabouts? Of course not. A library? No? Well then, a library."

Kate spoke up. "The Tom Gagliardi Library?"

Tom said to Alice, "Kate is telling me, in her gracious way, that I am building castles in the air. I have that tendency. But I was merely trying to demonstrate that it can be done. There are ways."

Lavinia started to stir in the stroller, and Alice bent down to untie her. Before she did, Lavinia began screaming, full blast. Zero to loud in two seconds. Alice picked her up, jiggled her up and down, and shouted over the din to Kate, "Could you hand me that receiving blanket there, in the diaper bag side pocket? Thanks. Oh, Lavinia, for god's sake."

Alice threw the blanket over her shoulder, adjusted her clothing underneath, and directed Lavinia's wailing head to her breast, a move which silenced her cries and replaced them with sucking noises.

Kate stood up. "It was a pleasure to meet you, Alice. Thank you for telling us about Oakdale."

"I liked meeting you guys, too. Not my everyday experience around here."

"Happy to oblige," Tom said.

"And let me know if your air castles turn into concrete ones, will you? Because if they do, I'd like to be involved."

* * *

In the car on the way to Hallie's house, Tom said, "That woman was laughing at me."

Kate smiled. "I liked her."

"Do you think all the inhabitants are of her ilk? Erudite university lecturers? Or are you sticking to your golf-playing, scotch-swilling theory?"

"If Alice belongs to a country club, I'm a religious Catholic."

After a leisurely drive around the area, Kate and Tom came to Hallie and Sam's stately Federal-style house, parked in front of the wide, expensively landscaped lot, and went inside. They had drinks, admired the two Orenstein girls until they were led away by a nanny, and sat down to eat in the dining room.

"I'm pleased to report," Hallie said, from the head of the table, "that I cooked nothing you see before you. Sam grilled the fish and the vegetables, the nanny made the potatoes, and I bought the salad ready-made. I know Tom doesn't approve, but we can't all be master chefs, now can we, Kate?"

"It's all delicious," Kate said. "The snapper is cooked perfectly, Sam."

"Thank you. I've rediscovered the satisfactions of cooking since I sold the business."

Kate said to Hallie, "And the house looks fantastic, everything in its place and all settled in. How did you do it?"

"It's amazing what can be accomplished when you're willing to write a cheque. And having Sam here all day to take deliveries and deal with the tradesmen makes everything so much easier." Hallie smiled prettily at Sam when she said this, and drank her wine, and Kate wondered if she was the only person present who heard the resentment in Hallie's voice.

"How are you adjusting to being at home?" Tom asked Sam. "How's the writing going?"

"I haven't done any writing since a month before the move."

"I'm sure you'll establish a routine now that you're settled," Kate said.

"I hope so."

Hallie was up refilling their wine glasses already, though Kate had hardly touched hers. "So what do you two think of Oakdale?" Hallie said. "Isn't it charming?"

Kate exchanged a glance with Tom. "You might as well tell them."

"Tell us what?"

"About my plan for Main Street," Tom had said.

And so had Tom's Oakdale involvement — what Kate was starting to think of as his own mid-life crisis — begun.

5

September 2010

Mary Ann had hoped she would run into Sam Orenstein when he was dropping his girls off at school, so she could casually invite him to the dinner club as if his presence weren't essential to its success. But she hadn't seen him, so she had to call him. Now, when the kitchen was tidied up after dinner and the kids were occupied upstairs. Now, when Bob wasn't home. *Now* now.

She picked up the phone, put a smile on her face so there'd be one in her voice, and dialled the Orenstein house. The phone rang three times, then went to voicemail, to Sam's relaxed voice on the outgoing message. There was the beep. Go. "Hi there, it's Mary Ann Gray calling, to invite you to the first meeting of a small dinner club I'm starting up — a glorified potluck, essentially, but we'd love you to be part of it. The first meeting's at my place, on September 25th. Come alone — no spouse, no kids. Call me to confirm, and we can discuss menu. Talk to you soon." Whew. That hadn't been so bad. She'd sounded cheerful and innocent, not like someone with designs on a married man.

When Sam had sold Samosa King, his little food company made good, and decided to try his hand at writing a mystery, he hadn't considered himself a stay-at-home dad. When the family moved from Philadelphia to Oakdale, and Hallie took the high-profile job at Morris Communications, Sam still thought of himself as a working man — one who wrote out of a home office.

At the beginning, to perpetrate this myth, Sam tried to keep regular office hours in his study, and he employed a full-time nanny/housekeeper whom he spent most of the day avoiding. She cared for the girls when they weren't barging into his office after school and demanding he settle an argument, give a hug, or help with some homework.

After that nanny quit to go work for an employer who wasn't home all day, Sam told Hallie he didn't want to hire another full-time person. Instead, he took over meal preparation, and child-ferrying and minding duties. He still had plenty of time to write while the girls were in school, and a cleaning woman came in twice a week to clean and do laundry during the hours when Sam was out walking Chutney the family dog, or buying groceries.

He hadn't intended to become a househusband, yet now he was on a joshing basis with the other moms and some of the nannies, he arranged play dates, he was up on little girls' fashion, TV shows, and music of choice, and he had a good grasp of playground gossip.

On the day Jessica and Annabelle had their first evening gymnastics class of the fall season, Sam picked them up from school at three-thirty, fed them dinner, calmed Annabelle's pre-class jitters, readied their gym clothes, cleaned up the kitchen, and made it to the community center in good time to cadge a seat on the sidelines with the other moms. With the other parents.

When he brought the girls home an hour and half later, Hallie had come home from work and was sitting in the family room, still dressed in her suit. She had a glass of wine in her hand, the TV was tuned to CNBC, and Chutney was asleep at her feet.

Annabelle sat down next to Hallie and leaned against her. "Mommy, Laura Wright was mean to me today at school, and I don't want to invite her to my birthday party anymore, but Daddy says I have to."

Sam straightened up the shoes and bags thrown down in the front hall while Hallie kissed and hugged the girls and listened to their stories about the day, and said most of the right things. When they'd gone upstairs to play on their computers, Hallie caught Sam's eye and said, "Another meeting was added to my itinerary in L.A. I have to leave tomorrow instead of Wednesday."

"But Jessica's soccer league starts tomorrow."

"What can I do?"

Sam and Hallie didn't have a chance to talk further until after Sam had supervised the girls' bedtime rituals and said goodnight. By then Hallie was on her second glass of wine and nibbling on her usual dinner fare — a breadstick or a carrot stick or a celery stick (anything but his stick, Sam thought). And other than complaints about a too-long meeting she'd attended that afternoon, and some details about her upcoming trip, the only other news she had was that she'd taken a phone message from Mary Ann Gray, who had invited her to join a dinner club.

Sam was on his hands and knees on the floor searching for the TV remote when Hallie told him this. "She invited *you*?" he said.

"Why wouldn't she? She's probably tired of all the soccer moms around here."

Sam must have spent too much time with the kids lately, because his first thought was that Mary Ann was supposed to be *his* friend.

"I checked my schedule and I should be home that night," Hallie said. "So I just may attend this occasion, take a walk on the dull side."

Sam gave up on the remote. His back hurt from bending over. Unless that ache was a prick of annoyance. From what? Some kind of childish jealousy of Hallie?

Hallie stood up. "I'm going to review my notes for my meetings tomorrow. Go to bed without me if you're tired."

"Don't go yet. Stay awhile and talk to me."

She sat back down. "About what?"

"I came up with a new idea for my novel today."

Chutney made a loud snuffling noise from where he lay asleep on the rug next to Sam.

"Feel like a brandy?" Hallie said.

"Sure."

She walked over to the bar they had set up on the far side of the room. "What's your new idea?"

"I'm still going with the restaurant cook main character, the guy who finds the body in the diner where he works, but —"

"Are you still setting the story in Philadelphia?"

"Yeah, why?"

"I think New York is a more exciting locale."

It wasn't enough that he'd agreed to her demand that the family move to the New York area when he'd sold his business, he was supposed to set his novel here, too? "A million novels are set in New York. And I know Philly better."

She brought over his glass of brandy, took a swallow of hers before she sat down. "Keep talking."

"Remember the hero's back story? That he'd taken a year off from college and gone to live in Nepal and teach English?" Similar to what Sam had done, when he was young.

Hallie didn't answer, just stared into her brandy glass.

"Do you remember his back story, or not?"

"Yes, I remember. I just said I remembered."

"No, you didn't. You didn't say anything."

"Yes, I did. You didn't hear me."

Oh. Maybe. "I was thinking today I might have him stay in southeast Asia after the teaching gig and spend some time in an ashram in India, in thrall to a maharishi. Did you ever know anyone like that? I did, in college. This guy went away one summer and came back a total convert, dressed head-to-toe in orange clothes. Which could be great background for the terrible secret that drives the mystery, don't you think?"

Hallie yawned. "What's the terrible secret, again?"

"I haven't decided. But it's definitely related to the samosa special that Simon —"

"Who's Simon?"

"He's the main character, the cook."

"I thought his name was Raoul."

"I changed it to Simon. But I still think the whole story should hinge on the samosa special that he offers on Fridays, off the menu, to impress the pretty young medical resident who drops in for breakfast after her all-night shifts at the hospital."

"Do you know anything about medical residents? About what they do, I mean?"

"Not really, but I might change her profession. Yeah, I probably will."

Hallie finished her brandy. "What's your title this week?"

"I'm debating between *Murder in the Kitchen* and *Samosa Special*. But what do you think about the maharishi idea?"

"It's not bad. Adds some cultural colour, makes your story more original. Are you going to work on it tonight?"

"I thought I might." He walked over to his desk, powered on his laptop. He'd stay up for a couple of hours and try for eight new pages. Or six. Four, even.

"Goodnight, then. That brandy really took the edge off. I think I'll pack and go to bed, review my notes on the plane." She got up, padded barefoot down the hallway, placed her glass in the kitchen sink, and left Sam alone with Chutney and the blank page on his computer screen.

Melina Pappas had grown up in the ranch-house subdivision part of Oakdale. She'd attended school with kids from the older, richer part, and befriended some, but she hadn't truly entered their world until she was fourteen and began babysitting for Mrs. Gray. Perky supermom Mrs. Gray, who liked her babysitters to be friendly and playful with children, and alert and competent with adults. Who said, the first time Melina came over, "Please call me Mary Ann."

Melina helped Kayla with homework, played video or computer games with Griffin, knew to leave Josh — who was only a year younger than her, and awkwardly so — alone. She served the kids meals like supermarket barbecued chicken, cut up, with mashed potatoes and frozen peas, ate a little herself, loaded the dishwasher after, rinsed the dishes first, wiped the kitchen table clean, and took neat, accurate phone messages.

With skills like these, Melina became a trusted and valued employee who kept babysitting the Gray kids even after she turned sixteen and could get a real job. And only partly because Mary Ann paid her double the going babysitting rate and gave her a hefty annual Christmas bonus. There was also the benefit that after the kids had gone to bed, Melina could do her homework in peace and quiet on an enormous dining table in an enormous dining room. And it helped that Mary Ann hadn't freaked out the day Melina showed up with her right eyebrow pierced.

Mary Ann had touched her own eyebrow. "Did it hurt?"

Melina wavered. She already regretted the piercing but she wouldn't be able to admit that for a while. Not after the scene her parents had made. "It hurt a little at the actual moment of piercing," she said. "But it doesn't hurt now."

Mary Ann came closer, examined the black-beaded ring. "A much better place for a ring than the nose, I'd say. I've never understood how people with nose rings deal with snot."

"I know. Or a tongue ring. How would you eat?"

Kayla came into the room then, and Mary Ann said, "Look, Kayla, see what Melina's done to her eyebrow? Isn't it cute?"

That kind of attitude made Mary Ann Melina's favourite babysitting mom, apart from Alice Maeda. Alice's daughter, Lavinia, was on the stubborn side, but looking after her was worth the effort, if only to get a taste of Alice's life, a life different from the Oakdale norm.

To start with, like Melina, Alice had a mixed ethnic background, being half-Asian and half-white. Unlike Melina's father though, she wasn't obsessed with her parents' cultures. Melina's father had never taken the family to Greece, but he made everyone shut up when anything Greece-related came on the news, and had insisted Melina learn Greek folk dancing when she was little. Melina doubted there'd be any heritage-related folk dancing in Lavinia's future, unless Lavinia demanded it.

Alice had travelled the world and lived in England for years, and yet she'd grown up right here in Oakdale. She was also living proof of a fact of life Melina had only recently begun to understand — that the rules taught in school don't apply to adults. Alice was a never-married single mother but she wasn't living on welfare or unemployed, she was a university professor.

Ethnic, but not obsessed with it, a single mother, a good job, and living in the better part of Oakdale — nothing about Alice added up to how things were supposed to be. Her appliances were old but she was in no hurry to replace them. She had no family room and an old TV. And instead of displaying museum Monet posters (Melina's mother's choice of wall art) or boring antique illustrations of pears and apples (Mary Ann Gray's style), there were framed black and white photographs up on the wall, photographs Alice had taken of strange and foreign places, places Melina hoped to visit one day, when she got out of Oakdale.

Melina told Alice she liked the pictures one weeknight after she'd babysat Lavinia while Alice stayed late in the city to go to a lecture.

"Thanks for noticing them," Alice said. "They're just some old snapshots I took or had taken years ago. Reminders of my youth. I dug them out and hung them up a few weeks ago on a night when I was feeling restless."

Melina walked over to the first photograph, pointed at it. "Where was this one taken?"

"That's Wroxeter, a Roman town site in England. I worked on those excavations for a couple of summers when I was in college."

"And the middle picture?"

"That's the temple of Apollo at Delphi in Greece. I never dug there, but I love those old Doric columns."

"It looks so ancient and old world," Melina said. "So unlike anything you'd find here." She moved to the third photograph in the series. "How about this one?"

"That's me in my youth. Nice hair style, huh? The picture was taken in France, at the site of a small Roman villa I helped excavate."

"You've been everywhere," Melina said.

"No, I haven't. I've never set foot in Asia or Africa. Or Australia. But I did spend a considerable amount of time in the U.K. and Europe before Lavinia was born."

Melina picked up her backpack. "I want to travel, too. I'm thinking I might take a grad trip next summer. Or even go to college abroad. You did that, didn't you?"

"Yes, I did, and loved it. I couldn't wait to get out of Oakdale when I was in high school. Where would you go?"

"I don't know yet. I'm still at the fantasy stage. But when I get to the planning stage, can we talk?"

"Sure," Alice said. "I could recommend a few destinations I'd go back to if I had the chance. More than a few."

6

June 1992

The wedding invitation listed the names of five different parents who requested the pleasure of Alice's company at the nuptials of Mary Ann and Bob, wording Alice suspected was meant to indicate how the wedding costs were being shared.

What she understood from it was that since their divorce, Mary Ann's dad had apparently married someone named Cynthia, and Mary Ann's mom had married no one at all. Also that Bob's real name was Robert, same as his dad. There was no explanation about why his parents had shortened Robert to Bob. Or why Bob had continued to call himself that, when he had a choice.

There was no explanation either for why, at the tender age of twenty-four, Mary Ann was throwing her youth away, marrying an investment banker, and committing to life as one of Them.

Alice's first stop on her arrival home for the wedding was her parents' house on Pine, where she endured the parental greeting, discovered there was no food in the house, and borrowed her mother's car to drive to McLean's, the local grocery store.

She'd picked out capers, olives, anchovies, and canned tomatoes to make a puttanesca sauce, and was searching in vain for a box of imported pasta when she was nudged by an oncoming shopping cart rounding the corner.

"I'm sorry," a woman's voice said, and Alice looked into the face of Mary Ann's mother.

"Hi, Mrs. MacAllister. It's me, Alice Maeda."

"Oh, hello, Alice. How nice to see you. Call me Sarah, please. When did you get in? Did you have a pleasant flight?"

Alice said she'd only just arrived, and asked after Mary Ann.

"Well, you know brides," Sarah said, though Alice didn't, not at all. "She's overseeing every detail. And she's brought a squad of her sorority sisters along to help. I can only take so much of them. This is my second trip to the store today."

Alice said, "So you couldn't talk her out of getting married?" She meant it as a joke.

Sarah's shoulders sagged. "You wouldn't have time for a coffee, would you?"

When they'd paid for their groceries, and sat down at Station Bakery on Main Street, Sarah said, "I think Mary Ann is too young to get married. But who knows? Maybe it'll last. Some marriages do."

"I was sorry to hear about your divorce. Has it been very difficult?"

"Yes and no. My real estate work helped me get through it. And I like living alone. Mary Ann doesn't understand that. Anyway. Are you coming to the shower?"

"What shower?"

"I mailed an invitation to your parents' house a few weeks ago. It's tomorrow evening. At my house."

"I've never been to a shower."

"This one's mixed — it's a Jack and Jill."

"And you're hosting it."

"It's what a mother does."

Alice tried to imagine her own mother hosting a wedding shower, but that meant imagining herself getting married. Both scenarios were too implausible. "Maybe I could help you with the food and drink. Make myself useful. What are you serving?"

"I'd love your help. It's going to be typical shower fare: a layered Mexican dip, a cream-cheese sandwich loaf, spinach dip in a bread bowl, a raw vegetable tray, some spiced nuts."

"I can't wait. I'm always up for new food experiences, and I've never heard of some of those things."

"Mary Ann wanted classic food. She's always been drawn to the conventional."

"What am I supposed to be showering the happy couple with?"

"Kitchen things, with a blue-and-white theme, for their new house in Oakdale. I brokered a deal for them on a big Colonial on Green Street, did you hear? It needs some work, but Bob's doing all right for himself. And they'll commute to the city."

"A husband and a Colonial house? What's happening here?"

"Mary Ann is trying to recreate her childhood. And conveniently forgetting that her father and I weren't happy for years before we separated." Sarah sighed. "I shouldn't have said that. Don't tell her I said that."

"I won't. But do you think that's how it is?"

"Why else would an intelligent young woman cling to these outdated ideas?"

Because, Alice remembered, Mary Ann had always wanted to fit in, and to succeed.

Sarah said, "Why don't you come back to the house with me now and see Mary Ann? If we're lucky, the sorority sisters will have gone."

* * *

"Look what I picked up at the store," Sarah called when they entered the house, and Mary Ann said, "What?" saw Alice, said, "Oh my god!" and ran to her.

Mary Ann's hair was blonder. That was the first thing Alice noticed. Blonder, and more done-looking. The face, too. More made up.

Mary Ann hugged her, though they had never hugged before, not that Alice could remember.

"You look just the same," Mary Ann said, and Alice couldn't bring herself to say, "So do you," so she just smiled, and nodded and said, "Well, well."

Mary Ann touched the curls at the back of her head. "You're probably thinking what's with the roller set, right? I've been trying out various hair options for the wedding. I can't decide. Should I wear it down, or up, with tendrils? What do you think? My friends just left, but they were definitely leaning toward up."

Before Alice could formulate a reply other than an incredulous "Did you say tendrils?" Mary Ann had moved on, prattling about her fingertip veil, and the rhinestone tiara that would hold it on her head, and her gown, which had cost a fortune, but was worth it because it was her dream dress, the one she'd always wanted, a Cinderella kind of dress, did Alice want to see it? And Alice had been led upstairs, to Mary Ann's old bedroom, where a huge white puffball hung on the outside of a closet door.

Alice said, "How do you sleep with it in the room? Aren't you afraid it'll come to life and eat you in the middle of the night?"

"Wait till you see the detail on it."

Alice sat on the bed, lit a cigarette, and watched Mary Ann use a fingering technique that she must have learned at wedding dress school to unroll the layers of plastic wrap that encased the dress.

"I won't take the cover all the way off, but what do you think? Can you see? It's made with Alençon lace. Do you love it?"

"It's beautiful," Alice said, and sneezed violently once. Twice.

Mary Ann replaced the cover with more intricate finger movements. "Are you all right?"

"I'm fine." Alice sneezed again, produced a tissue from a pocket, blew her nose. "It's probably an allergy. To American pollen."

"Don't give me that. You think I'm nuts to be getting married, don't you?"

Alice worked at keeping her face expressionless. "Not at all. What do you mean?"

"You and Mom both. I can tell."

"It's your life. What do you care what anyone else thinks?"

"That's the problem. I do care."

Alice looked around for an ashtray, didn't find one, went over to the window and cranked it open, ground out the burning cigarette on the brick sill. "Your mom told me about your new job — congratulations on that. I don't understand what software project management is, but it sounds impressive. I'm sure Miss Alexander would be proud."

"Thanks. I worked real hard to get it, and it's going to be tough. The company expects total commitment from their employees and long hours. But I'm looking forward to it."

"What about Bob?" It was a strain for Alice to say the name without putting ironic quotation marks around it, but she managed. "How will he feel about your long hours?"

"He works long hours too. We're going to be a real yuppie couple. He already has a BMW."

"No."

"Yes. Is that too gross for words?"

Alice smiled. "You're allowed."

Mary Ann hugged her again. "I'm so glad you came! How are your parents doing?"

"Same as always — lost in their music. If I know them, they've already forgotten I'm here."

"Don't you have their car?"

"Shit, I do. I should go." She got up and they went downstairs.

"You're coming to the party tomorrow, right?"

"Wouldn't miss it."

"Good. Bob and I thought having a pre-wedding party for all of our friends was a far better idea than having a separate stag and bridal shower."

"Men still have stags? I thought that went out with the eighties."

"They call them bachelor parties now. Bob's been to a few."

"With scantily clad women jumping out of cakes?"

"With strippers and gambling and dirty movies."

"Your party sounds much more grown-up."

"Thank you. I can't wait for you to meet Bob. I know you'll love him."

"And if I don't, that'll be okay, too."

Alice cleared the kitchen table of newspapers, magazines, and music scores, set it with three place settings, made a puttanesca sauce, served it over some linguine, and called her parents to come for dinner.

Her father came into the kitchen from his study, his eyes clouded, his mind still on the Chopin sonata he'd been playing, and her mother came from upstairs, where she'd just finished giving a violin lesson to an unfortunate child. When they were seated and eating, Alice said, "So, Mom, it turns out there's a wedding shower for Mary Ann and her fiancé tomorrow evening."

"That's nice."

"Mary Ann's mom says she sent me an invitation here, in the mail."

"Oh, Kenji," Alice's mother said, "that documentary on Yo-Yo Ma is on PBS tonight. At eight o'clock."

Alice's father almost spat. "You think I want to see Yo-Yo Ma?"

Forget the invitation. "Could you lend me something to wear to the shower? I only brought one nice dress with me."

"Sure. But all I have are my concert clothes. Would something like that be okay?"

"Black would be fine for the shower. It's like a cocktail party."

"Look in my closet and see what you can find. Will my clothes fit you?"

She didn't know? "I think so."

"Don't get me started on Yo-Yo Ma," her father said.

Wasn't it great to be back home.

Alice practised a fake laugh for the shower on the way over to Mary Ann's. To go with the phony smile she planned to use on Bob Gray, no matter how unpleasant or uptight he turned out to be.

She rang the bell, Mary Ann answered the door, and Alice handed her the gift bag containing the pair of blue-and-white hand-turned bowls she had spent the whole afternoon locating in the city.

"Come in, come in," Mary Ann said.

Alice entered, ready with the fake manners, but she didn't get a chance to use them, not at first, because Bob was on the phone in the front hall. A business call, Mary Ann told her, when she led Alice, on tiptoe, through the dining room — so as not to disturb Bob — and into the kitchen to say hi to Sarah.

Alice was left with a first impression of a tall, dark-haired man in a suit.

Mary Ann's hair was a mass of bouncy curls, and she was garbed in a flowered cotton poufy dress that was all pinks and oranges and yellows. In contrast to the severe black jersey number Alice had borrowed from her mother.

"Isn't the weather glorious?" Mary Ann said. "We can have the party outside." She pointed out the sliding glass doors to the flagstone patio, where several young women flitted about, arranging flowers, mixing punch in a big cut-glass bowl, speaking in high voices. "Come out and meet my college friends."

Fifteen minutes later, Alice retreated to the kitchen. Sarah was there alone, sticking stuffed olives into a big white brick of something on a serving platter.

Alice closed the sliding glass door behind her. "That was exhausting."

Sarah looked up. "You're too elegant to fit in with that crowd."

"Gee, thanks. But weren't you one of them yourself, in your day?"

"I'm afraid so. Chapter president. Just like Mary Ann."

Alice looked out the window at the scene in the garden. The girls were directing Mary Ann's brother in arranging garden chairs into conversation corners, whatever they might be. "Why are they all blonde?"

"They've discovered hair dye. And their natural colour isn't a beautiful deep shade like yours. More of a mousy brown like mine was."

Alice's took in Sarah's well-coiffed blonde head, thought of her mother's graying hair, long and always worn in a loose chignon, never noticed. "What can I do?"

"Come see this creation I've made."

Alice walked over. "It looks very neat. And rectangular. What is it?"

"It's a cream-cheese sandwich loaf."

"Please continue."

"Inside is a loaf of white bread, cut horizontally into four long slices. Between the slices lie three fillings: egg salad, tuna salad, and chopped pineapple in mayonnaise."

"Chopped pineapple? You don't say. Is that icing on it?"

"It's softened cream cheese. All that's left to do is complete the garnish. I think those olives look cute, don't you?"

"Very."

"Do you think I should add a heart shape, made of gherkins? In honour of the bride and groom?"

"Are you pulling my leg?"

"Maybe that's going too far."

"I don't know. With something like this, I don't think one can go far enough. Have you considered writing their initials in grated carrot?"

"The orange would be lovely against the white background."

"Within the gherkin heart."

Sarah smiled. "You're teasing me now."

"I'm not. I'm fascinated by this symbol of a foreign culture. And how often do I get an opportunity to do anthropological field work in my own backyard?"

"You're funny, Alice. Funny haha and funny strange."

"Tell me about it. And pass me the gherkins, please. I'd like to do the honours. Experience a cream-cheese loaf creation first-hand."

Some people at the shower seemed to think Alice was a waitress. Due to the black dress, the fact that she was handing around things on trays, the half-Asian face. She didn't care. She only minded people making ignorant assumptions about her when they were people she cared about. And this way, she could eavesdrop on conversations, make like a detective.

Which was how she heard two older women discussing Sarah. "Doesn't she look brave?" one said.

"Yes, but I wonder if she's been alone a bit too long."

"What do you mean?"

"A few weeks ago, I offered to introduce her to my brother-in-law's business partner. He's recently divorced. But she refused."

"She must not be ready."

"It's been four years since Jim left."

"That's not so long, when you haven't dated for twenty-five."

"Do you know what she said to me? She said, 'The last thing I want to do is start looking after another man.'"

"She said that?"

"Fairly nervy, I thought."

"I must call her. I know exactly what she means."

Alice also listened in on two young suited men who seemed to be Bob's work colleagues.

"How come there's no stag?" said the shorter one. "We've got to do something about this. Send the man out in style."

"Tonight?"

"After this thing's over. We'll get a few of the guys together, drive into the city, go to a strip club."

"Whoa, boy. The fiancée would not approve."

"So?"

"You're right. Let's do it."

After this, Alice wandered over to the girls' side to listen in on the sorority crowd, to see if they might be planning an equal-opportunity outing to a male strip joint for Mary Ann. But the only conversational topics she picked up on were career, honeymoon destinations, and china patterns.

When there was no food left to serve, and after Alice had tasted a slice of the cream cheese loaf and found it to be too exotic for her taste, the only thing missing from her shower experience was to meet the groom-to-be. From a distance, Alice had seen that he was neither handsome nor ugly, neither fat nor thin. He was pleasant-looking, but he was no Jake Stewart, which was not a bad thing. He seemed confident and outgoing — he worked the room, laughing with this group or that. He'd hardly given Alice a second glance when she'd come around with a tray of cheese balls. He hadn't wanted any.

About two hours into the party, after the toasts and the opening of presents, but before the drifting out had begun, Mary Ann took Alice over to him. "I've wanted you two to meet for so long," she said.

Alice shook Bob's hand. "At last I get to meet the famous Bob."

"And you're Alice." He made direct eye contact, but Alice saw no warmth there, only formality. "It was good of you to make the trip over for the wedding," he said. "I know it meant a lot to Mary Ann."

Alice said, "I had to be here to make sure Mary Ann wasn't making a big mistake. Another one of her jokes."

Bob's eyes went cold for a split second. There was no other sign of her comment having any impact. Other than Bob placing an arm around Mary Ann's shoulders, pulling her close to him, and saying, "As long as you don't feel displaced, Alice. Mary Ann has promised to put me first above everybody. Haven't you, honey?"

Before she could stop herself, Alice said, "That doesn't sound like a very modern attitude."

Mary Ann cut in. "Don't listen to him. He's joking. He has a great sense of humour."

Bob said, "I'm glad Mary Ann introduced us. All evening I thought you were the hired help."

That was the cue to pull out her ready-made smile. And to be relieved that no one present could read her mind.

* * *

Alice perfected the fake smile at the wedding. She held Sarah's hand extra long in the receiving line, raised her glass dutifully for the toasts, and couldn't wait to get out of the country club after the reception. Out of Oakdale, out of the U.S., and back to England, where she completed her master's degree, followed it up with a Ph.D., secured herself a lecturing job, ran archaeological digs during the summers, took lovers when she felt like it, and didn't get married.

And didn't return to Oakdale. Why should she? She saw her parents once a year when they came to London en route to concert destinations in Europe. Her friendship with Mary Ann became little more than an annual Christmas email exchange. Alice had her own life, thank you, the one she'd built all by herself, and it suited her just fine.

Until Lavinia came along.

7

September 2010

On the Monday before the first dinner club meeting, Mary Ann's son Josh came into the kitchen at eight a.m. and said, "Mom, can I use the car this Saturday?"

Kayla walked in behind him and sat down at the counter. "Could I have breakfast, please?"

Mary Ann passed a glass of orange juice and a bowl of cereal over to Kayla and said to Josh, "This Saturday? No."

"Why not?"

"For a variety of reasons."

"What was the point of getting my licence if you won't ever let me have the car?"

Mary Ann said, "I don't you want driving around with your friends on the back roads on a Saturday night."

"I'm glad you trust me, Mom." His voice rose in volume with every word. "But how about asking me why I want the car, instead of assuming the worst?"

Mary Ann shut her eyes a second, clenched her jaw, searched for patience. If she had any left after dealing with Griffin's truculence, Kayla's bossiness, the stresses of her new job, and the brittle shell that was left of her marriage. Not to mention the upcoming dinner club meeting. To Mary Ann's dismay, Hallie Smith had intercepted the invitation meant for

Sam, and accepted it for herself. Mary Ann couldn't very well disinvite her now. Maybe she could poison her wine on the night of, to make sure she wouldn't come back?

"Hello? Did you hear what I just said?" asked Josh.

"Of course I did. What *do* you want the car for?"

"To go to a movie at the mall after my basketball game. Is that boring and safe enough for you?"

"Who with?"

"FORGET IT, OKAY? FORGET THE WHOLE FUCKING THING!"

He stormed out, and Mary Ann busied herself putting away the box of cereal in the cupboard so that Kayla wouldn't see the tears pricking at her eyes and the smoke coming out of her ears.

When they'd heard Josh's bedroom door slam upstairs, Kayla said, "He wants the car to go out with a girl."

"He does? How do you know?"

Josh had been secretive about his dealings with girls, had not yet dated any one girl as far as Mary Ann knew. Though what did she know? Did kids date anymore? Or only hang out?

Kayla slurped the milk in her spoon. "He left his laptop on last night with his IM windows open when he took a shower, and I read the whole conversation."

"You shouldn't have done that, Kayla." Though Mary Ann might have done it herself, given the chance.

"Six of them are going — three girls and three boys."

Mary Ann leaned against the counter. "I see."

"How come you let him swear at you?"

"It's not a question of letting him."

"Dad would yell if Josh talked to him that way."

"Dad's not here right now. And how I deal with Josh shouldn't concern you."

Kayla pushed aside her bowl. "I'm going to brush my teeth. Don't forget I need money for the school photos."

Mary Ann tidied the kitchen, put an envelope with the school-photo cheque in Kayla's backpack, kissed her, and sent her out the door to be picked up by the carpool mother who drove Kayla on Mondays. How soon would Kayla give Mary Ann a hard time about every word she said? Thank god Griffin had already left for an early morning football practice. Thank god Bob wasn't around to complicate matters, either.

She girded her psyche, went upstairs, and knocked on Josh's door. "Josh?"

Angrily, "What?"

"Aren't you going to school today?"

"I have a first-period spare on Mondays. Don't you even know that yet?"

Mary Ann felt a wave of hurt ripple through her, and fought a strong impulse to kick the wall and slam a few doors of her own. "Could you just let me in for a second?"

He stomped across the floor, unlocked his door, stomped back to his bed, and flopped onto it.

She sat down in his desk chair and tried not to look at the mess of papers and books and bits of junk scattered across his desk. "I'm sorry about saying no to the car without hearing the whole story first. Let's start again."

He made no reply, but she couldn't hear any music coming from the headphones he wore — a promising sign. She said, "I don't know if you remember that I'm having the first meeting of my dinner club here on Saturday night."

"So you won't need your car."

"Not after five o'clock, no. But your basketball game won't be over until nine or nine-thirty."

"Nine-fifteen at the latest. It's only an exhibition game."

"I've arranged for Dad to take you to the game —"

"Why?"

"Why not?"

"Since when does Dad come see me play?"

"Josh —"

"Can I have the car after my game or not?"

She had to ask. "Are you going to drink or smoke weed that night?"

The look he gave her was filled with contempt. "No."

Maybe he hadn't started drinking or smoking yet. Not regularly, anyway. "Fine. You can have my car. After Dad brings you home from the game, and as long as you're home by midnight."

"Midnight? For fuck's sake, the movie won't be over by then!"

One more yelled statement and Mary Ann would snap in two. Her top half would topple onto the floor and roll over to rest beside Josh's bookcase, and her bottom half would stay sitting upright, like half of a Lego person, until Josh reached out with his foot and kicked it off the chair, too.

She pulled her halves together and cheered herself by thinking about the dinner club. In a few days she should be able, for one evening, to enjoy herself, to feel liked and sought after. Versus unwanted, witchlike, and hated. She said, "What time do you propose to come home?"

His eyes turned almost reasonable. "Two?"

He could have suggested three or four. She'd stayed out later at his age and been drunk and having sex besides. "Here's the deal," she said. "My final offer. No drinking. Seatbelts to be worn by all people riding in the car. And home no later than two."

"Fine." He still sounded angry, but less so.

She got up, considered and rejected the idea of suggesting he use his spare period time to study, and turned to go.

"I don't know why you have to make everything so hard on yourself, Mom," Josh said, from the bed. "Why didn't you just say yes the first time?"

When Tom Gagliardi had received all the necessary approvals to restore the Oakdale train station and develop Main Street, Alice had volunteered her time to the project as a historical consultant with the thought that she could easily fit an occasional meeting or site visit into her schedule. Silly Alice. The reality was that she could do very little in her post-Lavinia life without help.

That's how she came to be knocking on Sarah's door at six o'clock on a Tuesday evening after a meeting with Tom and the site manager. She was fifteen minutes earlier than she'd said she'd be when she'd asked Sarah to watch Lavinia, but she still felt guilty.

"Come in," Sarah called out. "Door's open."

Alice walked in, to the smell of fresh-baked muffins, the sound of one of Lavinia's CDs playing on Sarah's stereo, and the sight of Lavinia dancing in Sarah's living room.

Lavinia ran over and jumped into Alice's arms. "Mommy!" After a good long hug, she jumped down again, and resumed dancing and singing.

Alice said to Sarah, "Thanks so much for picking her up from daycare."

Sarah waved her thanks away, stepped into the kitchen, and started wiping the counter. "I'm happy to help any time you have a conflict, I'm not busy. I gave her dinner, by the way, some macaroni and cheese. I hope that's okay."

"That's terrific. Thank you."

"How was your meeting?"

"Short. But it was good to see Tom Gagliardi while he was in town."

Sarah pulled out a piece of aluminum foil and wrapped up some muffins. "What's he like?"

"A little eccentric, but a charmer."

"Will I meet him on Saturday night?"

"He's supposed to be there."

"Wasn't Mary Ann clever to organize this dinner club?"

"Yes, she was," Alice said, though she wasn't sure clever was the right word to describe Mary Ann's dinner club scheme. Devious, maybe. "I'm not sure I remember how to act in a social setting. Will you nudge me if I act gauche? If I put my feet on the table or start scratching myself?"

Lavinia danced over to Alice's side. "Can I build a fort in the living room?"

"Upstairs at our place, honey."

Sarah handed Alice the package of muffins. "It'll be good for both of us to go to a party, get out of our ruts."

Alice thanked her again, went up to her own apartment, helped Lavinia pile up the sofa and chair cushions in the middle of the rug, made herself a tomato sandwich, and sat down to eat it.

Was she in a rut? A rut implied boredom, and Alice wasn't bored. Exhausted and frantic and always running late and often certain she had forgotten to complete some vital task such as buying milk or doing the laundry so Lavinia's current favourite item of clothing was clean and dry and available for wear, yes. But not bored.

Alice washed and dried her dinner dishes, asked if she could inspect the fort, crawled inside and flicked on the flashlight, listened to Lavinia tell a silly ghost story punctuated with laughter, and felt a surge of affection for this child she'd built her life around.

All right, then. When was the last time she'd done anything new and different? Other than listening to Lavinia's music, reading new children's books, and learning the astonishing number of ways a four-year-old girl can adorn herself with hair accessories and nail polish? That Alice had recently splurged on some new underwear and socks probably didn't count. Either did ordering a tuna sandwich on multigrain bread for lunch instead of her standard deli salad. The dinner club could prove to be a novel experience, but only in a voyeuristic sort of way. And though she'd enjoyed working with Tom on the station restoration project, how much longer would it last? How long until the development would be complete and Alice would return to her same old routine of teaching, commuting, and Lavinia-raising?

Until she climbed right into that rut of hers and dwelled in it, in other words.

At five, Danielle served Alex a dinner of steamed rice, oven-fried chicken tenders with gluten-free breadcrumbs, and a Caesar salad without croutons. "And can I have a cupcake for dessert tonight?" he said. "Because Caitlin's mom brought in birthday cupcakes for the class today with gummi worms and icing and coloured sprinkles."

Danielle said okay fine, took one of his cupcakes out of the freezer, and reminded herself not to buy a Christmas gift for Alex's teacher. Rather than giving Danielle the list of birthdays she'd asked for at the beginning of the year, the teacher had suggested that a box of Alex's non-perishable, store-bought cookies be kept in the classroom cupboard instead. So that when the other children ate fancy decorated birthday treats, Alex could enjoy a nice, hard gluten-free biscuit.

At five-thirty, a hungry Ethan was dropped off from his karate lesson by a friend's mother. Ethan didn't like salad, so his vegetable of the day was steamed broccoli. His chicken was breaded with regular breadcrumbs, his rice the same as Alex had eaten — steamed. Danielle and Benny ate rice, too — arborio, cooked by Danielle into a saffron risotto with white wine and shallots and sautéed sage leaves. Alongside was a mash of rutabaga, carrot, and sweet potatoes made with brown sugar and butter. And a salad of strawberries, the last of the summer tomatoes, and some buffalo mozzarella, all drizzled with olive oil and balsamic vinegar.

When she'd cleared the kids' dishes, called Benny for dinner, and given Ethan, at his insistence, one of Alex's cupcakes, Danielle sat down at last to her own meal.

Benny said, "Great piece Adele had in the *Times* today. She made that new restaurant sound so good I was tempted to try it. And you know how I feel about restaurant food."

Danielle bit into some cheese and tomato, savoured the mingled tastes on her tongue.

"You talk to her lately?" Benny said.

"My mother? No. Why?"

"Just wondered. If I were you, I'd call and tell her when you like her column. I'm sure she'd love to hear it."

"But I don't like her columns. Did you see that crap today about her fond childhood memories of braised rabbit and sweetbreads? Read that and you'd think she'd grown up in France instead of Oklahoma."

Benny forked in some risotto. "I still think you should call her once in a while. Old people want to hear from their children. When Ethan and Alex are grown-ups I sure hope they call me every day."

Danielle said nothing. She'd heard and disagreed with Benny's views on this topic before, and there was no use repeating her belief that her relationship with Adele was her own business. So. Should she make succotash for the dinner club or glazed baby vegetables? The baby vegetables would be less work — on a cooking effort scale of one to ten, they'd rate about a four, versus the succotash's six. Though anything above a three was still more kitchen duty than Danielle could bear, ever since she'd passed about the five thousand mark in number of meals cooked. Or had the four thousandth meal done her in?

"When was the last time you saw Adele, anyway?" Benny said.

"I had lunch with her in the city in June." She would combine baby carrots and cauliflowers, some finger-size zucchini, cipollini onions, pattypan squash, and young Brussels sprouts, cook the whole lot in butter, glaze them with honey, sprinkle over some fresh thyme. Peeling the onions would be a bore, but worth the drudgery in exchange for a night out, a night off.

"Anyway," Benny said, "I'm sure you could cook circles around that restaurant chef, whoever he is."

"I could not."

"Yes, you could. I've never met the professional chef who can cook as well as you."

Too bad. Because if he had, they might eat out once in a while. She said, "That dinner club party is this Saturday."

"What time?"

"Seven, until I don't know, maybe ten?"

"So I'll have to put the kids to bed?"

"Guess so."

"And what about my dinner?"

"Your dinner?"

"And dinner for the kids. What will we eat while you're out partying in Oakdale?"

Was now the time to break the habits of eighteen years of marriage? Was now the time to tell Benny to look after his own dinner, for crying out loud, and feed the kids, too? Danielle put down her fork. "You could take the kids out to eat at the diner in town."

"And what about me? What am I supposed to eat?"

She pushed her plate away. "Do you think you could look after your own meal that night?" For a radical change.

Benny sighed. "If I have to, I have to. I just wish I knew why you want to go to this dinner club. Why suffer through everyone else's mediocre cooking when you could stay home and feast on your own?"

Two days before the first dinner club meeting, Tom told Kate that he hadn't yet decided what to bring. "What do you think?" he said. "Would a fresh ciabatta loaf from Sullivan Street Bakery do?"

Kate felt her shoulders hunch up at the mere mention of the dinner club. Or was it Tom's apparent eagerness to attend it that made her crabby? "Do that if you want people to think you can't cook. *I'm* the type who brings bread."

"Maybe I should make a coulibiac of salmon, with a whole salmon."

"Because that would take no time at all. Have you considered roasting a suckling pig?"

"Surely you jest."

"How about a baked Alaska?"

"Kate."

"You could always do individual wild rice timbales, with asparagus stalks sticking straight up out of the top."

"What bothers you about this?"

"Nothing."

"I can tell."

Why *was* she so bugged? "I just think that if these people lived in the city, they could find more meaningful activities to occupy themselves with than competing with food. They could go to a restaurant."

"You think that because you don't cook."

"I have better things to do."

"Speaking of people who don't cook, Hallie Smith appears to be attending the first meeting. Her name was on the reminder email I received today."

"She'll probably get her nanny to cook something."

"Perhaps I should make steamed pickerel with ginger and oyster sauce."

"Drive that out there and your car will stink for days," Kate said. "Now leave me alone. I've got work to do."

The next day, she called Hallie at her office. "Tom's been invited out to a dinner club in Oakdale this weekend," she said, "told not to bring me, and now he hears you're going."

"Tom's coming to Mary Ann Gray's dinner club? How bizarre. I assumed it would be only women."

"What's the story?"

"To tell you the truth, I was surprised to be invited. We working mothers don't mix much with the stay-at-home moms, and Mary Ann Gray is a real Mother Superior out here."

"Doesn't she work for Tom's computer guy?"

"Does she? I can't keep up with these women's little part-time jobs."

"Can you tell me what's she like, at least?"

"She's okay-looking, if you're into the hearty athletic type. Sam's friendly with her: they talk on the sidelines at soccer games."

"And what food are you bringing to this occasion?"

"Vietnamese salad rolls. There's a place near my office that makes them. I'll buy them Friday and bring them home, pass them off as my own."

"That's my Hallie."

"You're not worried, are you?"

"About what?"

"About a horny housewife making a play for Tom."

"I wasn't, no. Should I be?"

"No. Tom seems oblivious to the lure of extramarital sex."

"How would you know?"

"All I'm saying is that in general, his eyes don't rove. You know whose do, though? This Mary Ann's husband. His name's Bob, or Bill, or something. And he was giving me total bedroom eyes at the last country club dance. The guy has thinks-he's-a-player-but-he's-not written all over him."

That was her Hallie, all right. "So you represent the lure of extramarital sex? Is that what you're saying?"

"To people of a certain type, yeah. And Tom's not that type."

"Tom does have his little affectations of speech, that verbal overcompensation he makes for having grown up working class. Some women might misconstrue that as flirting."

"Tell you what. I'll keep an eye on him for you at the party. And if I see any predators closing in, I'll intervene. Though he's probably as innocent as Sam would be in that situation."

"I'm glad to hear Sam doesn't have a roving eye either."

"Of course not. He's married to me, isn't he?"

Alice joined the line for the supermarket express lane holding a basket that contained a carton of eggs, a package of sliced mushrooms, a bunch of arugula, and a tube of goat cheese. In fifteen minutes, she'd pick up Lavinia from daycare, take her home, whip up a mushroom omelette and a salad for them both, and dinner would be taken care of. Provided the lane would live up to its name and move along.

The man in front of her placed his one item, a cellophane-wrapped bunch of lilies, on the conveyor belt, and she caught a glimpse of his profile. He looked familiar.

He was bald, and fortyish, and on the thin side, and he was wearing a leather jacket over a T-shirt, jeans, and Vans. Was he a worker from the station site? A hardware store clerk? Her mailman, out of uniform? She took a step to the side, checked him out from that angle, and still couldn't place him.

When she finally figured it out, she stifled a gasp, leaned into his line of sight, and said, "Jake? Is that you? Jake Stewart?"

He turned around. "I'm afraid so. Hi." He smiled at her, raised his arm, and placed the palm of his hand on the top of his head. As if to see if any hair had grown back since the last time he'd checked.

That was why she hadn't recognized him right away — because he no longer had his flowing blond locks, his alpha male mane. That, plus he was twenty-odd years older. But did he remember her? "It's me, Alice Maeda," she said. "From kindergarten and elementary and middle and high school."

"I know who you are," he said.

"Yeah? Prove it."

"You were my partner in eighth grade for the deathless swing dance performance our class did to 'In the Mood.' The most awkward, embarrassing dance performance ever."

Alice had forgotten about the swing dancing until that moment, forgotten he'd been her partner. But as soon as he mentioned it, she remembered an old photo her mother had filed away somewhere. The picture was of a gawky, pre-pubescent Alice, in costume — wearing a sweater, a homemade poodle skirt, and white sneakers. Her eyebrows were thick and unplucked and caterpillarish, her hair untamed. How shy she'd been then, and how ignorant of tween social norms. How mortified to be partnered with Jake, who was already popular, to have to touch him, and pretend to be comfortable touching him.

But wait — he'd felt awkward and embarrassed too?

The cashier rang up the lilies. Jake handed over some cash, and he said, "I'm here to see my mother." He held up the lilies. "These are for her. What are you doing in town?"

"I moved back four years ago, from England. I work in Manhattan, and live out here with my daughter. I'm about to pick her up from the daycare at Oakdale Elementary."

"So you get to relive your life all over again through her? At the same schools, in the same neighbourhood? That should be a trip. I wonder if the middle school still makes eighth graders learn how to jive. Probably not, huh." His hair was gone, but he still had a mischievous grin.

Alice paid for her groceries, they walked out to the parking lot together, she asked Jake what he was up to these days, and he told her he lived in Brooklyn, and had a job leading bike tours in Europe and Asia for an adventure travel company.

"I haven't followed a typical or ambitious career path," he said, "but I like travel, and I've never wanted a desk job. Even if some people — most people — think I'm pissing my life away."

"Pissing your life away? It sounds to me like you're living the dream." And living a life that was better than being mired in Oakdale. Alice looked at her watch. "Shit, I have to run, I'll be late to pick up Lavinia. It was good to see you, though." She meant it. The years had tempered him well, softened his hard edges.

"Good to see you too." He touched his head again. "We should have lunch sometime, in the city, and continue the conversation."

"I'd like that."

They exchanged numbers — entered them into each other's cell phones — and parted, but not before he said, "You look great, by the way. And like you haven't aged a day since you were the pretty hippie girl who got suspended for smoking in class."

She warmed herself with that compliment all the way to the daycare and home.

Mary Ann called Alice at the five o'clock on the date of the first Dinner Club meeting. "Can you come over early," she said, "before anyone else?"

"As soon as Lavinia's finished eating her dinner, we'll leave. Are you okay?"

"No. I'm a basket case. I was never this nervous when I entertained Bob's clients. I've already sweat through two shirts."

"Take a few calming breaths and tell me: is the table set?"

"Yes."

"Is Melina on her way?"

"Due at six-thirty."

"Is Bob out of the house?"

"He's safely on the road to basketball with Josh."

"Are you buffed and polished?"

"I spent a full hour on the hair and makeup."

"And created a natural healthy glow?"

"No, I created a deathlike mask, what do you think? I didn't overdo it. Did I? Shoot. I'll go scrape off some foundation right now."

"Sounds like you have the situation well in hand, and there's nothing to worry about."

"Yeah, but am I a total fool to be doing this? Will either of the males present find me remotely attractive? Will Hallie Smith figure out that I meant to invite her husband, not her?"

"You're going to have a swell time." Alice crossed her fingers behind her back. "Everyone is."

"Just get here as soon as you can."

The First Dinner Club Meeting:
September 25th, 2010

Host: Mary Ann Gray

Menu

Hors d'oeuvres

Smoked Salmon Tortilla Roll-ups	Lisa Carsten
Vietnamese Salad Rolls	Hallie Smith
Squash, Goat Cheese & Toasted Pistachio Crostini	Tom Gagliardi

Mains

Glazed Baby Vegetables	Danielle Pringle
Chinese Noodles with Meat Sauce	Alice Maeda
Ceviche	Phoebe Morales
Grilled Shrimp with Pesto	Mary Ann Gray

Desserts

Raspberry Pie	Sarah MacAllister
Lemon Poppyseed Cake	Amy Millson
Beer & Wine	Drew Wacyk

8

Danielle had been apprehensive about the dinner club meeting — about what to wear and what to bring, and should she park the truck around the corner where no one would see it?

Benny didn't understand. "It's just dinner with a bunch of women," he said. "What are you worried about?"

Yes, Mary Ann was welcoming and warm when Danielle walked in — she oohed and ahed over her platter, asked where she'd found the beautiful baby vegetables, and expressed amazement that Danielle had grown them herself. But then she'd gone off to greet Lisa and Amy, two school moms so alike Danielle couldn't tell them apart, and left her alone, surrounded by interior-design-magazine décor and people wearing dress-up clothes. Danielle had known enough to leave her jeans at home, but she wasn't prepared for the chicness of Mary Ann and her friends, of the tall, elegantly attired man who could have walked out of the Sunday Styles pages, or the glossy blonde in business attire who Danielle ended up beside during the drinks part of the evening.

The blonde introduced herself as Hallie Smith, threw back some wine, and said, "Are you a stay-at-home mom?"

"Partly," Danielle said. "I also run a produce-growing

business. I just told Mary Ann about it. I've known her for years, and she never knew I had a farm."

Hallie smiled in a way Danielle didn't find friendly. "You're a farmer?"

"Of a kind. I grow heirloom vegetables, flowers, a variety of lettuces and greens. All organic."

Another gulp of wine. "How fascinating."

"It's satisfying work."

Hallie said, "I'm a firm believer in the rewards of hard work. I only wish Sam, my husband, felt the same way. He used to be in the food business. He was the Samosa King before he sold out."

Danielle wasn't sure she'd heard correctly. Sam the Samosa King? And sold out how? She pictured compromised samosas, stuffed with substandard fillings. "What does he do now?"

"Nothing. Hangs around the house all day and pretends to be writing a novel called *Murder in the Kitchen*. Stupid generic title."

Danielle wondered how Hallie's underlings handled being spoken to so dismissively. Because there had to be underlings. "And what do you do?" Danielle said.

"I'm the director of finance at Morris Communications." When Danielle showed no sign of recognizing the company name, Hallie said, "We publish magazines."

"How interesting."

"What did you say your job was again?"

Danielle stammered, "I grow vegetables. And lettuces?"

Hallie walked away. "Of course. Nice talking to you." She held up her glass. "I have to get a refill."

Mary Ann came up next. "Have you met people? I've been telling everyone you grew the food you brought. I can't believe I never knew you did that. Are you having a good time? Don't answer yet. Tell me after you've eaten."

Danielle said, "That woman Hallie said something about her husband that I didn't understand."

"He's Sam Orenstein. Do you know him? He's around the school a lot — he drives his kids to and from. They have two girls — Jessica and Annabelle. And a black Portuguese water dog."

"What did she mean when she called him the Samosa King?"

"That was the name of his company, out of Philadelphia. Still is, but it doesn't belong to him anymore. He sold it before moving up here. It produces a whole line of Indian foods — samosas, pakoras, breads, curries."

"And here I thought every man in Oakdale except Benny was an investment banker or lawyer."

"What does Benny do?"

"He's a vet, and a dog breeder."

"He is? I never knew that, either. Excuse me a minute, would you? It's almost time to serve."

"Can I help?" Danielle said, hoping not.

"No, I'm fine, thanks. But have you met my mother yet? She'd love to talk gardening with you, I'm sure. Let me introduce you."

Alice helped Mary Ann lay out the food in the dining room. "How are you holding up?"

"Okay so far." Mary Ann set down a large platter of shrimp on the sideboard. "Is my face flushed?"

Mary Ann's face *was* flushed. A bright pink spot of anxiety burned on each cheek. "Your face is fine," Alice said. "And the party is going well. People are talking to each other. I always find that incredible."

"Have you met everyone?"

"I think so. I like Phoebe. She's very direct."

"And young."

"Drew seems nice, too."

Mary Ann pointed to the dish Alice had brought — fine egg noodles, covered in a brown meat sauce and garnished with julienne slices of cucumber and carrot. "What's that called, again?"

"Chinese Noodles with Meat Sauce. I got the recipe from an English cookbook I bought years ago."

"What's in it?"

"Ground pork, ginger, hoisin sauce, and lots of garlic. You might want to avoid it if you plan to get close to Tom or Drew later."

Twenty minutes later, Alice joined the buffet line behind Tom and heard him introduce Drew to Hallie. "He's the local computer expert," Tom said. "When not busy with the set-up and maintenance of home and office computers, he consults for me on the Main Street project."

Hallie looked Drew over and placed a hand on his arm. "We've been having trouble with the kids' computers at home. I think they need more memory. Do you handle problems like that?"

"I could tell you what to buy and talk you through the installation over the phone."

"But that's not the only thing. My husband's printer is also acting up. Have you got your food? Come sit beside me at the table, we'll talk about it. Do you work weekends?" She led him away.

Alice and Tom reached into the basket of napkin-wrapped forks at the same time.

"What did you contribute to this bounty, Alice?" Tom said.

She pointed. "The noodles."

"Do you know I've been searching for a specific variation on that dish for years? It forms the basis of some Proustian memories of mine that were formed in a Szechwan restaurant in Montreal in the early eighties."

"Really? The closest thing I have to a Proustian food memory is the recollection of a very fine batch of fish and chips I once ate in an English seaside town. But I bet fish and chips are too mundane to qualify as Proustian, huh."

"You like to mock me, don't you?"

Alice winced. "No, I'm just bad at social chit-chat. That was my feeble attempt to be amusing. No mock intended. Let's change topics. Ask me about the station."

They made their way to the table and sat down where their place cards were set, side by side.

"How is the station faring?" Tom said. "I haven't been by in a few days."

"The drywall's all down, the plasterers are starting in a few days, and the clean-up crew found some seventy-year-old lost-and-found boxes tucked away in the basement."

"An archeological find, as it were?"

"Of a sort. I haven't gone through the boxes yet, but I thought I would see if there's anything interesting we might be able to set up in a display case once we're done. Like a first edition of an old novel, or a vintage sweater."

"Your noodles are delicious. Exactly how I remember them. The piquancy of the sauce makes a delightful contrast with the crunch of the cucumber."

"Thanks. Do I have the okay to go through the lost and found stuff?"

"Do you need my okay?"

"The building and contents belonged to you last time I checked."

"To the company."

"Same difference."

"You have my okay."

* * *

Melina was in the kitchen whipping cream to go with the raspberry pie when Mary Ann's husband came in the back door. He returned her hi, and said, "How's the party going?" but Melina could tell he didn't care.

"It's going great," she said.

He opened the fridge, pulled out a bottle of beer, said, "I'll hide out upstairs," and took off. Real personable guy. No wonder Mary Ann didn't include him in her social life and wanted to hang out instead with the likes of the tall distinguished-looking man and the hipster hottie guy Melina had seen earlier.

Josh came next, dragging a sports bag across the floor. He stopped when he saw Melina. "What are you doing here?"

"Helping your mom. How'd your game go?"

"We won by fourteen."

"Did you get much playing time?"

Josh sat down on a kitchen stool. "About twenty minutes."

"Good for you. You still going out tonight?"

He looked wary. "Why?"

"Your mom gave me the car keys and some instructions for you."

"Instructions? Shit. She won't stop harassing me about taking the car."

Melina ejected the cream-covered beaters from the stand mixer, held one out to him. "You want?"

He took it and licked the cream off and she did the same to hers. She had just figured out that there was something porny about them doing this together when Josh said, "So where are the keys?"

"Aren't you going to shower first?"

He pointed to his wet hair. "Duh. I showered at the gym."

So he had. And either the shower or the exercise or both had flushed his face, brought blood close to the surface of his skin, made him look vulnerable. And kind of sweet. "Okay, then." She picked up the keys from the counter, handed them over, pulled a piece of paper out of her jeans pocket. "I'm supposed to remind you that everyone has to wear their seatbelts."

"Yeah, yeah, and no drinking, and be home by two. I know."

"Where are you going, anyway?"

Josh dropped the licked beater into the sink. "To a movie."

Look at him: almost seventeen and awkward and about to go out with some younger girl who would probably act as thoughtless and immature as Melina had at that age.

"Be good, now," she said. "Don't be an idiot like I used to be."

His cheeks stained redder still and he smiled, and Melina noticed his good teeth, noticed the absence of the braces he'd worn as long as she could remember. When had they come off? Must have been a few years ago, now. But she couldn't remember the last time she'd seen him smile.

"I don't know why everyone's so convinced I'm going to do something stupid," Josh said. "I'm pretty boring."

"Don't call it boring, call it sensible. I wish I'd been more sensible a couple of years ago. I wish I'd gone to the movies with someone like you instead of doing some of the stupid shit that I did."

He fumbled with the keys, opened the door to go. "Tell Mom I'll do everything she says." He winked. "Maybe."

He wasn't a bad kid, that Josh. And nothing like his dad.

Alice came down from upstairs and found Mary Ann in the kitchen pouring coffee into a carafe. "I'm in shock," she said. "Lavinia fell asleep in Kayla's room."

"Why don't you let her stay over?"

"She's never slept away from me in her whole life."

"This can be the first time."

"What if she wakes up in the middle of the night?"

"I'll try to soothe her, and if I can't, I'll call you."

The idea of a night alone was vastly appealing, provided Alice could get over the feeling of guilt associated with it. "Are you sure?"

"Positive. Is Melina coming down?"

"Soon, she said. She's playing a video game with Griffin."

"Then while we're alone, I have to say that I couldn't believe how Hallie monopolized Drew during dinner, and how you cozied up to Tom."

"I was talking to him about the station."

"So it wasn't you who changed the place cards?"

"Someone changed them?"

"I didn't think you'd done it. Hallie must have switched them when she wanted to sit beside Drew. Good thing there's still dessert ahead, in case I want to make a move."

"I won't talk to any males for the rest of the evening, I promise."

"You know who I ended up spending some time with, though?"

"The one who brought the baby vegetables?"

"Yeah. Danielle. I like her."

"Does that mean you won't make a play for her husband?"

"I think I'll stick with Hallie's instead. And anyway, I've seen Danielle's husband. He's round and bald."

"Oh god. That reminds me."

"What? Let's take this coffee in."

Alice followed Mary Ann into the dining room. "You'll never guess who I ran into the other day."

Mary Ann set down the coffee, sang out, "Here's coffee. Anyone for tea?"

"Me, please," Alice said, and they returned to the kitchen, found Melina at the sink, rinsing dishes.

"Jake Stewart," Alice said.

Mary Ann plugged in the kettle. "I haven't seen him in years. How'd he look?"

"That's what made me think of him, when you were talking about baldness. He's extremely so. Hairline up to here." Alice indicated a spot on the top of her head.

"And the rest of him?"

"He's noticeably lined in the face. You know how some fair complexions go?"

"Like mine?"

"No, like his."

"You don't make him sound very attractive."

"On the contrary, I prefer him with no hair to fling around." Alice made eye contact with Melina. "Melina, this must sound awful to you, the way we're talking."

Melina closed the tap. "Sorry. What did you say? I couldn't hear over the sound of the water."

Alice said it was okay, never mind.

"Where'd you run into him?" Mary Ann said.

"At the supermarket. He was in Oakdale to visit his parents, but he lives in Brooklyn. We might go for lunch sometime."

"Is he single?"

"I didn't ask him, Mary Ann."

"Maybe I'll come along if you meet him for lunch. I'm curious to see how he's changed."

"Sure," Alice said, even as her subconscious mind startled her by saying not on your life, and, just in case, throwing up foot-thick walls around her thoughts about Jake.

9

June 1987

Alice sat on a wooden bench in Mary Ann's backyard, picked at the label on an empty beer bottle, and checked her watch for the tenth time since she'd arrived. It was only eleven o'clock, and she'd promised she'd stay at Mary Ann's grad party — "the last party of our high school lives!" Mary Ann had billed it, "the last chance to see everybody before you go to England!" — till midnight, at least. Make that till midnight at the latest.

Mary Ann had invited various athletic teams, most of the marching band, her student council buddies, and anyone else she'd run into during the last week of school, so the large crowd making too much noise around Alice was a strange mix of cool kids and misfits. When two of her nerdy pals from the history club drifted over, she chatted with them, asked about their summer plans and where they were going for college, and falsely promised to keep in touch.

She peeled the beer label off in one piece, crumpled it in her hand, and stood up on the bench, looking for Mary Ann. There she was, across the yard, with Davey and some tall guys who must be basketball players. Alice would go over there, say her goodbyes, slip out the side gate, and head home.

She navigated her way through several groupings of people

engaged in raucous conversation, and successfully avoided contact of the spilling or burning variety with the various drinks and spliffs that were waved around. She was halfway to Mary Ann when Jake Stewart loomed up in front of her and declaimed her name: "Alice Maeda!"

He stood very close to her and grinned drunkenly. He smelled of beer and smoke and aftershave and a primal maleness that the arty, intellectually inclined guys Alice usually gravitated toward did not tend to emanate. His good bone structure — he had a strong, straight nose, wide-set eyes, and a firm jaw — framed by his long hair, gone wavy in the summer heat, made him look roguishly handsome. If you liked that sort of thing.

"Hi," she shouted back. "And bye. I'm leaving." She tried to move past him but he didn't give way.

"Don't go yet," he said. He didn't sound *too* drunk. "I want to talk to you. I've been looking for you."

"Some other time, maybe."

"No, now. Please? Come." He reached for her hand and she let him take it — out of curiosity — and lead her through the press of people. What he could possibly want to say to her? She had known him since kindergarten, but they rarely spoke.

He led her in the back door of the house, through the crowded kitchen and dark dining room, to the empty living room. When they'd sat down on a sofa, side by side, she said, "So here we are. What's up?"

The sofa sagged slightly in the middle, and they were seated so close together on it that her thigh, under a thin cotton skirt, touched his shorts-clad one. But the novelty of the situation — that she was practically sitting in the lap of a species of male (genus golden boy) with which she was unfamiliar — intrigued her. So she did not inch away. She stayed put, curious to see what would happen next.

He turned toward her, reached over and tucked her hair behind her ear with his finger, traced the hoop of her earring. "Oh, Alice." He'd dropped his voice into a lower register. "Where have you been all my life?"

Alice laughed out loud. And said, "That was so cheesy it was funny."

He didn't smile.

"You meant it to be funny, right?"

"Yeah, of course. But hear me out." His right arm had somehow come to rest along the sofa back behind her, the soft hairs on his forearm tickled the nape of Alice's neck, and his hand cupped her shoulder. He was such a smooth operator, he seemed to invite her ridicule. Yet she found herself staring at his mouth, and wondering what he could do with it, wondering if he could tie a cherry stem in a knot with his tongue.

He said, "Do you realize that this is the last day of this stage of our lives, the last night before everything changes?"

He must have been talking to Mary Ann. Or he was the kind of guy who liked to express deep thoughts when he'd had a few.

"Nothing will ever be the same after this. We're all going to scatter, and go out in the world in search of adventure, and new horizons, and whatever the fuck else we find. But what if what we're looking for turns out to have been right here, under our noses, the whole time?"

Such bullshit he was spouting, and familiar-sounding bullshit, too — Alice had heard some of the same phrases in the valedictorian's speech at the graduation ceremony. Or maybe in the principal's remarks. "So what are you saying?" she said. "That we should seize the day?"

"Yes! You get it! That's totally what we should do."

"Like, seize the day and make out?"

He hesitated for a second, smiled, and said, "Exactly! Exactly." And he leaned toward her, his head tilted to one side, his eyes half-closed.

She was still amused, but she was turned on, too — yes, she was. His nearness, his rogue look, the attention he was paying her, his corny seduction techniques — her body responded to them all. The crotch of her underwear was wet, and her breathing had turned shallow.

She opened her mouth, loosened her tongue, and felt Jake's cheek against hers. When he pressed his lips against the tender skin below her earlobe, she gave in, let out a rapturous sigh, reached for his thick, rapidly hardening dick, and copped a feel through his shorts.

He moaned quietly in her ear, and said, "Let's get out of here, go over to my place. My parents are away, I've got the house to myself."

Hold on. That was a bad idea. A terrible idea. No matter how much she wanted to, she should not now go sleep with Jake Stewart. She did not want to become the latest notch on his belt, the last holdout at Five Oaks to succumb to his charms, the tawdry topic of conversation the next day among his friends.

From the back of the house, a male voice called, "Jake! Where are you, man?" And another voice, closer, yelled, "Yo, Jake!"

Jake muttered "fuck," removed his arm from the sofa back, and slid along the seat cushions just far enough away from her that when his buddies walked in a few seconds later they might not realize he'd been playing her like a goddamned violin, heavy on the vibrato. A casual observer might think they'd just been sitting and talking in the dark room, maybe reminiscing about their emotional elementary school music teacher, Ms. DaSilva, who had taught the fourth graders to sing "Both Sides Now," and wept when they performed it.

Two guys stopped in the doorway of the living room, their hulking bodies silhouetted in the light that spilled out from the kitchen behind them. "Jake, you coming?" one of them said.

"Give me five minutes."

The posse went outside, and Jake said, "I have to go out for a bit, but why don't you meet me at my house later?" He'd slid back close to her and his hands were on her again — one stroked the back of her neck, and the other rubbed her bare knee. It was an impressive display of ambidexterity, but the spell was broken. She'd remembered who she was, and how she didn't belong there, and where she was going.

"Thanks, but I don't think so." She smiled — no hard feelings. And no hard dick for her to play with either, unfortunately.

Jake stood up, and ran his fingers through his hair. "I'll leave the side door unlocked. If you want a night you'll never forget, come by."

She said, "You know what kills me? That your cheesy lines actually work most of the time. They do, don't they?"

He was at the door, on his way out. He pointed at her. "You know where I live? At 5 Forest Lane. I'll ditch the boys and meet you there in an hour. Hour and a half, tops."

"Goodnight Jake," she'd said. "Have a good life." And she'd gone home to lie in her bed, and toss and turn, and think for far too long about what might have been.

10

September 25th, 2010

When Danielle came home from the dinner club at ten-thirty, the kids were asleep. The kitchen was as clean as she'd left it after lunch, and the dishwasher wasn't full, wouldn't need to be run until the next day.

Benny was in bed, watching TV. "How was it?"

"I had fun. There was lively conversation and good food and I didn't lift a finger."

"I'm glad someone had a decent meal tonight. My stomach's upset after eating those greasy hamburgers."

"Did the kids like them?"

"Yeah."

There were so many caustic replies Danielle could have made to this, but the evening had put her in a mellow mood. So she said, "A couple of people were curious about the farm, including Mary Ann's mother. She wants to come out and see it."

"Could this lead to some new business for either of us?"

Danielle had the impression Sarah was just interested because she was interested, but who knew? "Maybe."

"In that case, I don't mind so much missing out on a home-cooked meal."

* * *

Sam was at his desk, on his computer, when Hallie walked in. "You're home early," he said.

She took off her jacket. "What a mistake that was. A group of more out-of-touch suburban moms you can't imagine. I bailed as soon as I could."

"How was the food?"

"There wasn't even a green salad. I had to eat one of the tasteless salad rolls that I brought because everything else was so high calorie or carby."

Sam was pretty sure he would have liked at least something on the menu. "Why did you go, again?"

"Every so often I get curious about what other women do for kicks. But no more dinner club for me." She walked into the kitchen, shook some ice cubes into a glass, ran the water. "Oh, by the way, I met a computer guy at the party, and I asked him to come out to the house some Saturday and check out our PCs, see if he can fix your printer."

"Okay. Are you going up to bed? I'll join you." He closed his document. It was time to shut down. He'd been struggling with an awkward transition passage in his novel for over an hour, since the girls had gone to sleep.

"I think I may work out," she said. "Run a few miles on the treadmill. Don't wait up."

Kate was in bed reading when Tom came home, at midnight. "So?"

"My crostini were enjoyed by all."

"And?"

"Most of the food was unremarkable, with the exception of a rustic Chinese noodle dish and some fragrant baby vegetables."

Kate took off her reading glasses. "Don't torture me with food talk. What were the people like? Who did you talk to?"

"I spoke briefly with Alice Maeda about the station restoration, and made small talk with some neighbourhood women who seemed to approve of the Main Street development."

"And nothing exciting happened?"

Tom sat down on a chair and untied his shoes. "Hallie was in fine form."

"Doing what?"

"She sequestered Drew in a corner to talk computers and appeared to be pressing her bony knee against his thigh."

"What's he like, this Drew?"

"He's young and sincere, has a beard, and dresses like a Brooklyn hipster."

"Knowing Hallie, she'll tell me he was all over her and she had to let him down gently."

"I would certainly call her the aggressor in this case."

"That may be, but you know how often she detects come-ons. What about you? Were any knees pressed against your thighs?"

Tom stepped into his dressing room. "Several limp hands were offered to me in greeting, but there was a distinct lack of lower body contact."

Could Kate trust him to tell the truth? Probably. But when he came out in his pajamas, she said, "I think I'd better go with you next time."

"I'm sure that can be arranged, but why?"

"So I can witness the soap opera going on over there up close."

On the one night that Alice had the whole bed to herself, with no threat of Lavinia coming in to sleep sideways across the mattress with her feet pressed against Alice's back, the one night when she had a chance at an entire block of uninterrupted slumber, she couldn't fall asleep. She looked out the window, found no solace in the nighttime gloom. She started to count backwards from one thousand and stopped, bored, at nine hundred and ninety-two. She tensed and relaxed her toes, her feet, her calves — and almost gave herself a cramp. How had she lulled herself to sleep pre-motherhood, when she wasn't always tired?

Ah, yes. Alcohol. Drinking had been a good route to oblivion now and then. Except that she'd drunk her share of wine at the dinner club, and the wine mixed with the rich food had made her stomach feel unsettled, which was having the opposite of a somnolent effect.

What else? There were times she'd sent herself to dreamland with visions of career fame in her head — remember those? She'd fantasized about news-making discoveries, about finding a well-preserved temple hidden in an underground cave, perhaps. How naive and deluded she'd been. And now the only finds she handled were from twentieth century lost-and-found boxes.

She rolled over. There must be another technique she could use. There had to be an alternative to her usual bedtime routine, which called for her to fall asleep in Lavinia's bed around nine, get up at midnight disoriented and stiff, stumble around the apartment turning off lights, drop into her own bed, and wake up again a few hours later to find Lavinia nestled in beside her.

What did normal people do at bedtime to send themselves off? Sex was a good soporific, she recalled. When she'd had any. She buried her face in the pillow, let her mind venture into the locked room where she kept her sexual memories, opened the creaky door with the rusty key, and relived a few of her archived good sex moments. Like the dirty weekend she'd spent with a Scottish student named Will, when she was nineteen. They'd fucked themselves silly in his flat during a winter

112

holiday break. He was into giving oral sex, and fond of getting on his knees on the carpet and going to work on her while she reclined in a leather easy chair, her legs bent at the knee like she was having a pelvic exam.

Going on. To Thierry, the digger she'd had outdoor sex with in a field in Brittany at high noon — the sun in her eyes, blades of grass under her head and in her hair, insects buzzing around while he described, in French, exactly what he was doing to her. My, my.

Then there was Lawrence, the married Canadian banker she'd met in London. Her afternoon guy, she'd called him, her hotel lover. He liked her to wear a dress or a skirt when they met, with no underpants on, and meet him in the hotel bar before their trysts. They'd sit in a booth, have a drink, discuss current events, and he'd use his well-manicured, nimble fingers — he had years of piano training — on her under the table, get her so hot she'd be tearing his clothes off in the elevator on the way up to the room.

She hadn't thought about any of them, or about any kind of sex, in ages. It was forever since she'd even … oh, hell. She reached inside her underwear, gingerly felt around. Now look what she'd gone and done.

She took matters in hand — quietly — though she barely remembered how. And she felt better afterwards, tired and loose. She curled up in bed, yawned, closed her eyes, and told herself this wasn't a slippery slope situation, a marijuana leads to crack progression. She was not becoming sex-obsessed like Mary Ann, and tomorrow she would return to her regular celibate routine and forget about this whole self-indulgent episode.

She fell asleep very fast.

11

October 2010

Sam had worked on (and procrastinated about working on) his mystery novel for three years and he was only at page 121 of his first draft. That is, he was stalled at page 121. His current excuse for his low rate of production was that he was having trouble with the main female character in his novel, his hero's romantic interest, a young woman he'd named Celeste.

He'd thought of making Celeste a librarian instead of a medical resident, but that seemed too much a cliché of the spectacled lonely spinster, unless he turned the convention around and made her a funky librarian with piercings and blue hair, which seemed like a reverse cliché.

If he could just get Celeste settled, finalize what she looked like, what her job was, then he would know what she would and wouldn't say or do. Having a specific mental picture had helped him with the other characters — the hero Simon resembled Sam, only taller and thinner and younger and more muscular. And the dead body that triggered the mystery was a ringer for the plumber who fixed the taps that sprung leaks on some sort of relay system at Sam's house, one every few months.

But all Sam knew about Celeste was that she was in her early thirties, single, and smart, she enjoyed sex but wasn't addicted to it or into anything too kinky, and she liked pancetta and avocado sandwiches with lemon mayo, Sam's current lunch of choice. Celeste liked food, in general. She wasn't leery of spice or afraid of fat on a piece of meat, not like some people. He'd already written a scene in which Celeste waxes poetic about the grilled octopus Sam had eaten on the Greek island of Hydra when he was a student. And so impassioned is Celeste's description of the octopus that the usually silent Simon character spins his own yarn about eating chapatis in Mumbai and reveals in the process that he's a good guy. Since only a good guy would remember chapatis so fondly, Sam figured.

But what if, instead of a medical student, Celeste was a computer expert? Like Mary Ann Gray. Mary Ann had mentioned at a soccer game that she used to be a computer person and was now doing similar work — project management of some kind — for Tom Gagliardi's Main Street development. Sam could easily imagine Mary Ann sitting at a computer, surrounded by blueprints and spreadsheets or whatever the job required. Maybe he should use her as a model for Celeste. Celeste was younger, and single, and not a mother, but Mary Ann did have a warm smile and a flattering way of making bright-eyed contact with him, paying attention to what he said, and laughing in the right places. Once or twice, he thought he'd seen her face light up with genuine gladness when she'd caught sight of him. Though maybe she was just that way with everyone, warm and friendly by nature.

Sam could make Celeste warm and friendly by nature, too. But if he wanted her to be proficient with computers, he'd have to learn a little about the field, get some terms down, do some research, see how he could work Celeste's skills into the story. He'd want to use her occupation to help solve the mystery of the ashram. Which might have to do with Alexander the Great, he thought. Possibly.

For now, he could ask Mary Ann for help with some jargon. The next time he saw her at school, he'd suggest they grab a coffee so he could interview her, make notes. That would be an easy way to get a better handle on Mary Ann, find out more about her. About Celeste, he meant. It would be a good way to learn more about Celeste.

On a Thursday evening, an hour after Lavinia had fallen asleep, Alice was sitting at home, reading, when Mary Ann, dressed in running gear, knocked on her front door.

"You busy?" Mary Ann said when Alice came to the door. "Can I come in?"

"Please do." Alice motioned her inside. "You all right?"

"I'm fine. I had to get out of the house."

"Who's with the kids?"

"Bob."

"Do you want tea?"

"No thanks. I just want to sit for a minute and yammer. May I?"

Alice led the way inside, sank into her reading chair. "Yammer away."

Mary Ann opened her eyes wide. "Get this: Drew said at work today that he broke up with his girlfriend. He's single."

"Is that good news?"

"Of course it is. He's more available now."

"So when do you make your intentions known?"

"I'm taking it slow. I don't want to get him on the rebound."

"Why not, if it's just an affair you're after?"

"Good point."

"So Drew's the one? I'm happy to hear it isn't Tom

Gagliardi. Or the husband of that Hallie woman. What's his name again?"

"Sam. And I didn't say I'd ruled anyone out."

Alice rearranged some books on the coffee table. "So, if Drew were the man you were after, what would you do to signal your interest in him?"

"Why?"

Because Alice was thinking about herself and Jake Stewart. And the vague, most likely insincere suggestion he'd made that they have lunch. "I'm curious. I haven't engaged in North American dating rituals for twenty years. How do I know what people do?"

"I haven't got the faintest idea. Lately I've tried to come up with lines to use on Drew. Or Sam, or Tom. But when we're alone in the office, and Drew leans over my shoulder and takes hold of the mouse to show me something on my computer, and I inhale his woodsy scent, and he's kind and patient and thorough, and I could just turn my head and kiss him — I don't know. I can't do it."

"Why not?"

Mary Ann sighed. "I guess I need him to make the first move."

"That does it. I'm having a cigarette."

"You've started smoking again?"

"Occasionally. After Lavinia's gone to sleep, I sit outside on the porch and listen to the night noises and puff away. Want one?"

"No thanks."

Alice brought out her smoking materials from their hiding place behind an atlas on her bookshelf, lit a cigarette, and opened the porch door a crack, held the cigarette outside. "What if you were to send him a clear message about being available and interested? Without saying the words."

"Go for the suggestive conversational topics and the expressive body language, you mean?"

"If only you could get him on a dance floor."

"I can just see him at one of the country club oldies dances. Boy, would he not fit in."

"Have you considered getting him drunk?"

"How? Pull a bottle of scotch out of my desk drawer and offer him a drink?"

"Maybe the real problem is that you don't see him in the evening. It's much easier to be romantic when it's dark out, and you stumble, he catches you, your body brushes against his, electric currents of desire run through you both — stop me before I get into this."

Mary Ann gave her an appraising eye. "What about you, Alice? How's your sex life?"

"What sex life?"

"What's the story?"

"There is no story."

"Since when?"

"Since I don't remember what sex is like."

"Come on. You've been back in Oakdale what, four years now? You can't tell me there's been no one all that time."

"Why would I lie?"

"No callow student in one of your courses? No baby-food-stained single dad from the daycare? No fellow faculty member with hair coming out of his nose?"

"Describe the men I meet that way, and no wonder."

"You haven't met anyone who's capable of yearning, is that it?"

Had she? "I don't know. I'm so tired all the time."

"God, Alice, what happened? You were such a ... you were so *active* in that area."

"I used to travel, too. Do interesting archeological work. Go out at night. Wear jewellery. I haven't worn earrings since Lavinia almost severed my earlobe pulling on one when she was a baby."

"You can't use Lavinia as an excuse for not doing things."

"Why not?"

"Because I could take her overnight anytime. My mom could watch her. Or your parents. Or a babysitter."

"Even if Lavinia were not the major complication that she is, there are other reasons not to enter the arena."

"Name one."

"Relationships are so draining."

"I must know someone who would be right for you. You still prefer guys who aren't good-looking, right? That should widen the field."

"I tell you what, I might — repeat *might* — try to line up my own someone if you promise not to matchmake me. I have a possible person in mind. A remote possible." Better not to mention that the possible was Jake Stewart.

"You get yourself rolling with someone new, and I'll do my best to engineer some action with one of my three guys. Any of them. Or all of them. Deal?"

"Maybe."

"I pledge that over the next few weeks, I will take a step toward seduction of each one of my candidates."

"How?"

"I'll approach Tom at work."

"Poor Tom."

"As for Drew, I think we're going to need a second dinner club meeting, go for the evening angle you suggested. I'll ask Lisa if she can host it. She just had her kitchen redone. She'll want to show it off."

"What about the third guy?"

"Sam? I'll make sure he comes to the dinner club next time, instead of Hallie. And I'll continue to turn on the charm with him at school. But he seems like the slow-burn type. A longer-term project."

"I don't know where you find the energy."

"Just remember I'll only be resolute about this if you keep up your end of the bargain and find yourself a guy."

Alice said, "What's in this for me, again?"

"Getting laid."

"Oh yeah."

Mary Ann was working at her computer in the office supply room, revising a schedule, and Phoebe was making photocopies nearby, when Drew stuck his head in the doorway. "I'm going out," he said.

Phoebe said, "When will you be back?"

"Don't know."

Mary Ann and Phoebe heard his heavy tread down the stairs, the squeak of the front door opening, the thud of its close. "Didn't he just get here ten minutes ago?" Phoebe said.

Mary Ann didn't answer, went back to work. The only sounds in the room for a few minutes were the hums and flaps of the photocopier until Phoebe said, "Drew seems to go out on these mysterious errands a lot lately."

"Does he?"

"You're here every day. You should know."

"Maybe he *has* been busier than usual the last couple of weeks."

The photocopier stopped. Phoebe collected her copies and straightened them out on the countertop. "Since he broke it off with Krista," she said, "I find he's gone all quiet. Has he clammed up with you, too?"

"Sort of."

"He was the one who did the dumping, you know."

Mary Ann looked up from her screen. "He told you that?"

"No, but I know because Krista left him a voicemail message to say she'd moved the last of her stuff out of their apartment. Her closing line was, 'I hope you're happy with whoever she is, you creep.'"

"He's seeing someone else?" Mary Ann had a queasy, passed-over feeling that felt all too familiar.

"I thought you might know who it is."

"Why'd you listen to his message, anyway?"

"She left it in the general office voicemail box. Drew always said she wasn't technically proficient." Phoebe came over to Mary Ann's desk. "And now he disappears all the time. Never says where he's going. If you ask me, I think he's sneaking out to meet his new hookup."

"But if he's broken it off with Krista, why would he need to sneak around?"

"Because his new girl is married, of course. Or spoken for."

"Oh." Another flare of nausea.

Phoebe said, "There were a couple of days when you and he went out around the same time, and I thought maybe you two had something going on."

Too quickly, Mary Ann said, "What an imagination you have, Phoebe."

"But twice now, you've been here when he goes out, and you're still here when he comes back, reeking of cologne. So I guess he's bonking some other girl."

Mary Ann couldn't keep a plaintive note out of her voice. "Do you really think so?"

Alice sat in her office, pretended to review her lecture notes, and fought off sleep. She'd been up at three a.m. the night before, trying to convince Lavinia to spend the night in her own bed. And now, with the sunlight streaming in her window, and her notes on the desk in front of her, it would be so easy to drop off in her chair. She wouldn't even need to lie down; all she'd have to do is close her eyes.

The ringing of her cell woke her.

Alice jumped, picked up the phone, said her name, and heard a male voice claiming to be Jake Stewart say hi and ask how she was doing. She wiped some saliva off her face, pulled her voice up to a more alert-sounding pitch, and said, "Fine, thanks. How are you?"

"I'm good. I'm calling to set up that lunch we talked about, if you'd still like to go."

"Yes, I would, very much. Like to go. I was going to call you, suggest the same thing. Let me get my book. When were you thinking of?"

"I only work till noon on Fridays when I'm in the office. So Friday could be good."

Alice stared at her appointment book. Today appeared to be Monday. "This Friday?"

"Sure. I know a nice restaurant in the West Village with a Mediterranean vibe, if you'd be into that."

Alice rubbed sleep from her eye. Had Mary Ann infected her mind, or was this sounding like an actual date? "That would be lovely."

Mary Ann found an opportunity to announce the next dinner club meeting when Phoebe, Drew, and Tom were all in the office. "It's October 23rd," she said, "at Lisa Carsten's place. Do you remember her from the last time? She was the tall woman with short auburn hair."

"Oh yeah," Drew said, "I remember."

Phoebe said, "Do you know her *well*, Drew?"

His confused *no* was overrun by Tom saying, "I'm not sure I know who she is."

Mary Ann said, "She brought those smoked salmon roll-ups with cream cheese and green onions in them."

"Ah yes," Tom said. "An ordinary combination of elements, but not without a certain bourgeois charm."

"Lisa, or the appetizers?" Phoebe said.

"I was speaking of the food."

Phoebe winked at Mary Ann. "Just checking."

Tom said, "I wonder if I could presume on the dinner club's hospitality to bring my wife Kate to the next occasion. I praised the fascinating company and sumptuous fare at the first meeting so highly that she has expressed a desire to make all of your acquaintance."

Mary Ann thought fast. If Tom brought his wife, Mary Ann could hardly court him at the party, but that was okay. It was Drew she'd targeted for this particular outing. "I guess we could make an exception, for you only, since you asked so nicely."

Drew pulled his phone out of his shirt pocket, and opened a calendar app. "Other than Tom's wife, will it be the same people in attendance as last time?"

"Pretty much."

He keyed in the date. "I'm free that day."

"Yeah," Phoebe said, "but are you available?"

Mary Ann sure as hell hoped so.

Alice ran into Macy's to buy some on-sale T-shirts for Lavinia, and on the way out she slowed down in the cosmetics area, with the idea that she should buy a new lipstick or eyeliner or mascara in preparation for her lunch with Jake.

"Can I interest you in our skin-care products today?" a sales clerk said, and Alice looked into the meticulously made-up face of a woman whose nametag identified her as Suzanne.

"Skin-care products?" Alice said. "I wanted makeup." She peered at the coloured bottles, jars, and tubes on display in front of her, and saw that the fine print on the labels all contained words like cream or tonic or treatment.

"Our makeup line is on the other side of the counter," Suzanne said and stepped over to a different multicoloured display. Alice already wanted to leave, but she followed along. She would fake interest for a few seconds, and make a break for it.

Suzanne placed a large oval mirror on the counter in front of Alice. "What specific type of product are you interested in? Eye shadow, lipstick?"

The reflection Alice saw in the magnifying mirror looked like an illustration from a medical textbook on skin disorders. "My god. What's happened to my face?"

"You *are* showing a lot of pigment."

Alice stared in the mirror. "Pigment? Is that what you're calling those brown spots?"

"Do you have children?"

"One. Why?"

A knowing nod. "Child-bearing leaves marks. Do you use sunscreen?"

"In the summer, when I'm outside."

"Someone with your skin type needs sunscreen every day, all year. Our day cream includes thirty SPF sunscreen. Forty dollars for one and a half ounces."

"Forty dollars?"

"You could try foundation, too, to cover it." Suzanne came closer, examined Alice's pores. "You'd need full coverage." Her hand disappeared underneath the counter and reappeared holding a tester bottle of foundation. "This would be your shade — beige umber. You want to try some? Here." She produced a Q-tip, dipped it into the bottle, spread some liquid across Alice's cheek, blended it with a small sponge. "There. Take a look. What do you think?"

She was lucky not to have a magnifying mirror at home, is what Alice thought. "Maybe I'll just go into hiding," she said. "Or hibernation."

"I also recommend a skin-lightening cream. You apply it at night, before bed. After about a month, you'll see the difference. This one is sixty dollars for a half ounce, but it's to be used sparingly."

"What's in it? Bleach?"

"No, no. It exfoliates to make your skin lighter."

"Lighter as in whiter. Are you suggesting people with pigment should try to be whiter?" Maybe taking a little racially motivated offence was the key to escaping this situation.

Suzanne shrugged. "You complained about your brown spots. I'm telling you what your options are."

"I'm sorry," Alice said. "This has been an upsetting experience for me. I don't think I can buy anything today."

"Suit yourself," Suzanne said. "You want to show your face out in public looking like that, you go right ahead."

Mary Ann said, "Sam, you know that dinner club meeting I had at my place, the one that Hallie came to?"

They were standing outside the school, being whipped by a wind that wasn't doing Mary Ann's hair any favours but was tousling Sam's curls and ruddying his cheeks becomingly.

"Chutney!" he said. "Don't do that! Sorry, Mary Ann."

Mary Ann pushed aside the dog's head with her knee, fought off the urge to touch Sam's face.

"What about the dinner club?" he said.

Mary Ann settled for touching his arm. "There was a bit of

a mix-up there. I meant to invite you. Hallie must have heard my phone message and just assumed. I was happy to have her, but I thought you should know for next time."

"Down, Chutney. Who trained you, anyway?"

"So you'll come the next time? It's on October 23rd. At Lisa Carsten's house."

"Isn't the dinner club a women's thing?"

"No, it's a cooking thing. And I'm dying to try yours."

Sam tugged on Chutney's leash. "I guess Hallie mentioned that the computer guy was there last time, and Tom Gagliardi."

"Yes, Tom was there, being his suave self and charming all the ladies."

"I'm sure he did a better job of it than I would have."

"But I don't want you there to charm the ladies. I want you there so I can feast my eyes as well as my tastebuds."

Sam looked so startled by these words that Mary Ann laughed, and touched him again, and said, "Do you always blush like that when someone pays you a compliment?"

On the phone, Alice said, "You sleazebag, you. What did he say?"

Mary Ann leaned back in her chair, put her feet up on her desk. "He chided the dog for trying to hump someone who walked by. And I'll bet his dog wasn't the only one with a hard-on."

"Don't be disgusting. But how do you talk like that to someone? That's my question. Where'd you learn how to do it?"

"My college sorority gave out booklets on man-baiting techniques."

"I knew it. You were trained."

"I'm kidding. And you think I don't feel like a total ass when I say these things?"

"Well, don't stop now. You've got him going. Keep at him."

"Do I hear actual encouragement from you?"

"I have to admit: the affair concept is starting to grow on me."

"How are you doing with your mystery guy?"

"I've arranged to meet him for lunch."

"I count on you to tell me every detail."

Alice scoffed. "Don't. And there'll be nothing to tell anyway."

"Should I run over right now and slip the man-baiting tips through your mail slot?"

"Goodnight, Mary Ann."

12

October 2010

On the day Sarah came out to see the farm, Danielle and Benny had exchanged a few heated words. And Danielle was upset enough that after she'd shown an admiring Sarah around the greenhouses, introduced her to the workers, and taken her past the dog kennels, through the kitchen garden, and into the house for a cup of coffee, she told her about the fight.

Benny's family tradition, she explained, was for a large extended group to get together every October to celebrate a cluster of fall birthdays and anniversaries. The host duties rotated, this year was the turn of Benny and Danielle, and the dreaded day was looming when Danielle not only had to prepare food for hordes of people, she had to accommodate Benny's father, the original picky eater.

Murray Pringle was in good health for his age (seventy-six), a state he attributed to the dietary regime he followed, his never-eat-raw philosophy. All food prepared for Murray had to be overcooked, since anything served al dente — be it animal, vegetable, or grain — was considered indigestible. Murray never ate fish, due to a traumatic fish-bone incident in his youth. He didn't eat butter or oil either, unless they were baked into a cake. Murray made an exception for cake.

"I want to pull out the stops with the family party this year," Benny had said to Danielle that morning. "No fried chicken and potato salad like Eva and Chris served last year. Don't you agree?"

With barely concealed irritation, Danielle had rhymed off her preliminary ideas about the main meal, which would be served at lunchtime. A gravlax appetizer to start, she thought, with a sour cream dill sauce. Spaghetti for a main course, sauced with her own tomatoes, some white wine, and fresh herbs, and topped with steamed fresh clams and mussels. On the side, a cold salad of her greens in a blood-orange vinaigrette, and a warm salad of fava beans with feta in a mustard and mint dressing. For dessert: five kinds of berries with vanilla whipped cream.

"My mouth's watering already. But what about Dad?"

"If he doesn't want to eat what I make for the adults, there'll be good bread and cold cuts laid out for the kids, some plain pasta with tomato sauce, and grated Parmesan. And make-your-own ice cream sundaes for dessert."

"And cake?"

"One of your sisters can bring cake. All of your sisters can bring cake. You can buy six cakes at the supermarket bakery. I am not baking any cake."

"You're awfully touchy."

"I'm not touchy. I'm describing a very nice menu, and all you can say is, 'What about Dad'?"

"I want him to know what a wonderful cook you are."

"I'm not a wonderful cook," Danielle said. Snapped.

Benny came over, put his arms around her. "What's wrong? What's going on?"

She shook him off. "Nothing. Don't."

"You will serve some more meat than just cold cuts though, right?" he'd said. "Maybe some steak?"

Danielle refilled Sarah's coffee cup. "Have you ever heard anything so aggravating in your life?"

"Your father-in-law sounds difficult. I pity his poor wife."

"Would you put up with this?"

Sarah smiled. "No, but I'm not you."

"Murray and his stupid cake."

"Where will you find the time to prepare this elaborate meal, when you have to run your farm and care for your children?"

"Where does any working mother find the time?"

"I know of a good divorce lawyer if you ever want one."

"I'm not at that stage. I mean, Benny's good points outweigh his bad ones, I know they do. I've made a list, and tallied them up. I only wish …"

"What?"

Danielle took a big quavery breath. "I only wish I never had to cook again. There, I said it. And I don't care if I sound petty."

"Petty? Who's to say what's petty? We're each allowed to be unhappy in our own way. Take me: I'm financially secure, retired by choice, healthy, my children and grandchildren are safe and well. I have nothing to complain about, yet I'm not the most contented person on earth."

"What do you wish for?"

"Nothing in particular."

"Are you sure?"

Sarah lifted her coffee cup to her mouth, said from behind it, "I could use more to do, I suppose, since retiring from real estate. A part-time occupation."

"Too bad we can't switch places for a while."

"When's your family party?"

"A few days after the next dinner club meeting, in late October. Why?"

"How about if I bake the cakes your husband wants? I like to bake."

"Oh no, Sarah, please. I wouldn't dream of asking you. And I don't care about providing Benny's family with dessert."

"I make a nice fluffy banana layer cake. Does your father-in-law eat bananas?"

Alice dropped Lavinia off at daycare, ran to her car, started it up, and hit the road. Was she imagining things, or had Lavinia been extra clingy during their goodbye today? As if she somehow knew her mother was going for lunch with a man. Everyone else sure seemed to have caught on. Like Sarah, who'd been sitting on her porch, reading her morning paper, when Alice and Lavinia left. "Don't you both look pretty this morning," she said, and made Alice regret trying to dress nicely. Made her want to rip her silver hoop earrings right out of her ears. She might have, too, if it hadn't taken her a good ten minutes of basically re-piercing the holes by hand to get them inserted.

Then at Lavinia's daycare, one of the teachers said, "You're all decked out. Big meeting at work this morning?"

Alice could only hope that Carl Somers, the foreman on the train station restoration job, wouldn't notice any difference when she came by. Or wouldn't comment if he did. Damn. She shouldn't have agreed to meet Tom at the site before she headed into the city, not today.

She drove past the subdivisions out by the school, and turned on the car stereo. NPR was running a discussion on the economy that required argumentative panelists to maintain extreme positions and interrupt one another whenever possible. No thanks. Alice switched the stereo to the CD player and let it play.

Lavinia's musical preferences had recently evolved from classic Raffi kids' tunes to pre-teen pop music, under the influence

131

of Mary Ann's daughter, Kayla, who was something of a tween music expert. The current CD, Kayla's birthday gift to Lavinia, was the product of a group called the Bad Boys, though the image they presented was fresh-scrubbed and clean-cut, from their gleaming teeth and product-heavy hair to the brightly coloured boxer brief waistbands that showed above their skinny jeans.

Kayla had explained to Alice the attributes of each Bad Boy, had delineated the differences between the Cute One, the Young One, the Dreadlocked One, and the One Who Wore Glasses. "If Lavinia wants to pick a favourite, she should go for the Young One," Kayla said. "Seeing as he's closest to her age."

Lavinia had not shown interest in any particular Bad Boy, thank god, but she liked the up-tempo rhythms of the music and requested the CD be played often in the car. A few weeks of this total immersion and Alice had learned all the lyrics — every single hey baby/you make me crazy/you know I love you/what will I do? one of them.

For any given line in a song, Alice could identify which member of the group was singing. On a few of the numbers she raised the volume before Lavinia asked her to. And she had begun to listen to the CD when Lavinia wasn't in the car, to tap out the rhythm with her left foot while she drove, and sing. She'd gone so far as to pick her own favourite Bad Boy — the One Who Wore Glasses. Though at least, she said to herself, when she thought about it, when she acknowledged how absurd and borderline sick it was for a fortysomething, university-educated, worldly woman to take an interest in a twenty-year-old member of a slickly marketed money-making machine — at least she'd chosen him as an object of her attention for his vocal talent, rather than for his youthful swagger or cut abs.

The One Who Wore Glasses — Alice preferred to think of him as the Voice — was the most beauty-challenged member of the bunch, face-wise. He might not have qualified for admission to the group at all if he weren't the possessor of a husky, full-throated instrument that imparted undeserved shades of meaning to the insipid lyrics he sang. His voice soared above the layered musical arrangements, cut through the generic pop hooks and spoke — to Alice, anyway — of sweat-soaked passion and steamy sex.

Alice didn't know which had come first — the insistent pressure of the Voice's purring, Mary Ann's outlook on life as one big affair opportunity, or her sex drive awakening from its years-long postpartum sleep and whispering its own *Hey, baby* lines in her ear. What she did know was that she was a little too primed for her lunch with Jake Stewart.

She parked in front of the train station building, ducked inside the plastic sheets that covered the scaffolding around the door, and heard Mary Ann say, "Gosh, Tom, when you talk like that, it takes me right back to the 1870s. As if I'm wearing a corset and my proximity to the sweating labourers is making me feel faint. Do you have any smelling salts?"

Oh, great. Mary Ann had chosen today to practise her bizarre brand of flirting on Tom.

Mary Ann saw her and waved. "You don't mind if I tag along on your site inspection, do you? When Tom told me he was meeting you here, I begged him to let me come." Before Alice could answer, Mary Ann said, in a drier tone, "You're looking good this morning."

"Thanks." Alice gave Mary Ann a warning glare. "You look nice too."

"We've only just arrived," Tom said. "Carl's upstairs. He said to 'holler up' when we're ready."

Alice hollered, "Hey, Carl! We're here," and they started up the back staircase to the second-floor gallery, Mary Ann in lead position, next Alice, Tom last. Halfway there, Mary Ann started fiddling with the silk scarf tied around her neck.

"Does anyone else find it warm in here?" she said, pulled the scarf off in a stripteasey manner, and tied it to her purse. Next came her jacket, but underneath was only a V-neck sweater. Nothing racier, Alice was relieved to see, despite the earlier talk of corsets.

Carl came down the attic stairs, greeted them, and stared at the spectacle of Mary Ann fiddling with a pendant on a chain around her neck. She dropped it into her cleavage, pulled it out, dropped it in again. He didn't seem to notice how Alice was dressed, or that she was even present, until she said, "So, Carl, where shall we start?"

He tore his eyes away from Mary Ann. "With the roof. You go ahead, Alice." He reached out an arm to steady Mary Ann's progress. "Watch your step there, Ma'am."

Alice turned around on the narrow steps to shoot Mary Ann a look and caught a wink from her.

Tom said, "Permit me to point out the fine brick and tile work on the turrets up here, Mary Ann. The degree of care and pride with which the craftsmen of old approached their work was such that they exacted the same standards of perfection on every part of the building, including sections that no one but roof repairmen would ever see up close."

"I bet they worked nice and slow, too," Mary Ann said. "Made sure they did it right, and didn't rush. I hate it when men rush."

Alice thought she heard Carl chuckle, but Mary Ann affected not to notice. Her performance was all for Tom.

"Why," Mary Ann said, "I wouldn't be surprised if the workmen made better love to this building than they did to their wives."

Alice suppressed a groan and led the way onto the roof, where they all squinted in the sunlight. Except for Mary Ann, who had brought sunglasses in her purse. She put them on, raised her head, and pointed her chin at the sky. "What a beautiful day!"

The two men obediently looked upward, and Alice said, "How's it going with the replacement roof tiles, Carl? Any luck finding some to match?"

Carl and Tom turned to Alice and Carl answered her question. But Mary Ann kept her head thrown back, in contemplation of the clouds, for a full minute.

Alice called Mary Ann when she arrived at her office. "What was that act at the station?"

"What act?"

"Come on. The disrobing, the cloud gazing, the double entendres — what gives?"

"By the way, I know who you're after, and it's okay. I can keep your secret."

"What?"

"Your mystery guy is Carl, right? The foreman?"

"No, Mary Ann."

"I could tell you'd gone to extra trouble with your appearance — the earrings and all — and he's not bad if you're into tool belts. Which I didn't think you were, but that's okay. People change."

"Carl is not my guy."

"Then who is?"

"I can't talk about him yet. I don't want to jinx it. And my skin's probably too pigmented for a relationship anyway. But what about Tom? Did your heavy-handed wiles work? Did he jump you on the way back to the office?"

"You've never seen anyone so businesslike."

"What was the routine with your neck, anyway?"

"That was throat-baring."

"I'm sure it was, but why?"

"I learned about it on a wildlife documentary. When you expose your most vulnerable body part, you imply your willingness to submit sexually."

"That's funny."

"I think Tom may prefer a more dominant type."

"Carl seemed like he might be interested in having you submit."

"At least I went after Tom like I said I would."

"And what comes next?"

"Drew. At the next dinner club meeting."

13

October 2010

The Mediterranean restaurant had rough plaster walls, rustic wooden tables, big windows that opened onto Cornelia Street, and it was peopled with well-heeled West Village types who made Alice feel, as usual, that she didn't fit in, that she was a refugee from her own planet, but Jake showed no such discomfort.

His tone with the hostess was engaging, he ordered a half bottle of red wine with a confidence that wasn't overbearing, he won over Alice and the waiter both with his easy informality when they made their choices. And was it the wine, or her excitable state, or was the food incredible? Sweet sautéed cauliflower with pine nuts and raisins. A plate of crisp fried artichokes redolent of a good, green olive oil.

"The food's so good," she said to Jake. "I don't usually eat this well at lunchtime."

"Me either. Except when I'm on a bike tour. Our customers like their food high end."

"How did you end up in that line of work, anyway?"

Jake filled her in on his past, on his three years at UCLA, his realization that he was not academically inclined or gifted, his failure to graduate, the extended period he spent leading excursions out of a bike shop in San Francisco, his travels in

Europe, his eventual return home, and the job with the tour company based in New York.

He spoke, and Alice pictured him, younger, riding a bike on a river path, his long blond hair flowing behind him, a blue bandanna tied around his forehead. He wore a faded T-shirt, baggy shorts, and hiking boots, and his long leg muscles flexed as he pedalled. He made a joke and laughed when he passed the other riders, and his easy grace made every woman on the trip want to sleep with him.

"A lot of aimless wandering is what I've been doing," Jake said. "And somewhere in there, I lost my hair and forgot to become very good at any one thing. What about you?"

Alice woke from her daydream of the Jake that was, and faced the current Jake, bald and self-deprecating.

"Tell me your life story," he said. "I'll bet it's been more directed than mine."

Alice had thought she could handle being a single mother. When, at age thirty-eight, she'd discovered she was pregnant — the result of a one-nighter with a Danish colleague at a conference in Berlin — she'd worried and wondered, weighed the pros and cons, and decided to keep the baby, to embark on a new kind of journey.

She was living in England still, teaching at the University of Leicester and directing archeological digs with student labour between terms. But she'd gotten a little old to be living in a caravan beside a dig site during her summers. And she didn't much like the image of herself she sometimes caught reflected in the wavy glass window panes of the classroom doors — of a no-longer-young woman in reproduction Roman-style earrings who eyed the visiting scholars and new professorial hires each year in search of a keen mind and an unassuming smile to sleep with for a term or two.

The pregnancy that would be Lavinia felt right, true, fated, the solution to her perpetual I-can't-imagine-living-with-anyone-but-do-I-really-want-to-be-alone-forever? dilemma. So she quit smoking, started eating right, and breezily informed her faraway parents and local friends of the impending event. She saw no need to notify her already forgotten lover of the conception, and she sailed through the pregnancy with an air of pleasant anticipation. She took birthing classes with a friend from the university, and outfitted her flat with the necessary equipment. She read baby books — British and American ones both. She was prepared.

No, she wasn't. Who could be prepared for a baby who alternated between adorable and deplorable, who cried for hours on end, who wouldn't lie still in her stroller for more than a minute, who wouldn't sleep if you laid her down, who drove Alice insane?

She got through the first few weeks of Lavinia's life without realizing how difficult and all-consuming single motherhood was. Her mother came over for ten days to help out, and Alice leaned on her, and was distracted by her friends' drop-in visits, by the congratulatory emails and phone calls, by her physical recovery from the unremarkable but nevertheless exhausting childbirth she'd experienced. By week three, though, after her mother had left, Alice leapt at the offer made to her by retired Mrs. Willoughby from the downstairs flat. "You can always leave the little darling with me for an hour if you need to run down to the shops, dear," she said. "I'm happy to mind her."

Alice did leave Lavinia. Started looking forward to leaving her. Began to build her entire day around the high point when she could drop Lavinia with Mrs. Willoughby, walk away, and go outside to breathe the air of freedom, of childless people, if only for a short time.

When Lavinia was five weeks old, Mrs. Willoughby took sick — nothing serious, a head cold. She wouldn't be able to mind Lavinia for a few days. So sorry, dear. And Alice found herself slumped in a chair in her sitting room, holding Lavinia in her arms, and sobbing at the thought that her future consisted of dependence on inconstant babysitters, of being chained to this needy creature, of an end to the now-guilty pleasures of solitude.

She loved Lavinia, but she couldn't manage her alone.

Once she put her mind to the task, moving back to Oakdale wasn't difficult. An American archeologist she'd dug with in France was at NYU and recommended her for a teaching job there that would allow her to do some low-level research if she would take on a dreary freshman-level ancient history survey course. There was an infant daycare attached to Oakdale Elementary School that took babies as young as six months. Her flat in Leicester fetched a fair price, enough that she didn't need to worry about moving expenses. Her parents offered to have her move in with them (she declined, with a shudder) and graciously pretended they had no need for their five-year-old Honda, were about to buy a new one, could give her the old car.

All she needed was a place to live. She emailed Mary Ann's mother, Sarah, and asked if she knew, through her real-estate brokering, of any available flats in a house with a yard. And she felt like she'd won the lottery when Sarah wrote back to say she'd recently sold her family house, and moved into a duplex near the park. The second-storey apartment in the duplex was vacant and the rent was reasonable. She had some furniture leftover from the old house, too, that she could use to furnish it, if Alice wanted.

Lavinia, meanwhile, became more human with every passing week. She began to smile, to emit a gurgly laugh, to lay her head on Alice's shoulder, and cling, sighing, when Alice held her. All of which led Alice to love Lavinia more than she had ever loved anyone.

Lavinia fussed and fussed during the transatlantic flight over. Alice offered her frequent access to the breast for soothing purposes, her fellow passengers be damned, and Lavinia grabbed at it every time, only to spit out Alice's chewed nipple in anger and disgust a few seconds later. The sequence was repeated so often over the eight-hour flight that Alice came close to screaming. Was appalled to find herself snapping — a whisper-snap, but still a snap — at Lavinia, "What the fuck do you want?" in the angry, I'm-losing-it tone she hated to hear herself use, the tone whose too-frequent appearance had spurred her to make this trip, to go home, for Christ's sake, to boring old Oakdale.

Where much had changed, she saw when she arrived. The traffic lights were bigger and bolder, the street signs were new, made up in an unfamiliar typeface and colour. Many of the old houses were done over, remodelled.

Sarah welcomed Alice and her suitcases and car seat and stroller at her door, invited her to sit in a wicker chair on the front porch, took Lavinia and exclaimed over her at length, offered Alice lemonade and homemade peach cobbler. "Run inside whenever you're ready and take a look at the apartment," she said. "I'm sure you want to see it alone first — I know what it's like to have a landlady hovering."

After consuming a delicious bowlful of peaches and cream, Alice accepted Sarah's offer, excused herself, opened the unlocked apartment door, and climbed the narrow steps to the second floor. The house was not as old as some in Oakdale — it dated from the nineteen-twenties. Much of its interior was original, including hardwood floors, white plaster walls, and a large bay window. The light in the living room was indirect (there was a screened porch at the front, above Sarah's) but bright enough.

A cross breeze blew through open windows. The kitchen contained old but sparkling appliances — a gas stove, a fridge that was all curves and chrome trim. The bigger bedroom featured more wood floor, a big bed and boxspring, a painted white dresser, and muslin curtains pulled back from two windows that overlooked the yard. Lavinia's bedroom adjoined, small and square, and was already set up with the crib and changing table Alice's mother had ordered for her from Sears.

Alice ran downstairs and onto the porch. "It's lovely," she said. "Thank you."

"If you don't like the furniture, or if there's anything you want to add —"

"Nothing but the few boxes of linens and keepsakes I've got coming over from Leicester."

Sarah said, "I feel awkward saying this, but I'm afraid I have a few house rules, and I think we should review them at the outset."

"Let's have them."

"Sound really carries in this house, so I'll have to ask you not to play music loudly."

"That's fine. Loud music is best enjoyed in a closed car, don't you find? But if the floors are thin, I worry about Lavinia's crying. She does go on. Often in the middle of the night."

"I can live with that. Don't feel self-conscious about it. I'm not much of a sleeper anyway."

"Insomnia?"

"Call it what you want. I put it down to age. I end up watching television at four a.m. more often than I'd like."

"Any good programs on then?"

"No."

"Not in England, either. Four a.m. tends to be one of my bad times with Lavinia."

"It must be difficult being the only parent."

Alice couldn't withstand Sarah's sympathetic gaze for more than a few seconds without wanting to bawl like Lavinia. "One makes one's choices."

"Coming back was a good choice."

"You're very kind."

"Enough of that. It pleases me to have you here."

"Thank you."

"No more thanking."

"Okay. I'll stop. What are the other rules?"

"Those were the only two. No loud music and no excessive thanking."

Alice smiled. "In that case, I think I'm going to like it here."

The next day, Alice spent some time with her parents, who doted on Lavinia, served Alice a simple lunch, and made it clear that while she could call on them in an emergency, their lives were regimented and full, and their available babysitting hours were few. Though a regular two-hour stint every Monday evening from six to eight might work, what did she think?

The day after that, Alice took Lavinia, in a stroller — she could last short walks now without major crying jags, as long as she was recently fed and the weather wasn't extreme — to visit Mary Ann.

She felt a twinge of anxiety on the doorstep of the grand house on Green Street. What would she and Mary Ann talk about? And what were the chances that there remained a square inch of common ground between them? Since Mary Ann had become the sort of prosperous wife and mother of leisure who busied herself with decorating projects and volunteer committees.

They could always talk about the baby, even if this one courtesy visit proved to be their last for the next twenty years. Adult company was adult company — better than being alone with Lavinia, staring at the walls in the new flat, and worrying that the decision to move home had not been a solution to her single motherhood problem at all, but was a compounding of her original mistake.

Since they'd last met, perky young blonde Mary Ann had become a perky middle-aged dyed blonde who proclaimed joy at the sight of Alice with babe in arms. "You're so thin!" she cried, when Alice had struggled inside the house with all her gear.

"Caregiving has had that effect on me. The draining of my life forces effect. Did it you, as well?"

"I wish. I've carried around ten extra pounds since Kayla was born. I'm so happy to see you! Come on in."

"Thanks for inviting me." Alice switched the bundle that was Lavinia from one arm to the other and followed Mary Ann into a large sitting room that was joined to her large kitchen. "I hope I'm not keeping you from something."

"Not at all. I've got loads of free time this month, with the boys away at camp, and Kayla doing the tennis program at the club. How often can I reorganize their dresser drawers or get a pedicure? Another few weeks of this and I might have to consider doing something meaningful with my life."

Alice smiled uncertainly. Was that last comment meant to be a joke?

"Please have a seat anywhere," Mary Ann said.

Alice bypassed two loveseats and crouched down on the area rug between them. With one hand, she eased her diaper bag off her shoulder, extracted a receiving blanket, and began to lay it down.

Mary Ann reached out. "Can I take her?"

Alice handed Lavinia over and smoothed out the blanket. "Put her down any time you want to. She's usually good for at least two minutes before she needs to be picked up again."

Mary Ann held Lavinia in the crook of her arm. "There's coffee made if you want some. And I baked some Stilton short-bread for you. Gosh, she's beautiful, Alice. Look at those eyes. And her eyelashes."

"She has her moments."

"She's heavy, isn't she? Solid."

"I know. My back kills. Would you mind if I made myself some tea?"

Mary Ann said of course not, told Alice where to find things, stayed put, cradled the baby.

"This is quite the house," Alice said, when she'd put the kettle on. "It's like something out of a real estate porn website."

"Bob calls it my never-ending project. I work hard to keep it looking good, but I'm embarrassed sometimes when people without money see it."

"People like me, you mean?"

"I'm sorry. How insensitive of me. Are you broke?"

"No, I'm not. The move was a little costly, but I've saved some, all those years of being single and childless. Mind you, I'll never afford a palace like this, not in my lifetime."

Mary Ann grimaced. "Do you take one look around and feel the urge to man the barricades?"

"No, but I never aspired to this. Not that there's anything wrong with people who did. Who do. Help me pull my foot out of my mouth, will you?"

"I guess I did aspire."

Alice let the "did" go by without comment. "Do you miss your kids when they're away?"

"Less this week than the week before. It's strange how quickly I get used to not having them here. Considering that my life revolves around them the rest of the time."

A pause followed, during which Alice made her tea and hoped the meeting wouldn't be full of awkward silences, and

Mary Ann cooed to Lavinia.

"Go ahead," Alice said, when she'd sat down with her mug. "Ask me what you want to ask me."

Mary Ann set Lavinia down on the blanket. "What do you mean?"

"What's making your forehead wrinkle up?"

Mary Ann tickled Lavinia's foot. "Okay, I'll ask. What about the baby's father? And custody? How did he feel about you moving here with her?"

"What custody? Lavinia's mine. The father doesn't even know she exists."

"Is that why you left England? So he wouldn't find out?"

"There's no intrigue. I wanted to raise her here, where I'm less alone, that's all."

Mary Ann got up, grabbed a dish of shortbreads and green grapes from the kitchen, and set it on the coffee table, which already held dessert plates, grape shears, and pretty patterned paper napkins. "And how are you coping with motherhood?"

"Not so well." Shit. Alice's voice had caught on her words. In keeping with her postpartum tendency to cry at the drop of nothing.

Mary Ann said, "It'll be better when you're working and not with her all day. I went back full-time five months after Josh was born, and it was such a relief to get away from that demanding little creature, I can't tell you."

Alice smiled. "I think that may be the most comforting thing anyone's said to me about motherhood so far."

"Are you being sarcastic? No, you're not." Mary Ann gently poked Lavinia's belly. "Do you like to drive your mother crazy, Lavinia? Do you?"

Lavinia gurgled and kicked the air.

"When do babies become manageable, then?" Alice said. "At one? Two?"

"Try five or six. If I were you, I'd keep working until she's at least in first grade. The ideal time to begin devoting yourself to her full-time is when she's in school all day. Then you can become a tennis-playing, car-pooling housewife like me."

"No tennis for me. And no income to live on if I don't work."

"Maybe you'll find an income-earning husband here."

"I doubt that, since I have no interest in romance. Or sex. I'm never having sex again."

Mary Ann scoffed. "Famous last words."

"I mean it. I've had sex once since Lavinia was born, and it was so awful, so painful, that I can't bear the thought of repeating the experience."

"What happened?"

"All was well until the moment of penetration. But the pain when the penis went in! The burning and chafing! My vaginal walls are seizing up as I speak at the very thought."

"Oh, Alice," Mary Ann said, and laughed as if she found Alice genuinely funny.

"Did the same thing happen to you?"

"No, not really. Bob didn't want to have sex while I was nursing, and I breastfed each of the kids for several months, so that was that. Would you like some shortbread?"

"Yes, please. How is Bob?"

"He's okay. He travels a lot on business. While I run this house."

Alice tasted a biscuit. "This is lovely. You baked it yourself?"

"Yes, from my mom's recipe. Is that what they say in England? Lovely?"

"Sorry. It's delicious. How's that?"

"Say lovely if you want to, I don't care. And tell me if it brings back any memories."

"Should it?"

147

"Think back," Mary Ann said. "Our senior year of high school. You came over for dinner. We did the telepathy experiment and ate Stilton shortbread."

"I remember the mind-reading, but I can't say I recall the menu."

"Try harder."

Alice's mind whipped through years of memorable moments: the day she'd uncovered the edge of a Roman-era mosaic floor in a farmer's field in Normandy. Her first glimpse of the Parthenon. Dancing all night in a disco in Nice when she was twenty-four. The first article she'd published in an academic journal. And overshadowing all, Lavinia's birth. "Sorry. I don't remember."

"Hold on a second." Mary Ann shut her eyes and scrunched up her face into an expression that reminded Alice of pushing scenes in baby-birthing films she'd seen. She watched in some fascination and ate another piece of shortbread until Mary Ann opened her eyes and said, "So?"

"What?"

"I was trying to send you a thought-picture."

"I didn't get anything."

Lavinia whimpered. Alice produced a pacifier from her pocket and stuck it in Lavinia's mouth. "You didn't really expect we could still communicate like that, did you? After all this time?"

Mary Ann's tone was light. "Just thought I'd try."

Lavinia spit out the pacifier and started on a moaning sort of cry. Alice picked her up, stood, rocked her. "About Lavinia, I was hoping you might be my guide on how to cope with babies."

Mary Ann passed over some stapled pages that lay on the coffee table. "I thought you might want some tips, so I prepared a contact list for you. There's info here on a baby gym class you could try, a mothers' group that meets at the church, the name of a store that sells used baby stuff. We could go there together, if you like. And I've given you the phone number of my favourite teenage babysitter, a girl named Melina Pappas."

Alice took the papers, looked at the first page. "This is wonderful. Thank you."

Lavinia started to cry, full blast. "Oh, all right," Alice said, "you can be fed." She sat down in a wing chair, pulled up her T-shirt, adjusted her nursing bra, settled Lavinia on her breast. "There you go." To Mary Ann, she said, "Breastfeeding is quite the physical rush, isn't it? I wonder if heroin feels like this."

"Heroin?"

"That feeling when she latches on, and the milk lets down — it's so intense, there's such a surge. She starts sucking, and I find myself sticking out my tongue, as if I've fallen into some sort of ecstatic trance. Like this." She acted it out — tongue lolling, eyes shut, head thrown back, neck and breast exposed. Then raised her head and sat up. "Know what I mean?"

Mary Ann laughed another peal of delighted laughter. "I'm so glad you're back," she said. Alice had been glad, too.

To Jake, Alice said, "So I live with my daughter in a duplex owned by Mary Ann MacAllister's mother. I'm in the top apartment, Mary Ann's mom is in the lower. Do you remember Mary Ann?"

"Yeah, sure. Blonde and into sports? Mike Reynolds' girl. She still lives in Oakdale, too?"

"I know. Sometimes I feel like I suffer from a severe case of arrested development. All these years later and I'm still sneaking cigarettes and hanging out with Mary Ann."

"What's she up to now?"

Other than coordinating a dinner club to enable her extra-marital affair? "She's married with children, and she's working for an IT guy who's part of the Main Street development team."

"Yeah, my parents mentioned that big changes are coming to Oakdale."

"I'm consulting on the project, too."

The waiter cleared their plates, Jake pulled a crumpled pack of cigarettes from his jacket and offered her one, they stepped outside to smoke on the sidewalk, and she told him a little about the station restoration, and the lost-and-found boxes.

"Before I opened them," she said, "I had visions of lost love letters, or an engraved pocket watch. I had my heart set on a dog-eared book of poetry with key passages underlined in fountain-pen ink."

"And there was nothing like that."

"No. Only some umbrellas and hats, a set of rusty keys, and a pair of plastic sunglasses. No museum-quality finds."

"And no romance."

"Which was fine, because I don't go for romance, in general. My idea of an exciting evening is to read in bed with my socks on. How about you? Get out much?" She instantly regretted how defensive she'd sounded, but he didn't seem put off.

He said, "I live a fairly simple life, too, when I'm home. I work, I work out, go to an occasional movie." He exhaled a long plume of smoke. "And I smoke too much — my one vice. It's totally fucked up my breath control. Though I think it may have improved my voice."

"Your speaking voice?"

"My singing voice. I sing in a band. A would-be R&B band. Purely recreational. Once every couple of months we get a gig at a wedding or at a small-town bar."

Alice stubbed out her cigarette, though it wasn't half done. "Sorry," she said. "I'm not used to smoking in the daytime. I'm starting to feel woozy. And I seem to be hearing things." She waved aside a veil of smoke. "Or did you just say that you sing?"

Kate called Hallie at her office. "I've invited myself to the second meeting of this Oakdale dinner club. Will I see you there?"

"No. Sam's going this time. Once was enough for me."

"What should I expect?"

"Housewives who've put too much time into their cooking. Someone's retired mother. A tarty young receptionist. No one of interest."

"You make it sound so appetizing."

"You might keep an eye out for Drew Wacyk, though."

"The computer guy?"

"Yeah. Make sure no one flirts with him."

"Why?"

"Because he's mine."

"What do you mean?"

"He's my boy toy, no one else's."

Kate swivelled her chair away from her desk. "My god, Hallie. You're not actually —"

"It's nothing. I had him over one Saturday to fine-tune our computers, one thing led to another, and now and then I use him as a pick-me-up. He worships me. And work's been tense lately, my boss is a total prick. I need to be worshipped."

"Just to be clear: you're having sex with him?"

"Yes, Kate. It's mostly oral sex, but yeah, we've fucked too."

"I don't know what to say to that. Except, really?"

"I didn't ask you to approve. I asked you to protect my interests."

"When do you see him? Where do you see him? No, on second thought, don't tell me. I don't want to know. What about Sam? Does he know?"

"Of course not. And don't you tell him."

"Believe me, I won't."

Kate told Tom, though, in the car on the way out to Oakdale, and when she'd finished the story, she said, "I don't know if I'm shocked by this news, or completely not shocked."

"I'm more surprised at Drew than at Hallie," Tom said. "If he wanted to have an affair with an older woman, why would he choose that ectomorph iceberg Hallie? Why not Mary Ann Gray?"

"What body type is she — hourglass?"

"She's neither voluptuous nor starved, she's in-between. And she's far warmer in personality than Hallie."

It took some effort, but Kate refrained from comment on the insufferable-sounding Mary Ann.

Tom said, "Is this serious? Do you think Sam and Hallie will divorce?"

Kate couldn't help herself. "Forget about Hallie and Sam. Are you saying that if you were Drew, you'd sleep with this Mary Ann person?"

"The only person I want to sleep with is you."

"Good answer."

The Second Dinner Club Meeting:
October 23rd, 2010

Host: Lisa Carsten

Hors d'oeuvres

Potato-Egg Tortilla	Phoebe Morales
Endive Stuffed with Brie,	
Prosciutto & Pea Shoots	Danielle Pringle
Pork & Chive Dumplings	Sam Orenstein

Mains

Mango Chicken	Alice Maeda
Torta Rustica	Tom Gagliardi
Rice Pilaf with Almonds	Lisa Carsten
Greek Salad & Oatmeal Bread	Amy Millson

Desserts

Chocolate Orgasm	Mary Ann Gray
Apple Tart	Sarah MacAllister
Beer & Wine	Drew Wacyk

14

Alice was closest to the front door when the bell rang to announce Tom and Kate's arrival, and Lisa was busy in the kitchen, demonstrating the hydraulic lift on the built-in spice racks in her new cabinets. So Alice was presented with two bottles of cava by Kate. "My contribution to the dinner," Kate said. "I don't cook."

"Aren't you thoughtful, they're chilled. But you didn't need to bring anything extra. Tom's pie looks amazing."

"It's a torta rustica, not a pie, he'll have you know. And something fizzy seemed appropriate to mark the occasion when I meet the pillars of Oakdale society."

Shit. Had Kate caught on that one particular pillar had designs on Tom? Alice said, "You won't find too many pillars here, just us regular folks." What on earth was she saying? "Let's open one of these bottles right away, shall we?"

Alice poured the wine into flutes Lisa retrieved from her new walnut-faced cabinets, left Tom in the kitchen to tend to his torta, walked Kate through the ground floor, and made introductions, ending with Sam. "I met Sam for the first time tonight," she said, "but you know him already, don't you?"

Kate kissed him hello and put her arm around him. "Sam!

How *are* you? You look great. The kids are well? And your writing? What exquisite food did you bring?"

Alice moved off and left Kate acting all warm and sympathetic with Sam, as if someone had died. What was the story there? Was it possible that Kate knew Mary Ann had Sam in her sights, and Tom too?

It was possible, but not likely, Alice decided, that anyone might have figured out Mary Ann's agenda. And at least Mary Ann had no major campaigns planned for either Sam or Tom that evening, so Kate's suspicions shouldn't be aroused. Mary Ann was occupied right now, in fact, having a tête-à-tête with Drew in the backyard. Drew had dressed up, was wearing a sweater with black jeans. The close-fitting knit suited his lean body and outlined his pecs, a feature Alice was sure Mary Ann would appreciate. Whereas what Alice would appreciate was another glass of wine.

In a corner of the great room, Danielle said to Sarah, "That businesswoman isn't here tonight. Hallie."

"She didn't seem very happy last time," Sarah said. "More of a dieter than an eater, I thought."

"And I see a few new faces — some people must have brought their spouses."

"Would you have liked to?"

"Not at all. I mean, this is my night out, away from my family." And she refused to feel guilty for enjoying it.

"I agree," Sarah said. "And I loved your stuffed endive."

"Did you? Thank you. I had trouble deciding what to bring."

"Have you decided what kind of cake I should bake for your family reunion?"

"I can't take a cake from you."

"What'll it be? Banana? Carrot? One of each?"

Danielle assessed the degree of determination in Sarah's eyes. "Is there any point in continuing to refuse you?"

"No. I'd just drive something out to your farm on party day, anyway."

"In that case, I'll accept your offer with thanks. Bake me whatever you feel like. I'll send Benny to pick it up from you that morning, and I'll wow his relatives with it. Though they don't deserve to be wowed."

"Done."

When she found herself alone in Lisa's garden with Drew, Mary Ann seized the opportunity to try flirting with him, but Drew did not respond to any of her wiles. So she was feeling a little discouraged when Phoebe pulled her aside after the hors d'oeuvres had been passed and said, "Have you identified any-one who could be Drew's married girlfriend?"

"No, Phoebe."

"He's drinking a lot, and he looks depressed. You know why? Because he can't openly declare his love."

"Shush. Here comes Tom's wife."

"Hi, again," Phoebe said to Kate. "Where's Tom?"

"Having a tour of that enormous kitchen."

"In that case, why don't you give us the dirt on him? We've often speculated in the office about what living with Tom could be like. Haven't we, Mary Ann?"

"Phoebe —"

"Does he read the dictionary every day? That's my question."

"Don't mind her," Mary Ann said to Kate. "She's still young enough to have a naughty streak."

Kate regarded Mary Ann. "And you're not?"

"Me? God, no. The soul of propriety, that's who I am. Tell her, Phoebe."

"Mary Ann's life *is* pretty boring," Phoebe said.

Kate said, "And here I thought non-stop hanky-panky went on in the suburbs."

Mary Ann avoided Kate's eye. "That's pretty much a myth."

"Drew's life is probably the most exciting in the office," Phoebe said.

Mary Ann said, "I don't know where she gets these ideas."

"Where is Drew?" Kate said. "I haven't met him yet."

"We'll go find him." Phoebe took Kate by the arm. "Do you know him well?" And behind Kate's back, she mouthed to Mary Ann, "Maybe she's the one."

Mary Ann twitched at the touch of Tom's hand on her elbow. "Where's Phoebe taking Kate?" he said.

"Kate wanted to meet Drew. And Phoebe's in a mood to stir up trouble. She's seeking scandal."

"Kate will like that. She's of the opinion that Oakdale is rife with illicit activity. She posits infidelity everywhere."

Mary Ann tried to think of a response that would make her sound cynical, amoral, and available, but her lack of a low-cut top and fuck-me heels limited her to a squeaky, "Infidelity? In Oakdale?"

"Kate plays at being suspicious, but in her heart, she knows I'm immune to the appeal of an affair. Even if a beautiful, charming woman were to express interest in me, or make advances that were genuinely enticing, I wouldn't stray."

Mary Ann stared at him a second, understood his message, admired the tactful way he'd communicated it, and fought to contain a look of consternation that would reveal she'd received it. "You're just a classy but staid guy, I guess."

"Staid, anyway. Now, would you excuse me a moment? I must go compliment Danielle on her delectable hors d'oeuvres."

* * *

Alice was fielding questions from Sam about Alexander the Great's campaigns in Asia — research for his novel, he said — when Drew walked by.

Sam interrupted himself. "Hey, Drew. Our computers are running so smoothly at home since you fixed them, we don't get to see you anymore."

Drew stopped and mumbled "yeah" in a manner that struck Alice as shifty.

Sam said, "Drew — do you know Alice? She and Mary Ann have been friends since high school."

Drew nodded at Alice. Furtively. "We met last time. When I met Hallie."

Drew's moodiness aside, Alice realized she was standing with two of Mary Ann's prospective guys, and here was her opportunity to further the cause. "So, tell us, Drew," she said, "what's it like to work with Mary Ann? Sam and I don't see her work side. I bet she's very competent and organized. Is she?" Help. She was making Mary Ann sound like a drone. "In an attractive way, I mean."

"Mary Ann at work? Yeah, she's good. Excuse me, guys. I need to get another beer."

He walked away, and Sam said, "It's true what you say about Mary Ann. She does seem competent, and together."

"And attractive."

"Yes, that too. So how far into India proper do you think Alexander the Great went?"

Kate joined the buffet line behind Sarah, who was taking very small amounts of food: the thinnest sliver of Tom's torta rustica, a tablespoonful of rice. Kate was following suit when Sarah stopped and said to Mary Ann, across the table, "Sorry, dear, what did you bring again? I've forgotten."

"I brought a dessert called Chocolate Orgasm."

There were a few titters at this announcement, and a woman whose name was Amy or Lisa, Kate couldn't remember which, asked Mary Ann how a Chocolate Orgasm differed from the usual kind of orgasm. Was it easier to achieve? Kate did not find that comment or question humorous, and neither did Sarah, from the weary look on her face. Everyone else laughed, though, and listened to Mary Ann explain that she'd found the recipe in a new cookbook she'd bought called *Cooking for Lovers*.

"So if you're in the mood for excitement," Mary Ann said, "do try a Chocolate Orgasm."

Later, Kate would ask herself why she'd felt compelled to speak up, where her words came from, and why couldn't she have just risen above, but she said, "You'd better save some for Tom and me. After twenty-five years of marriage, we could use a kick-start." And turned away to avoid being on the receiving end of a what-the-fuck look from anyone.

"What did you think?" Tom said to Kate, in the car on the way home. "Did the evening meet expectations?"

"Yes and no. For one thing, I failed to see the appeal of Mary Ann."

"I must say — her cake did not strike me as very orgasmic."

"Me either. I thought it was more like its maker — pleasant but a little dull."

"What about Sam? For a cuckold, he seemed in good spirits."

"That's because he's oblivious to Hallie's misdeeds. Though Drew isn't. The only time his gloom lifted was when I told him I'd known Hallie in college."

"It's not our place to intervene in their lives, Kate."

"I won't intervene. But I wonder if there's some strange behaviour-altering contaminant in the air or the water out there that's made Hallie do what she did. Or maybe in the food."

Mary Ann and Alice did the dinner club post-mortem by phone the next day.

"How'd it go with making your move on Drew?" Alice said. "He seemed a little out of sorts."

"Forget about him. I got him alone in the garden before dinner and tried every trick in the book, even resorted to a repeat performance of throat baring, and it was like trying to seduce a chair. What's the point of suggestive talk if he's not listening?" Mary Ann sighed. "Tell me the truth, Alice, am I ugly?"

"Of course not. You're very attractive. Repeat after me: I'm very attractive."

"Phoebe thinks he's involved with a married woman."

"He is?"

"I don't know. Or care. I've crossed him off the list."

"And Tom?"

"Also eliminated. You were right — the wife does seem smart and with it. And he can be a bore — that way he talks. And I didn't think much of the pie he brought."

"No? I liked it."

"But I loved those dumplings Sam made. Very toothsome. Like him."

"You're back to him now?"

"He's my last chance."

"Can I suggest you forego the throat-baring move this time?"

"I have a better idea. I've decided to get a dog."

15

October 2010

For Benny's family party, Danielle had her farm workers clean up the kitchen garden and set up the outdoor
furniture on the lawn, and enlisted one of them to help peel
tomatoes, beard mussels, and chop onions. But it still took her
two solid days of work time to get ready for the damn cele-
bration, two days when she could have put together her new
seed order, helped Ethan with his homework, or laboured on a
project of her own choosing.

On the first full day of party prep, she was shelling fava
beans in her kitchen when an unexpected Mary Ann tapped
on her screen door. Benny stood behind her. "And the last stop
on our tour," he said, "is the kitchen: Danielle's sanctuary."

Sanctuary? Try prison. "Mary Ann!" Danielle said. "What
brings you out here? If I'd known you were coming —"

"You'd have baked a cake?"

"No, but I might have tidied up a little. Come on in, and
don't mind the mess." Danielle smiled a welcome, and silently
cursed the house, her hair, and her apron for being in disarray.
Bad enough she lived out on the country road, did she have to
look so much the part? "Would you like a coffee?"

"No, thanks. And don't stop what you're doing. I just wanted
to say hello. I came out to see the puppies." Mary Ann pointed to

the mound of beans sitting on the counter. "Having company?"

Benny said, "We're hosting a big family party on Saturday. Twenty people for lunch. Danielle's going all out for it."

A bean slipped out of Danielle's fingers and across the floor. She picked up another. "I'm not going all out."

"Sure you are," Benny said. "You should hear the menu, Mary Ann. It's good enough to be written up in the *Times* by Danielle's mother, Adele Beaumont."

"Adele Beaumont is your mother, Danielle? No wonder you're such a talented cook. But I thought she was from France. Are you French?"

"No, and neither is she. She pretends to be, though. She likes to pepper her conversation with French words. It drives me crazy."

Benny said, "Adele will be so impressed by the lunch you're making, she'll declare it *magnifique*."

Danielle stopped shelling. "What do you mean, she *will* be impressed? Don't you mean that she *would* be impressed, if she were here, which she won't be?"

Benny wouldn't meet her glare. He picked up a pile of bean casings and dropped them into the compost bin. "I forgot to tell you. She called this morning when you were in the shower, and I invited her to come out Saturday for lunch. She hasn't seen my family in years, since our wedding."

"You invited her out here to eat a meal I'm going to cook? When I've never ever cooked a meal for her?"

Mary Ann said, "I should be going. I'll let you know about the puppy, Benny."

Benny held the door for her. "I'll walk you to your car. And feel free to bring your husband out to take a look before you decide."

"Not my husband, but thanks, I may bring the kids. Bye, Danielle. Good luck with your party."

The screen door closed behind them, and instead of throwing a cleaver at the wall Danielle ran her bean-scented hands up and down her face.

Sam still wanted to quiz Mary Ann about her computer background for the Celeste character in *Samosa Special* (a more distinctive title than *Murder in the Kitchen*, he'd decided), but it was hard to know how she'd take a request to meet him for coffee to talk it over. He'd gone to her dinner club feeling like he was her special guest after she'd made a suggestive comment about wanting to eat him with her eyes. Had he misunderstood? Maybe. At the party she'd seemed quite chummy not only with Tom, but with Drew. On separate occasions, Mary Ann had been tucked away with each of them, heads bent together, close.

His uncertainty about her motives was part of the reason why, though he'd seen her at school several times since, he hadn't raised the subject of his research. Also because there was always someone else around, or one of the kids needed attention, or Chutney had to be controlled. How convenient instead that she called him on a cold Friday morning, when he was at home working on his outline, and thinking about making aloo gobi for his lunch, which meant he would have to go buy potatoes and cauliflower, and chop them, and toss them with spices and oil, and roast them, and there would be the morning gone.

"I'd like to get some advice from you," she said.

"I want to ask you something too, but you go first."

"No, you start. What is it?"

"I need some research information about working with computers for my novel. Nothing too complicated, just background. I thought I might buy you a coffee sometime, ask you some questions about the field."

Her voice was cheery, enthusiastic. "Sure. I'd be happy to tell you anything I know, which isn't much. And I want to talk to *you* about dogs. Kayla's been bugging me to buy one for months and has sworn she'll walk it, so I went out to the Pringles' farm to see their puppies. But before I make the purchase, I thought I'd see if someone sane who had a dog could talk me out of it."

"In that case, how about we have that coffee, and talk about both topics?"

"What do you say to lunch instead? Today. The kids are having pizza lunch at school, so you're free, right? Or is that too short notice? I'm thinking we could try the new Italian sandwich place that's opened up in Pembroke."

Sam's heart was beating fast, he had no idea why. "Uh, sure," he said. "Lunch today would be great. Should we take one car or two?"

Sam's shirt and jeans were clean and pressed, which Mary Ann regarded as a good sign: he'd wanted to look nice for her. Except that he chose a table by the window, in full view of passersby, which indicated that he didn't consider their meeting to be in any way clandestine: a bad sign. Unless what he was really saying was that he was unsure of Mary Ann's intentions. Time to clarify them.

When they were seated with their sandwiches, Mary Ann said, "How's the writing going? Are you churning out pages daily?"

"Not exactly, no."

"Why not?"

"I get distracted a lot. By the arrival of the morning mail, by cooking shows on TV, by sudden overwhelming urges to nap." He opened his notebook. "But talking to you is a step

165

forward — I need to gather some substantive details that I can work into the story."

Mary Ann imagined Alice making a joke about some substantive details that Mary Ann could work into *her* story and hid a smile. "Okay," she said. "Ask me questions, and I'll try to answer them." She bit into her sandwich.

"Let's start with training. Where would an IT person of today have been educated, what would she have studied?"

Twenty minutes later, sandwiches and computer questions finished, Sam said, "It's your turn to ask me about dogs. What do you need to know?"

"My family had one when I was a kid, and I remember it being such a pain to walk him that I wonder if getting a dog now would be a mistake. Do you regret yours?"

"I have mixed feelings. Chutney can be a nuisance, but he's very good at unconditional love and acceptance. No matter what I do or don't do all day, he loves me just the same."

Now there was an interesting response, heavy with subtext. But how to pick up on it? Mary Ann said, "I suppose we can all use more affection."

"What kind of dogs do the Pringles breed?"

"Golden retrievers."

"I think they need a fair bit of exercise."

"Who walks the dog in your house?"

"Me. The only person with idle time in his schedule. I walk him three times a day. Three times a day I go outside, clear my head, and think about whether this novel is a lost cause."

"If writing is what you want to do, what you believe in —"

"Yeah, but is it? That's the question." He balled up his napkin. "I keep doubting myself, and wondering if my story and character hang together. Take my female character Celeste, for instance. I've been wrestling with her motivation, trying to figure out what would make her go for the hero, Simon.

He's no handsome devil, he doesn't talk much, he has a shady background. He's a cook in a diner, for god's sake. And she's supposed to be outgoing, pretty, and smart. Why would she like him?"

Here was Mary Ann's in. "Maybe," she said, "she could fall in love with the food he cooks for her. Or with the line where his jaw meets his neck, right there." Mary Ann pointed at Sam's chin. "Maybe she doesn't get enough affection in her life either, and longs to be held in his arms."

Sam leaned back in the spindly chair, almost tipped it over. "You make my story sound like a romance."

"Isn't it a romantic mystery?"

"I wish I knew."

Mary Ann called Alice late that evening. "So Sam and I went for lunch today, and I think we're talking genuine affair potential."

"Why are you whispering?"

"Josh is still up, and I don't want him to hear."

"Where's Bob?"

"I don't believe anyone by that name lives here."

"He's moved out, and you forgot to tell me?"

"He's in Australia. Or Hong Kong."

"Don't give me that. You know what country he's in."

"He's away for three weeks. You want me to check his itinerary, tell you exactly which city he's in today?"

"Sorry. It's none of my business."

"Wrong. Our love lives are each other's business. And now that mine has passed the all-important lunch stage, soon to be followed by the meeting to go buy a puppy stage, what's happening with yours?"

"Mine?"

"Have you had lunch with your guy yet?"

"Yes."

"And?"

"I should probably make the next move."

"You have to. You must. The timing is right. I can feel it. The planets are moving into a favourable alignment."

"Favourable for what?"

"Good sex. Which I think I can expedite for at least one of us if we convene another meeting of the dinner club, at your house."

The morning of the family party day, Danielle had a long list of last-minute things to do, and had expected Benny to entertain Ethan and Alex while she did them, had thought he would keep them out for a few hours and give her some quiet time. Not just drive them to their soccer games, pick up the cakes from Sarah, and bring the kids home right after, to get underfoot.

Alex walked in the house in his muddy soccer cleats. "I'm hungry. Can I have a snack?"

Danielle put down the lettuce she was washing and dried her hands. "Take off your cleats and tell me what you'd like. A rice cake with cream cheese? An apple?"

"Crackers and cheese, please. With orange cheese."

Ethan came in, sat down next to Alex at the counter. "Me, too. I want a snack, too."

It was just past eleven. The guests would arrive in an hour. If Danielle could feed the boys a snack and sit them down in front of the television, she should still be able to get everything done in time. She pulled out Alex's rice crackers from the cupboard, Ethan's wheat crackers, laid out six crackers on separate plates for each child. She found a clean cutting board and a knife, pulled a hunk of cheddar out of the fridge, started cutting thin slices off it.

Alex said, "Kayla Gray said at soccer she's going to buy a puppy from us. But she can't take Hero, right?"

The knife slipped, cut Danielle's finger, left a half-inch-long gash. "Shit!" she said, and dropped the knife, sucked at the wound, tasted blood.

Ethan sang, "You said shi-it, you said shi-it."

"Shut up, dickhead," Alex said.

Danielle took her finger out of her mouth, watched the blood ooze up. "Stop it, both of you." She turned on the cold tap, let the water wash over the cut. "Stop it right now. And don't swear like that in front of the family today, please." Her finger throbbed. She held it aloft, bent down, and reached with her free hand under the sink for the box of Band-Aids she kept there.

"But Ethan *is* a dickhead!" Alex said.

"Mommy said shi-it, Mommy said shi-it."

Danielle screamed, at top volume, "SHUT UP!"

Both boys were stunned into silence.

"I can't take this crap right now," Danielle said. "Any of it. Where's Daddy?"

Alex said, "He's out with the dogs. And Kayla can't have Hero."

Danielle pulled the Band-Aid tight around her finger, slid the snack plates toward them, took milk out of the fridge, schooled her voice, made it calm. "Daddy and I haven't said for sure that you can keep Hero."

"Ow!" A cry from Alex. "Mommy, Ethan kicked me!"

Danielle banged the jug of milk on the counter, and a big plop of milk spilled out. "That's it. I'm going upstairs to lie down. Do what you want. Kick each other, eat your snack, swear your heads off. Just don't bug me."

The bed was soft. A cool breeze blew in through the open window. Danielle lay down — just for a minute — and closed her eyes. She was so tired. She'd been up late the night before, corralling plates and cutlery and glasses and vases.

She still had to preheat the spaghetti cooking water, finish washing the lettuce, find some more serving dishes. There was no time to rest, but her body sank into the bed and dreams began to seep into her mind. She unwrapped her Band-Aid — she'd put it on too tight, her finger was pulsing painfully. Blood still oozed from the cut. She floated downstairs, held her finger above the simmering pot of pasta sauce, watched blood drip into the pot, stirred it in with a long wooden spoon.

Alex's warm hand touched her arm. "Mommy?"

She woke. Alex was standing by the bed. Her bedside clock showed she'd slept for ten minutes. She sat up, unfastened the Band-Aid, refastened it looser.

"I need a hug," Alex said. He climbed onto the bed and put his arms around her neck. He was a good hugger, always had been.

She hugged him back. "I'm sorry I yelled at you."

"It's okay," he said. And after a second, "Grandma Adele is here."

This time, Danielle didn't swear. She released Alex from the hug, and told him nicely to go play. She swung her legs over the side of the bed, slipped into her shoes, went to the bathroom, brushed her teeth, brushed her hair, applied eye pencil and lipstick.

She went downstairs and outside and greeted Adele, who stood on the grass in front of the house, dressed in her idea of country clothes — a Barbour jacket over pressed chinos and leather lace-up shoes, accessorized with a walking stick.

"Hello, darling." Adele kissed her on both cheeks. "It's so thoughtful of you and Benny to include me in this party. I rarely have the chance to experience life *à la campagne*."

"Weren't you visiting friends in the Hamptons this summer?"

"Yes, but that's not the real thing. This is far more salt of the earth." She gestured with her stick toward the peeling wood fence around Danielle's kitchen garden, the stacks of plastic planters lined up beside the nearest greenhouse.

"I hope you're not expecting an elaborate meal."

"Oh no. I came out here for the company, and the fresh air. I rarely eat lunch these days. It becomes so difficult to keep one's figure." She patted her stout waist, the same stout waist she'd had for years.

"You came all the way out here and you're not going to eat?"

"Maybe a nibble. When Ethan and Alex have stopped running around in circles like little *cochons*, would you bring them to me to say hello?"

Benny stepped in then, forestalled the rude retort Danielle had been about to utter, took Adele on the farm tour, offered her a glass of wine, and installed her in a chair under a shady tree that afforded a view of the arrival of Benny's relatives up the driveway. There was no question of Adele helping Danielle in the kitchen. Adele didn't help in her own kitchen.

Benny's sisters helped, though. Or rather, planted themselves on Danielle's side of the counter, hands full of jumbo-size Tupperware containers stuffed with cake and jello, and said, "What can I do?" and, "Are those mussels? My Joe doesn't touch shellfish," and "Everything looks good, but what's Dad going to eat?" They polished off the gravlax and pumpernickel in minutes, got in her way when she was trying to drain the spaghetti (three pots of it), asked her could she set aside some plain noodles for little Clarissa, and was there any white bread one of them could slice — you know how Dad likes his bread — and a cutting board, and a bread knife, and by the way, did that good-smelling pasta sauce have wine in it, because Joe didn't touch wine, either.

Somewhere in there, Benny's parents arrived. They did not come in to say hello first. Benny's mother Margaret sat Murray down alone at the head of the long outdoor table, placed his napkin in his lap, found Danielle, and said, "Is lunch ready? Murray likes to eat promptly at noon."

"The food's laid out buffet-style inside," Danielle said. "You can help yourselves."

"I'll make Murray a plate," Margaret said. "Show me where."

In the serving area, Benny's sisters were running amok. "I hope you don't mind," one said. "The kids were hungry, so I took the plastic covering off the platters, and told them to go ahead. Did I miss anything?"

Danielle hid her irritation and checked the buffet. Everything was out that should be — the plain food for the kids and whoever else wanted it, the spaghetti mixed with the sauce and piping hot, dishes, serving utensils, napkins, drinks. All that was missing was Alex's food, which was hidden away, so that people who could eat anything on the table wouldn't grab his gluten-free items and leave him with nothing. It had happened before. Alex's food and the salad were all she needed to get. She asked Benny to look after Alex, and she emptied the prewashed greens into a restaurant-sized salad bowl, tossed them with the blood-orange vinaigrette, and brought the bowl outside.

At the table, she noticed that Murray's plate was filled with cold meat, cheese, and bread, looked to see if Adele had taken a large portion of pasta (she had), saw that her kids were content, and tried not to scowl when Benny stood up and tapped his water glass with a knife.

"Now listen up, everyone," he said, and people laughed because the dogs picked that moment to bark, in chorus, from the kennels. When the barking had died down, Benny said, "I'd like to read a poem I've written in honour of this meal."

"But please eat the hot food," Danielle said, "before it gets cold."

"Yes, don't stop eating, just listen," Benny unfolded his piece of paper. "Are you ready?"

"Ready," someone yelled, and Benny's sister Theo leaned over and said, "This salad is absolutely divine, Danielle."

"Okay," Benny said. "Here goes: The day is fine / The sky is blue / My beautiful wife / Has cooked for you."

The family broke out into applause and bravos, aimed in Danielle's direction.

She lied. "It was my pleasure."

Benny held up a finger. "I'm not finished. There's another verse: We may not be rich / But when we eat like this / We forget our troubles / And know the meaning of bliss."

"Amen," Murray said, amid more applause, as Benny mouthed the words thank you to Danielle and sat down, and Adele directed a condescending smile into her wine glass.

Theo said, "Has everyone tried the salad? These greens with this dressing are amazing! It's the best salad I've ever eaten. You have to try it."

Murray shook his head. "I don't eat raw food." As if no one knew this already.

Adele didn't know. "Why is that?"

Murray launched into a speech about his dietary beliefs, and Theo passed around the salad bowl until it was empty.

"Is there any more inside?" Benny asked Danielle, at the same time as Ethan asked for more apple juice, and Alex announced that he wasn't hungry, but could he still have dessert later?

Danielle took the salad bowl and Alex's plate into the kitchen, fetched some apple juice for Ethan, and found more greens, unwashed, piled up in a strainer on the counter. To wash them and spin them now, and dry them — by the time she did all that, lunch would be finished. Of course, she could always go out and admit that there was no more. Publicly reveal herself as an incompetent meal planner, in other words. Or she could simply shake the greens — they weren't that dirty — pat them dry with paper towels, throw them in the bowl, toss them with vinaigrette, take the whole mess outside, and hope no one would notice.

When she walked onto the lawn with a glass of apple juice in one hand and the replenished salad bowl in the other, she heard Adele say, "But surely you're sacrificing a wealth of taste experiences based on unfounded superstitions. Are you willing to spend the rest of your life eating grey vegetables and stewed fruit? Are you willing to never again know the crunch of a raw apple, the snap of a fresh snow pea?"

Murray's jaw jutted forward. His bushy eyebrows lowered. He made a low rumbling sound that might have signified he was clearing his throat.

Danielle held up the bowl. "Anyone for more salad?"

"Give me some," Murray said.

Margaret waved her hands back and forth in front of her. "No, Murray! You can't eat that."

"I'll try some, and we'll see what happens," Murray said. "We'll just see."

A trick of the mind took Danielle back to her dream. She saw herself standing over the pasta sauce, dripping blood from her finger into the pot. The scene changed, and she dreamt that Murray brought a forkful of salad up to his mouth. A few clustered leaves of mache went in first, followed by a dangling piece of pale green frisée from which a large potato bug hung. Danielle gasped, then laughed when the bug hopped off the frisée and onto Murray's chin. She laughed out loud, the hearty laugh of a sleeping dreamer. But her laugh was cut off by screams. From where?

Oh. From everyone who stood around the table, yelling and gesticulating. In the real world.

16

November 2010

Melina hadn't applied to any big deal, hard-to-get-into colleges. There was no point, since her grades had slipped during her junior year, when she'd gone a little alternative and partied too much. Both Mary Ann and Alice had been cool about it, and acted as if they hardly noticed the changing colours of Melina's hair, makeup, nail polish, and clothes. An attitude Melina's parents should have adopted if they'd wanted to lower the stress level at home.

Now that she was back in the land of the semi-normal, her hair dyed to a shade of brown found within nature, her grades were good again, her SAT scores were better, and she was applying to some colleges not too far away, like Syracuse.

She told Alice about her applications when she came to babysit on a Saturday night. Alice was on her way out to a movie with Mrs. MacAllister from downstairs.

"But why so close to home?" Alice said. "I thought you wanted to go away. Why aren't you applying out of state?"

"I wouldn't be living at home in Syracuse. And going out of state isn't exciting. I've been to South Carolina. It's the world I want to see."

"So why don't you attend college out of the country?"

"We can't afford it. Just to live in residence at Syracuse, I'll need to use all my babysitting savings, work at a real job in the summer, and work part-time next year."

"Weren't you saving your babysitting money for a graduation trip to Europe?"

"Yeah, but things changed." Melina didn't feel like going into the details her dad had told her about their financial position — the mortgage, the insurance costs, how they needed to replace her mom's car, how business at the hardware store had declined since the discount superstore had opened up a half-hour drive away.

"I wish I could help you somehow," Alice said.

Melina wished so, too.

In the car on the way to the movie theatre, Sarah said to Alice, "Thank you for doing me a favour and coming out tonight."

"I owe you many favours, I know, but I'm doing this because I've resolved to go out more than twice a year. From now on, I'm going to make an effort to indulge in an occasional diversion."

"That's a good goal. But if you want some advice, choose your diversions with care. I recently joined a dance committee at the country club for something to do, and after one meeting, I'm in despair."

"Was it that bad?"

"You should have seen the committee members: there was a pushy, know-it-all, retired businesswoman who squirmed out of taking on a single task. And an Idea Lady, who proposed one outlandish suggestion after another, then complained when they were rejected. And the shady operator, a man who had a friend who could supply a sound system, a cousin who could underprice the caterer, and a son who could take photos for cheap. Too late I remembered that one of the best things about working in real estate was being on my own."

Alice signalled her turn into the theatre parking lot. "I'm not too keen on meetings, either. When I'm forced to go to them, I'm always trying to move them along, speed them up, get them over with, so I can go back to my office and be alone."

"Oh, Alice," Sarah said. "We always were alike."

At noon on the Sunday after Benny's family party, Danielle answered the phone.

"Hi, Danielle, it's Mary Ann. How'd your party go?"

"It went well. Except for the part when a bug crawled out of the salad and onto my father-in-law's face."

"Really? What a scream."

"People *did* scream."

"And you laughed, I hope."

"I started to, but I had to stop myself when I saw the horrified faces all around me."

"I'll never forget making barbecued corn one time — in the husk — and serving it to a client of Bob's. The guy was a real pompous ass. I had laugh behind my napkin when he unwrapped his corn and found a worm wriggling inside."

"Did the client think it was funny? Or your husband?"

"No, but I did."

"Well, it took me a whole day of apologizing, but by the time the family left they'd resumed speaking to me." Though Danielle's favourite part of the day had been right after lunch, when Adele had told her that she couldn't remember the last time she'd enjoyed herself so much at a party.

"And will you still be speaking to me if I come out there this afternoon with my kids to choose a puppy? Say no if you can't stand the thought of any more people traipsing through after yesterday."

"By all means, come over. And if you like clams and mussels, I've got leftovers you could take home."

Benny and the boys went down to meet the Grays in the driveway. From the doorway of the house, Danielle recognized Kayla, saw two older boys who must be her brothers, and last out of the car was a man Danielle had met briefly at the second dinner club evening, and whose name she'd forgotten. Danielle walked over, wearing a hospitable smile. Later, she'd ask them to stay for ice cream.

Alex said to Kayla, "You can't have Hero, we're keeping him."

Benny said, "I'm afraid one of the puppies is accounted for. But there are five others to choose from."

"Hi, Danielle," Mary Ann said. "You know Kayla, these big guys are Josh and Griffin, and Sam is an experienced dog owner, so we brought him along as a consultant."

So that was his name: Sam.

He said, "Great place you've got here, Danielle. Mary Ann was telling me about the produce-growing operation on the way out. I'd love to take a look at it later, if you don't mind."

"Sure."

"But first, to the kennels!" said Benny and led the kids off around the side of the house.

Danielle brought up the rear with Mary Ann and Sam, realized who he was, and said, "You're Sam the Samosa King!"

"Now dethroned. How did you know?"

"Your wife told me." Danielle looked at Mary Ann. "That woman Hallie is Sam's wife, isn't she? Or am I mixed up?"

Mary Ann said, "You know, Sam, I'm not so sure you should have left the food business. Did you try those dumplings Sam made at the last dinner club, Danielle? They were scrumptious."

All five kids were inside the kennel now, being jumped on by the puppies. Mary Ann, Sam, and Danielle stood outside, leaning on the fence.

"I enjoyed cooking for the dinner club," Sam said, "but I feel pretty far removed from the prepared-food scene these days."

Danielle stared over the fence, unseeing. "Prepared food is such a wonderful concept. What could be more like paradise than not having to make dinner every night?"

"Even more so nowadays," Sam said. "That segment of the market has really grown."

Kayla called out, "Mommy, all the puppies are so cute! I can't decide." Even her surly brothers were down on their knees in front of the dogs, letting their faces be licked.

"The problem is," Danielle said, "that every time I bring home purchased food, Benny doesn't like it. He says I could make it better, he thinks it doesn't taste right, or it upsets his stomach. So he won't eat it. Unfortunately."

Sam said, "A connoisseur of your cooking, is he?"

"Uh-oh," Mary Ann said. "Sam is getting that how-can-I-use-this-in-my-novel look. Watch what you say, Danielle, unless you want to read about yourself in Sam's book when it's published."

Book? What book? Then Danielle remembered Hallie dismissing it, calling it "*Murder in the Kitchen*, or some awful thing."

"If the book's ever published, you mean," Sam said.

Mary Ann gave Sam's arm a playful slap. Or was it a loving tap? "Don't say that! It will be."

"Mom, come see," Kayla said. "Help us choose."

Mary Ann and Sam entered the fenced area, waded into the dogs and kids.

"It's the best idea," Danielle said, "to have someone else prepare your meals. The best."

But what with the kids' voices raised in excitement, and the barking of the dogs, no one heard her.

Alice called Jake, got tongue-tied, left a lame message saying she wanted to know how he was and could he call her when he had a chance. And she did not jump every time her phone rang for the rest of the day. She busied herself with work instead, so she wouldn't be sitting and waiting for a call like a desperate single woman in a bad romantic comedy. She took care of some paperwork, checked her emails, and opened one titled "Silver Lining" from her former colleague in England, name of Roger.

Roger's message was excited, full of exclamation marks. A medieval church in a Tuscan village had been destroyed by fire — a tragedy, of course, in terms of the loss of the building and the priceless frescoes it contained — but a godsend to Roger, who had been wanting to excavate the site for years, since theorizing in his doctoral dissertation that a long-lost Hellenic shrine to Apollo had stood on the same ground.

He wrote:

> In case you were wondering, I did NOT arrange for the fire to be set! But if I can slash my way through the government red tape, my excavation of the site will start next summer. Care to join me for it?

Alice read the message once, twice, and quit the mail window without replying. Of course she couldn't go. Much as she'd love to. Did anything sound better than a summer in Italy, an exciting site, her old digging friends, a farmhouse they would rent for the season, an outdoor garden where they could drink wine and eat good food after a hard day's work? Was that the life, or what? Her former life. Her before-Lavinia life.

As soon as the waiter had taken away their menus, Tom said to Kate, "I may have erred in my order. Do you think the chef here truly comprehends ossobuco?"

"Probably. How was work today?"

"We closed the deal on the New Jersey mall."

"Congratulations."

"It's not what I'd call thrilling news."

"No? What would be?"

"Nothing I can think of at the moment. How was your day?"

"The usual. But then, I'm not seeking thrills."

"Perhaps I should have ordered a veal chop. Veal chops require less understanding."

"Are *you* seeking thrills?"

"If I were running this restaurant, I'd have had the table next to us cleared five minutes ago."

The waiter brought over a square glass vase filled with rosemary crackerbread, Tom asked some questions about the ossobuco that were answered to his satisfaction, and the waiter left.

"Maybe you should open your own restaurant," Kate said.

"Am I obsessing too much about the food? I apologize. I'll desist."

"You used to talk about going into the restaurant business, years ago. Do you ever wish you had?"

"No. I think my passion for good food can only remain alive at a remove from the industry of its production. I'm far more suited to be a demanding consumer than an accommodating proprietor. Wouldn't you agree?"

Kate broke off a piece of crackerbread. "Maybe."

"Would you like to open a restaurant?"

"Me? No. Never."

"Why are we talking about this, then?"

"Oh, look. Here come our salads."

Danielle came by to return Sarah's cake stands and brought with her two pots of flowers as a thank-you gift.

"What beautiful nasturtiums!" Sarah said. "And so late in the season."

"Isn't the colour strong and bright? I thought you might like them — to look at, or to eat."

"Thank you. As long as they bloom, I'll feel I've kept the cold weather at bay. I'm dreading winter this year." She set the pots down on the porch, on either side of the door. "Won't you come in?"

Danielle followed Sarah inside and placed the cake stands on her kitchen counter. "I can't stay, but thanks again for the cakes. They were a big hit. My mother asked what bakery they'd come from — she was shocked to find such quality out here in the country."

"Isn't she kind? I do enjoy baking. I volunteered to bake for the New Year's Eve dance I'm helping organize at the country club, but the committee said no. All the food has to come from the caterers."

"Someone from your committee called me to ask about flowers for the dance. Was that your idea?"

"Yes." Sarah had stepped behind the counter and was cutting into a pan of lemon squares. "That would be Sandra. I gave her your name. I wanted to help with the decorations, but Sandra has been in charge of flowers for years. I'm glad she called you, at least."

"If they wouldn't let you do decorations or food, what are you looking after?"

"Here's a joke for you — I'm in charge of music. I have CDs to listen to from the bands I'm supposed to be considering."

Danielle tried and failed to imagine having the spare time Sarah had to volunteer for tasks like this. "How are they?"

"Terrible. And the committee insists on a live band to maintain the club's party-giving standards. Honestly. If retirement means I have to spend all my time with people so set in their ways, I'll have to go back to work."

"And what will you do about the music?"

"Wait until the last minute and book the best of the worst, I suppose. But how are you now that your family party's done with? How's business? How're the kids?"

"We're all good, thanks, but I should get going. I have to pick up some groceries. And cook them."

Sarah handed her a baggie containing four lemon squares. "Let me give you these to take home. In case you want to let your family eat dessert for dinner."

Danielle sighed. "If only."

17

November 2010

Alice may have been the nominal hostess for the third meeting of the dinner club, but Mary Ann set the date and ordered the plates, silverware, and glasses from a party-rental store — her treat. She coordinated the menu, notified the guests, and provided babysitting for Lavinia and the Orenstein girls in the form of a slumber party at Mary Ann's place, to be presided over by Melina.

"Here's how we'll do it," she said to Alice a few days before. "I'll spend the afternoon at your house on Saturday helping you set up, and drive home around four-thirty or five to get myself ready."

"The whole afternoon? You think it will take that long?"

"Yes. At six o'clock, you come to my place, drop Lavinia off with Melina and my kids, and drive me back to yours. We get there at six-fifteen, the guests arrive at seven. And have you considered inviting your mystery man? That would spice up the proceedings."

"Forget it." Jake had not called Alice back, the bum. And she'd been trying very hard to paint over the picture that had become her mind's constant companion since their lunch, the image of him singing, on stage, head thrown back, eyes closed.

"What do you say to a double date sometime?" Mary Ann said. "We could go park by the river, make out in the car. I could really get into making out in a car."

Any fantasies Alice had done her best not to entertain had centered on smoky nightclubs, nowhere near cars. "We're not teenagers anymore, Mary Ann."

"Maybe you're not. But I'm sure as hell going to act like one, at your place, on Saturday night. And no more playing Betty. From now on, I'm Veronica."

"Bob's still away?"

"So is Hallie. Why do you think I picked this specific Saturday? Not to mention booked Melina overnight. And arranged it so I won't have my car?"

"I'm standing here in awe."

"Thank you. All accolades on my organizational skills will be accepted. And with Lavinia sleeping over at my house that night, this could be your big chance, too. If you don't want your new guy to come to the dinner club, why don't you make a date with him for after?"

"You have this way —"

"Of solving all your logistical problems? That's what I'm good at, darling. That's what I do."

"Darling?"

"I'm practising new endearments in anticipation of seeing some action this weekend. Did it sound natural?"

"Goodbye, Mary Ann."

"See you Saturday, babe."

Jake called Alice on the Thursday night, at nine-thirty, just after Lavinia had fallen asleep. He sounded casual, friendly, and made no mention of the message she'd left him over a week before. "I'm in the neighbourhood, at my parents' place. I thought maybe you could come out for a cigarette, walk around the block with me. Or have you already smoked your quota for the day?"

Thoughts bumped around in Alice's head. Like, *How do I look?* And, *What if Mary Ann decides to drop over unannounced?* And, *If he knew he was coming out here, why didn't he call in advance?* Plus the omnipresent, *What about Lavinia?*

"Sure," she said. "I mean, I haven't had a cigarette today. But we'd have to do it here. On my porch. Smoke, that is. I have to stay with Lavinia. She's asleep."

Jake seemed to understand this sorry attempt at communication, and said he'd be over in twenty minutes, giving Alice just enough time to comb her hair, decide against eyeliner (too contrived for the hour), brush her teeth, wash her mouth out with orange juice so she wouldn't smell like toothpaste, pick up the clothes lying on the floor and shove them into Lavinia's room, take a few deep breaths, and remind herself that she wasn't sex-crazed like Mary Ann.

When she opened the door she hoped to hell her smile wasn't tremulous. She winced when she heard how much noise he made coming up the stairs behind her — what would Sarah make of that? She offered him a beer.

He accepted, she handed him a cold one, grabbed herself a jacket, an ashtray, and her smokes, and led him out to the porch, which was storm-windowed for the winter, but unheated.

And drafty. When she couldn't light her cigarette off his lighter on the third try, he held her hand to steady the flame, and she felt minor sparks that she tried to ignore. "It's cold out here," she said.

"Nice and quiet, though. And peaceful after my parents' place. Man, they're irritating."

"What'd they do?"

"Nagged me about when am I going to find someone and settle down. At my age. My mom just doesn't understand how anyone could not want to live the whole homogeneous married suburban bullshit dream." He blew his smoke out sideways, away from her face. "No offence."

"What do you mean? I don't live that life. I may be back in Oakdale, but I take major stands against its dominant culture on a daily basis."

He grinned. "Like?"

"Like that I'm a single mother, my child's in daycare, I don't own diamonds or cashmere, I live in an apartment, my car's old. And I'm extremely principled about not joining the country club. I'm less principled about going there on a guest pass."

"Why are you single, if you don't mind my asking?"

"It's an aptitude thing. You're either suited to marriage or you're not. I'm not."

"Clearly, I should have paid more attention to you when I was young and had hair."

"I like you better without hair."

"Yeah, sure you do."

"And there *was* that one time you hit on me in high school."

"I did? When?"

"At a grad party at Mary Ann's house."

"Why don't I remember this?"

"Because nothing happened. You made an overture, and I passed on it."

"Let me guess: I acted like an entitled jerk."

"You were very smooth, actually. In an annoyingly cocky way." No need to let on how close she'd come to going over to his house that night, jumping into his arms, and fucking him all night long.

"And now?"

"Now the only source of possible cockiness is this singing that you do."

"A source of humiliation is more like it."

"How? I picture you coming off stage and being mobbed by groupies."

"Groupies? We barely draw an audience. You should see the venues we play in. And I'm nobody anyway. The star of the band is a young guy named Tristan. He has the best voice of any of us. He's good-looking too, and built. Goddamn guy is twenty-six years old."

"What's your band called?"

"Rhythm and Blues. A real original name."

"I'd like to come see you sing sometime."

"Yeah? We're playing this Saturday night at a bar in Booth — our first gig in months. Remember that honky-tonk joint, Chuck's? It's still around, and it's the reason I came out to Oakdale tonight. To bring down our amps. On Saturday, I'll drive out the rest of the equipment."

"Not this Saturday?" The night of the dinner club meeting.

"If you have other plans, that's cool."

"My other plans shouldn't go too late. Maybe I'll come by after. Would you introduce me to Tristan if I put in an appearance?"

"I'd tell him to wear a tight shirt so you can see his awesome body."

"I'm kidding about him."

"Yeah, but did you mean it about my hair?"

Alice reached over and touched the top of Jake's bare head for a second. "I meant it."

A fraught pause, then Jake stood. "It's late. I should be going. It's a long drive home."

Alice showed him out, didn't ask him to stay, didn't linger in the doorway, offered no cheek for kissing, was breezy and off-hand, said she'd see if she could make it Saturday night, she wasn't sure.

But tomorrow, she would go buy condoms. First thing.

* * *

There'd been much discussion about the naming of the new puppy in Mary Ann's house. Kayla wanted to call her Bridget, after the heroine of a book she was reading. Griffin wanted to call her Sport. And Josh, who had become, since turning seventeen, the family member least likely to express himself on any topic, surprised the rest of them by coming out strongly in favour of the name Honey.

"I don't mind that," Mary Ann said to him. "But what made you think of it?"

Josh bent down and petted the dog. "I don't know. Because she's the colour of honey."

"I guess Bridget is more of a person's name," Kayla said.

Griffin knelt on the floor and held out his arms. "Come here, Sport. Here, boy!" The dog didn't move.

Kayla said, "She's a girl, stupid, not a boy."

Mary Ann rubbed the dog's head. "Let's try Honey for a few days, see how it goes."

Alice went to a drugstore she'd never set foot in before, ten blocks away from her office, walked in, located the condom display, and stood staring at the array of choices available, none of which looked familiar. Had safe sex always been this complicated? All the options sounded awful. She didn't want thick, ribbed, lubricated, or hot — hot, for god's sake? Though maybe lubricated with spermicide might be good. Yeah. She needed protection from pregnancy *and* disease. And she'd buy some spermicidal foam for good measure. Where was that? Down on the lower shelf. How much was it? Fifteen dollars? Expensive. Oh well. She picked up the foam box, dropped it into her shopping basket.

So. Back to the condoms. How many? Twelve? Twenty-four? An urge to flee was pulling her away from the shelf. She forced herself to focus. Okay. A lubricated with spermicide twelve-pack. Only nine bucks. Cheap. She placed the condom box in her basket, walked quickly to the front of the store, paid the cashier, and left, convinced her purchases were unnecessary.

She didn't need twelve condoms. She didn't need one. The only sex she was going to have would be in her mind.

"But Mommy," Kayla said, "I don't want to walk Honey now."

"Kayla, you agreed when we got the dog that you'd walk her every day. Get moving."

"I'm about to beat the game I'm playing. Can't I go later?"

"No."

"It's too boring, walking Honey."

"I'll come with you."

"I'll still be bored."

"Thanks a lot."

"Can't you take her by yourself?"

"No."

"Can I invite a friend along, at least?"

"Don't make such a big deal of this. Let's just — someone like Jessica Orenstein, maybe?"

"Okay."

"Jessica, I'll allow. Go call her. Tell her to bring her dog, meet us at the park. She could bring her dad, too, if she wanted. So *I* won't be bored."

Late in the day, Alice and Tom walked through the station building. The restoration — its conversion to a library — was almost finished.

Alice said, "It's amazing how quickly the project was completed once construction began, isn't it? Thanks to you, I guess, Mr. Expert Developer."

"If the job was completed on schedule, it's because it's easier to marshal a labour force, to coordinate the trades, when they're all on contract to one employer."

Alice looked up at the vaulted ceiling, the carved mouldings, the intricate woodwork on the railings. "I love the idea of kids like Lavinia growing up in this kind of library. Associating reading and learning with beauty and history. It's a fine thing you've done, Tom."

"We still have to complete the rest of the Main Street job and find more tenants for the new retail spaces."

"And then?"

"There will be other projects to work on."

Alice sat down on one of the old railroad station benches. "Do you like your work, Tom? Find it fulfilling?"

He sat next to her, not too close. "Some projects more than others. How about you?"

Alice shaded her eyes from an incoming shaft of sunlight. "I heard from a former colleague of mine the other day. He invited me to be part of the crew for a site he's going to excavate in Italy next summer."

"That sounds exciting."

"I can't go. Because of Lavinia."

Tom crossed his legs. "She'll grow up one day, and move out. And you'll be able to do anything you want again. Having collected years of love and affection in between."

Alice turned to look at him. "You have kids?"

"Didn't you know? Twin boys. They're in college." He told her where they were, what they were studying, about their passions for sports over anything arts-related.

Alice digested all this, said, "And you keep on being a

developer so that you can pay for their education?"

"No, Kate and I have invested safely over the years — those expenses are covered."

"So when do you start doing what you really want to do?"

"What would that be?"

"I don't know. I thought everyone had something they'd rather be doing."

Tom pulled a handkerchief from his pocket and rubbed at a spot on the arm of the bench. "When I started the Oakdale job, I thought it would be different from the others. I hoped that the preservation of some of these fine architectural specimens might prove to be more stimulating, more satisfying an undertaking than my usual projects."

"But no?"

"It's been a fascinating job in many ways, and has allowed me the undeniable benefit of making your acquaintance, and that of the other Oakdalians, but — as you so succinctly put it — no."

"What's missing?"

"I wish I knew."

"Maybe we've all just become bored and boring."

Tom folded his handkerchief. "Forgive me if I've bored you."

"Oh, Tom. That's not what I meant. You know what you and I need? To be more like Mary Ann. When she's unhappy about something, she acts on it. She makes a change, makes things happen."

"Like the dinner club? She sent me a reminder about the meeting tomorrow night, at your apartment."

"You and Kate are still coming, right?"

"We're looking forward to it."

* * *

Mary Ann and Kayla met up with the Orensteins at the park. "Why don't you girls go over to the playground?" Mary Ann said. "Your dad and I will walk the dogs around a bit and meet you there."

"So," she said to Sam, when the girls had gone off, "What are you cooking for dinner tonight?"

"I'm ordering in pizza. You?"

"Grilled cheese for the kids. For myself, I made a minestrone soup with kale."

"Will you sprinkle fresh Reggiano on top?"

"I will. And I'll have a ficelle from the new bakery alongside."

"Sounds much better than pizza."

"Good, because I brought you some." Mary Ann opened a bag she held and showed Sam the container inside.

"For me? You shouldn't have. But thank you." He took the container and eased it into a big side pocket on his coat.

"You're welcome. Are you ordering in because you had a good writing day and didn't have time to cook?"

"No. Because I had a demoralizing day, spent reading over the two hundred pages I've written."

"And?"

"I think the draft might contain one or two salvageable sentences."

"It's better than that."

"How do you know?"

"You're better than that."

"Are you this nice to your husband? If you are, he's lucky."

Mary Ann bent down, took Honey off the leash. "I'm not this nice to him. We barely speak. Go on, girl."

Sam released Chutney, watched him bound off after Honey, and said, mildly, "Hallie left for a business trip to London today."

"Yeah. Bob's been in Asia since last week."

The pause that followed should have felt awkward, but

it didn't, not to Mary Ann, who used it to breathe deeply, in and out.

"Can I tell you a secret?" Sam said. "Sometimes I like being a single parent for a few days. When there's no one around to disapprove of me ordering pizza."

"Don't tell me Hallie expects you to cook nutritious dinners for the kids every night."

"Not exactly, but she doesn't like it when they eat junk food. Or cheese."

"I know what you mean about being able to call the shots. Bob travels a lot on business, and I've become totally used to running the home front on my own." So much so that she couldn't imagine how she'd cope if he became part of her life again in any real way.

Neither one spoke for a minute. Mary Ann because she'd realized that she was ready to split up with Bob and get a divorce. And that being a single mom would not be so terrible, nor so different from her current life.

Sam said, "Annabelle has been talking about nothing but this sleepover you've arranged for tomorrow night. She's excited about having a party with the big girls."

"Good. And a night out should cheer you up, too. Even if it is only with the dinner club."

"No crowd I'd rather be with."

Mary Ann's hopes lurched forward. "It'll be a good time," she said. "I promise."

18

November 20, 2010

At two o'clock on dinner club day, Mary Ann came up Alice's stairs carrying pressed tablecloths wrapped in dry-cleaning bags. "We've got two hours," she said. "Let's get busy. Hi, Lavinia."

Lavinia didn't look up, kept playing with her dollhouse.

"Say hello, Lavinia," Alice said.

Lavinia kept her head down, murmured a word that might have been hello.

Mary Ann threw her coat and purse on a chair, draped the tablecloths over the back of the sofa. "Shall we rearrange the furniture? I think these chairs should be pushed back against the wall."

"Why?"

"To create conversation corners."

"Oh, right."

"Have you really never entertained before?"

"Never."

"Not once?"

"Does cooking dinner for a boyfriend count?"

Mary Ann glanced at Lavinia and whispered to Alice, "What boyfriend? You've cooked for him?"

Alice shook her head. "I was talking about someone in the past. But I do have something to tell you about the present."

"Help me move this table on an angle while you're talking. There. See how we've opened up the space?"

"Hold on, Mary Ann." Alice held out a hand to Lavinia. "Come on, Lavinia. It's time to watch your movie in my room."

When Alice returned, Mary Ann was spreading a cloth out on the table. "This must be good if you had to remove Lavinia from the room before telling me. Spill."

Alice told Mary Ann about Jake — about the lunch and the drop-in visit, and about his band's gig at Chuck's that night. When she was done, Mary Ann said, "I hardly know what to say, Alice. Friendships have ended for less."

"Are you serious?"

"Semi. Why didn't you tell me any of this before now?"

"I don't know. I'm sorry. I should have. I didn't think I had much of anything to tell."

"What I can't really get over is that you — the person who hates conceited guys — are seeing Jake the Snake Stewart."

"I'm not seeing him, not yet. And he's different now. Less generic, more humble. More individual."

"Probably still has a big dick though."

"Mary Ann, please."

"Okay, I'm feeling optimistic about me and Sam tonight, so I'll forgive you."

"Thank you."

"And I love the idea of taking the dinner club dancing. I can't wait to get Sam on the dance floor."

"What?" Alice said, weakly.

"Continuing the dinner club party at Chuck's is a super idea. Where do you want to set up the dessert table?"

* * *

After Mary Ann had left, Lavinia came into the living room and stopped short when she saw how it had been transformed — the tablecloths, the gleaming rows of glasses, the stacks of plates, the rearranged furniture.

"What do you think?" Alice said.

"Is tonight the night I'm sleeping over at Kayla's?"

Alice bent down, put her arm around Lavinia. "Yes, sweetie. And Melina's going to be looking after you and the other girls."

Lavinia said, "I like Melina."

"Me, too."

"She has an earring in her eyebrow."

They'd done this dialogue before. "Would you like an earring in your eyebrow?"

"Nooo!"

Alice hugged her. "How about in your belly-button?"

Lavinia giggled. "Nooo!"

"Your nose?"

Suddenly serious, Lavinia said, "Do you have earrings in your ears, Mommy?"

"Yes, I do."

Lavinia lifted Alice's hair above her ear, felt for Alice's right earlobe, touched one of the hoops Alice had taken to wearing daily.

"Careful," Alice said.

Lavinia let Alice's hair drop, reached for her own ears. "When can I have my ears pierced?"

"When you're fourteen. Let's pack your bag for the sleepover now."

In the car on the way out to Oakdale, Tom said to Kate, "You're not coming tonight to keep an eye on me, I hope."

"No. I'm coming for the entertainment value these evenings afford. I trust you. Everyone else may be giving in to temptation, but you will no doubt continue to remain unmoved by even the fetching Mary Ann Gray."

"You don't seem too pleased by my steadfastness."

He had a point: it was churlish of Kate to be bugged by Tom's rectitude. Or was it his complacency she minded? She let a mile go by before speaking. "Do you remember when we moved in together? In that awful apartment in Chelsea? Your hair was long, you were the maître d' at that chi-chi uptown restaurant, you were doing your master's degree. A responsible dreamer — that's what my dad called you. A wonderful combination, I thought."

"And what am I now?"

"Still responsible. Isn't this the turnoff coming up?"

Melina sat at the kitchen counter listening to Mary Ann's instructions. She'd seen Mary Ann dressed up before, but never looking so sexy. The fitted wrap top, the swingy black skirt, the shiny stockings, the strappy heels. What was going on, with her husband out of town?

"So," Mary Ann said, "you've got the four girls to look after. Kayla and the Orenstein girls are upstairs, and Lavinia is being dropped off any minute."

"Okay."

"Griffin's sleeping over at a friend's, so you don't need to worry about him."

"Uh-huh."

"As for Josh …" Josh had wandered into the kitchen and opened the fridge door. "Josh, are you going out tonight or not?"

"Not sure."

"Well, if you're home, stay out of Melina's way. And leave

the girls alone. They have exclusive rights to the family room and the big TV."

"Yes, Mrs."

"If you do go out, don't be too late."

"Yes, Mrs."

"And close the fridge door if you're not having anything."

"What's in this big pot?"

"Soup for the dinner club. Hands off."

Josh took out some milk, closed the fridge door. "Yes, Mrs."

Mary Ann said to Melina, "He started calling me Mrs. as a joke when he was eleven. Now he only does it when he wants to annoy me. Don't you, Josh?"

Josh looked up from pouring cereal into a bowl. "Honestly, Mom. How could you suggest such a thing?"

Mary Ann said, "The girls could bake some cookies if they need an activity. There's a mix in the cupboard. Or they can have microwave popcorn when they watch the movie."

"Okay."

Josh sat down at the kitchen table and started to eat his cereal.

"You should aim for lights out for the girls at ten," Mary Ann said. "To start the process then, anyway."

"Sure."

"And the guest room's made up for you to sleep in. I'll be late or I might stay at Alice's."

"I brought my overnight bag."

"If there's an emergency, you can call me on my cell phone. The number's on the fridge."

"Say yes, Mrs.," Josh mumbled, his mouth full of cereal.

"Josh, I don't want Melina to have to wonder about you coming home. Are you going out or not?"

"Probably not. I have a history assignment to do."

"Okay. You don't mind him being around, do you, Melina?"

"He's no trouble."

There was a knock on the back door, Alice walked in with Lavinia, and Melina saw that Alice had also dressed up — in a Boho-style top and skirt, chunky beaded necklaces, and boots. When everyone had said hello, and Lavinia had been helped out of her jacket, Mary Ann said, "Oh, shoot. I almost forgot something. I'll take you up, Lavinia. I won't be two seconds, Alice."

Alice kissed Lavinia goodbye, leaned against the kitchen island, and watched Mary Ann lead Lavinia away.

Melina thought she saw concern on Alice's face. "Lavinia will be fine."

"Melina's an excellent babysitter," Josh said. "Mom always says so."

"I know," Alice said. "And I appreciate you doing this, Melina, looking after all the girls."

"It'll be easy. They're good kids. And Mary Ann's paying me big bucks to stay over."

Alice said, "We're lucky to have you. When I was your age, spending a Saturday night babysitting was the last thing I wanted to do. Brooding in my room and plotting my escape from Oakdale was more my speed."

Melina smiled politely at this, but Alice said, "Oh my god. Did I just utter the words 'when I was your age'? I did. Shit. This is why I have to get out more."

Mary Ann came into the kitchen. She carried a tote. "Okay. Lavinia's settled. I'll grab my soup and we'll be off."

"Have a good time," Melina said. "You two look so nice."

"Thank you, Melina." Mary Ann pulled the soup pot out of the fridge. "Josh, don't forget to take Honey out for a pee before you go to bed."

"Yes, Mrs.," Josh said. "Now will you go, already?"

* * *

In the driveway, Alice opened the trunk of her car, waited while Mary Ann placed the pot inside, and said, "Hey. I just figured out that you named your dog after Melina."

Mary Ann closed the trunk. "What do you mean? Josh named her Honey because of the colour of her coat."

"Yeah, but in Greek, Melina means 'sweet like honey.'"

"Josh doesn't know Greek."

"Okay, whatever." They settled into the car, and Alice backed out of the driveway.

"Look what I almost forgot," Mary Ann said. She waved a foot-long cellophane strip of candy-coloured condoms in the air. "You want some?"

19

February 2010

On a cold weekday morning, Mary Ann was puttering at home when she noticed that Bob had forgotten his laptop in the front hall.

She stopped with one foot up on the stair. It was just like Bob to forget something — she was no longer amazed that a man who earned a high six-figure salary and commanded staff could waste ten precious minutes three days out of five looking for his coat, his keys, and his phone — but rarely did he leave the computer behind.

She picked up the laptop case and carried it upstairs. She'd been having trouble with the email program on her desktop and she might be able to fix the problem if she could see the settings Bob was using.

In the study, she turned on Bob's computer and found that access to his email account was controlled by a password. Not a problem. Mary Ann entered Bobby2728, the same password and PIN he used for everything. He could only remember one four-digit number, he often said. Which usually prompted Mary Ann to say, "And to think I married you anyway." Haha.

Her eyes ran over the subject headers for the twenty-two new messages in Bob's inbox: Sanderson Fund Draft Prospectus. Dublin Conference Itinerary. Associate Performance Review

Procedures. Minutes of Jan. 11 Management Committee meeting. And so on. Except for the sixteenth message, sent by someone named Zoe Bennett, and titled Last Night. Mary Ann clicked on it before stopping to think about whether she should.

The message was dated that morning at nine a.m — fifteen minutes before. It was accompanied by an instrumental music track of a mellow jazz tune, heavy on the saxophone. It said:

> I haven't texted because my phone died but I had to tell you that just thinking about everything we did last night makes me wet all over again. Can you meet me for lunch?

Dismay surged through Mary Ann's body. She blinked a few times, swallowed down the rising swell of her breakfast, and read the message over twice more before she thought to turn down the volume on the annoying wail of music. How the hell did one attach music to an email, anyway? She read the message a third time, and a fourth, and tried to remember where Bob had claimed to be the night before. At dinner with clients? At a Knicks game? She didn't know, hadn't retained the details of his whereabouts beyond the fact that he'd arrived home around midnight (when she was already in bed) and left that morning at six-thirty, like always. Except without his laptop.

She pushed back her chair, bent over, rested her head between her knees, and attempted to breathe not in gulps and gasps, to stay calm. Maybe this was a joke. Someone like Bob's golf buddy Ron would think sending a fake email like this would be a hilarious prank. In keeping with the stories he'd told Bob about his own adulterous exploits — weekly escapades, if Ron were to be believed, with any number of willing partners, in the unlikeliest of locations. When Bob had passed the stories on to Mary Ann, she'd said, "I don't believe a word of it," or, "What's with people?" and been glad Bob was not like that. Glad Bob wasn't the affair type.

Why, Bob had liked to repeat to her — in addition to the bit about remembering one password — that while there might conceivably be some cheap thrills to be found with a stranger, he was content with the tried and true sex he had with Mary Ann, sex honed to his exact specs after years of repetition. And Mary Ann's take on the subject was more or less the same. There was something to be said for practice making perfect in the orgasm department, for a partner whose frequency and variety of needs had seemed to coincide with her own. Provided she could ignore the way Bob's hand brushed against the tender spot near her hipbone that she'd always hated having touched. And how he dug his chin into her shoulder when he was on top. And how he — never mind.

She pulled Bob's laptop toward her, searched his emails for more from Zoe Bennett, found only work-related ones, and determined that Zoe was an attorney working on a deal with Bob. A young, pretty attorney, according to the picture of her that appeared beside her profile on her law firm's website.

Mary Ann tried to ignore the deafening roar made by the walls of her life crashing around her, closed the computer, and sat, staring out the window and seeing nothing, for some time.

There were scenes. Whispered screaming matches between Mary Ann and Bob after the kids had gone to bed. Suspicions were confirmed, doors slammed, recriminations hurled, tears shed by Mary Ann. Many tears.

The worst part was that Bob wouldn't stop seeing Zoe after he was found out. Couldn't stop. "You don't want to hear this," he said. "But I love Zoe. She makes me feel alive and young and happy. Happy!"

"You're right, I don't want to hear that."

"I love you and the kids too, though. I don't want to break up the family. I don't know what to do."

She wasn't stupid. She heard how he'd lumped her in with the kids, that he loved the four of them as a unit, and not her alone. That hurt. But did she love him? There was a question that was hard to answer honestly. In case the answer was no, she didn't. In case all she'd ever loved was the concept of she and Bob as a couple, the two of them good-looking, popular, and success-ful, living in their very nice house, on Bob's very nice income, with their very nice, good-looking, and popular children.

Bob said he needed time to figure things out. Time to keep seeing Zoe in the city, while pretending his marriage was intact in Oakdale. Time to keep their marital strife hidden from the kids, and live the lie.

And Mary Ann had agreed to this mortifying, soul-destroying, eat-out-her-insides plan because it was better than the alternative: to kick him out, start divorce proceedings, become a broke single mom.

Mary Ann had confided her troubles in Alice and no one else, and eventually picked herself up, dusted herself off, and gone to work for Drew. Only to have Bob come home with news one night soon after she'd settled into the job.

The younger kids had gone to bed, and Mary Ann was working on some status reports in the study when Bob came in the front door, ran up the stairs, stood in the doorway, and with great drama, announced that the affair with Zoe had ended, and Zoe had transferred to Chicago.

It took Mary Ann a minute to find the right reply. A min-ute during which she located the affair topic on the back shelf of her mind, hauled it up front, gave it a cursory examination, and said, "So now what?"

"So now what?" Bob said. "Is that all you have to say? Aren't you happy? Isn't this what you wanted?"

"Yes, I wanted you to stop seeing her. But am I happy? I wouldn't go that far."

Bob sat down in the visitor's chair on the other side of her desk. "Don't you want to know how I feel?"

Did she? "How do you feel?"

He slumped forward, buried his face in his hands. "Like a total douche. I can't believe what I've done. What a jerk I've been." He looked up. "But at the same time — I'm destroyed that it's over."

Mary Ann got up from her chair. It wasn't that late — Josh might hear their voices. She shut the door, sat back down, and waited for Bob to calm himself. Mary Ann would stay with him for now, stay married, until she got her bearings and found her footing. But she would neither forgive nor forget. And when she was ready, she'd get hers.

The Third Dinner Club Meeting:
November 20th, 2010

Host: Alice Maeda

Menu

Hors d'oeuvres

Engorgeous Soup	Mary Ann Gray
Artichoke Dip & Crackers	Phoebe Morales

Mains

Maple Glazed Salmon	Alice Maeda
Creamed Spinach	Lisa Carsten
Eggplant Towers	Sam Orenstein
Pommes Anna	Tom Gagliardi
Flower and Baby Lettuce Salad	Danielle Pringle

Desserts

Trifle	Sarah MacAllister
Chocolate Napoleons	Amy Millson
Beer & Wine	Drew Wacyk

20

The dinner club meeting was in full swing in Alice's apartment and, to her amazement, it was going smoothly. The only explanation for that state of affairs was that Mary Ann, AKA the Great Arranger, had organized everything. Including the invite she issued to the group, before Alice could stop her, to come along to Chuck's later.

"Attention, please!" Mary Ann said, when everyone had arrived. "Before you stuff yourselves with food, I wanted to mention that Alice has a friend playing in an R&B band over in Booth tonight, and she was hoping we could all go there later, cheer him on, and dance."

"You can count me out," said Mary Ann's friend Lisa, who was standing near Alice. "I don't dance."

"Me neither," Danielle murmured.

And Amy said, "Don't you have to be under thirty, or drunk, to dance in public?"

In the ensuing conversational buzz, Mary Ann did not appear to catch the reproving, thanks-a-lot look Alice gave her.

Now Mary Ann was carrying around a tray of soup-filled shot glasses, offering one to each guest in turn. She'd made the tackily named Engorgeous Soup from a recipe in her lovers' cookbook. "Mmm, it's good," Alice heard Danielle say. "Velvety

Kim Moritsugu

and rich." And Mary Ann whispered something to Danielle that made her laugh. Something dirty, no doubt.

Alice watched Mary Ann sidle over to Tom and Kate, who were standing by the fireplace. *Careful now. Put on a friendly smile, don't be afraid to look them in the eye. They don't know you contemplated rolling around naked with Tom, climbing up and down that long body. "Hi, guys. You up for some soup?"*

Alice shivered. Hold on a second. Mary Ann was on the other side of a noisy room, facing away. Alice couldn't have heard her offer soup to Tom and Kate. And where had those thoughts about climbing Tom's body come from?

Alice put down her glass of wine on a side table and covered her face with her hands. Was she hearing voices, or was the telepathy coming back? It couldn't be, could it, after all this time?

She turned her back on the room, closed her eyes, concentrated on tuning in Mary Ann's brainwaves, and got — nothing. She must have imagined hearing Mary Ann's thoughts. All she could hear now was static, and all she could see was a blurred collage of sexual images that had to be the product of her own fevered mind, the result of too much anticipation of tonight's rendezvous with Jake, and too much time spent listening to the Voice croon in her ear.

She walked over to the drinks table, took an ice cube out of the bucket, popped it in her mouth. She had a long night ahead. She should keep calm. Stay away from the wine. Be a good host, forget about long-lost mind-reading powers.

Tom came up, having survived the soup tasting. "I hope you don't mind," he said. "I took the liberty of giving myself a tour of your apartment. It has great character. And the way you've let the house's personality shine through by keeping the wood floors uncovered, by painting the mouldings white — the effect is very serene."

Good old Tom. And good thing Mary Ann had given up on pursuing him. Though spoon-feeding the aphrodisiac soup to Sam, as Mary Ann was now doing, seemed almost equally indiscreet.

Better Tom didn't see. Alice bit down on the ice cube. "Can you come with me a second? I need some help in the kitchen. And thanks about the apartment. I had very little to do with it — Sarah set it up for Lavinia and me."

"Lavinia is not among us this evening?"

They stepped into the kitchen, and Alice picked up some serving spoons from the dish rack, found a clean dishtowel, and asked Tom to dry them. She also raised the sash on the window, propped it up with a piece of wood, leant down, and tried to inhale the cold outside air. "If Lavinia were here tonight, you'd know. She's being babysat elsewhere."

"By your au pair?"

Alice reached for her oven mitts. "I don't have an au pair, or a nanny. Lavinia is a daycare child. She's with a teenage babysitter at Mary Ann's house."

"I should have known. If you had an au pair, you would be arranging to take her with you to Italy on that excavation."

"There's people who have staff, and there's me, is how it works."

"I understand. And let me bring us back to where I started: your apartment is charming."

Would he think it charming when Mary Ann led Sam onto the floor for some dirty dancing at the bar? Alice pulled her dish of salmon out of the oven, laid it on a trivet. "About the announcement Mary Ann just made? Please feel no obligation to come to the bar and see my friend's band. I'm happy to go by myself." She would *prefer* to go by herself.

"But Kate and I love to dance. You're looking at a former disco king."

Alice tried to picture Tom in a white suit, pointing to the sky. "I can't see it."

"I'm several years older than you, don't forget."

"Anyway, I'm not sure this band covers disco music. I think they're more into classic Motown-type material."

"Even better. Wait till I tell Kate."

After the main courses had been consumed, Sam said to Danielle, "Your salad was exquisite. I'm starting to see why your husband only wants to eat your food."

"Gee, thanks, I guess."

"You're still not too keen on food prep?"

"It's the cumulative effect, I think, of having done it non-stop for twenty years."

"Have you considered the alternatives?"

"Like?"

Sam pulled a small notebook and a pen out of his jacket pocket. "When I was in business school, I was taught a problem-solving method using numbered alternatives. Shall we apply it to your wish not to cook?"

"It's not exactly a business problem."

"Neither was the writing of my novel, but I used the approach on my plot. For example, what should be the ultimate fate of my hero? Should he A1: die, A2: live happily ever after with the pretty girl, or A3: jump into a raging river, disappear, and return in a sequel?"

This was why Danielle was here tonight. So she could have a funny conversation like this instead of talking about dogs and plants and kids every evening of her life. "What did you decide for your hero?"

"Maybe that wasn't a good example. Let's return to yours. You're fed up with your cooking, so your alternatives would be something like, A1: your husband takes a turn, cooks for the next twenty years." He made a note in his book. "By the way, I do the cooking at my house, and I enjoy it."

"You don't understand. Benny is hopeless. He can't boil an egg."

"And you want to stay married to him?"

"Well, yeah."

"Okay, then." He made another note. "A2: You eat out every night."

"Benny would die of heartburn, indigestion, and sheer grumpiness."

"A3: You jump into a raging river and return in a sequel?"

Danielle laughed.

"Okay, seriously now," Sam said. "A4 would probably be that you hire a cook."

"I don't mean to be negative, but that won't work either. We can't afford help like that."

"Don't apologize. You're exposing my method, my entire post-graduate education, in fact, for the trickery that it is. And now that we've eliminated the obvious solutions to your problem, we must come up with something — dare I say it — creative."

He thought for a few seconds. "I've got it. What number are we at? Five? A5: an acquaintance of yours who used to be in the prepared food business, and who has recently come to the painful realization that he is no novelist, re-enters the world of commerce with a boutique operation on Main Street, a pre-pared food outlet called Danielle's Kitchen. A cook is hired and trained to replicate your recipes and techniques exactly, so that all you need do each night is choose which item from your own repertoire you wish to take home and give to your family. Served with each meal are perfect little side salads made of heirloom lettuces and edible flower petals, supplied, of course, by you." He grinned. "Go ahead. Shoot it down."

"Not Danielle's Kitchen, please." She liked this game. "How about we name it The Oakdale Dinner Club? And get Sarah to do some baking for it, and some of the other members to provide their best recipes."

"You're right. We should draw on the wealth of available talent. Mary Ann could teach the cook how to make soups, for instance. Her soup tonight was stupendous."

Danielle said, "If only it would work."

"Why couldn't it?"

"We'd need capital, food industry experience, commercial kitchen facilities."

"Got it, got it, can get them."

"Where would you find cooks willing to cook someone else's recipes?"

"This would be a dream job for some cooking school graduates. Far better than an institutional gig."

"There'd have to be more than one potential customer willing to pay for my food."

"That shouldn't be difficult. You're a proven crowd pleaser. And I have a hunch you're not the only person in Oakdale who's sick of making dinner."

Danielle saw a distant look in his eye, something like the one Mary Ann had said meant he was thinking about his novel. "This is all just party talk, right?" she said. "You wouldn't actually consider doing this, would you?"

"Wouldn't I?"

Mary Ann was in Alice's small kitchen washing a few dishes when Phoebe walked up to her and said, "Come with me for a minute?"

"What for?"

Phoebe made a shushing sign, pulled Mary Ann away from

the sink and down the hallway into Alice's bedroom, and closed the door behind her. "Guess what?" she said. "I found out who the other woman is."

Mary Ann checked her reflection in the mirror hung above Alice's dresser and finger-combed her hair. "Are we talking about Drew now?"

"Yes. The married woman he was boning was Hallie Smith! That stuck-up blonde."

Mary Ann stopped in mid-comb. "What? Are you sure?"

"He told me the whole story out on the porch before dinner. She broke it off yesterday when he offered to fly to London and meet her there."

Drew and Hallie? How and why had that come about? More importantly, how did this news affect Mary Ann's plans for the evening? "Does that mean she might come back early from her business trip?"

"If I were her, I'd try to stay away longer, give him a chance to get over her. Though I don't know what he saw in her to begin with. I thought she was a bit of a bitch."

Mary Ann imagined herself being rejected by Sam at Chuck's later, after all her efforts, and her shoulders sagged in empathy. "Poor Drew."

"I've talked him into going to the bar where Alice's friend is playing," Phoebe said. "The guy needs to have a little fun, and see that there's other fish in the sea. You'll help me cheer him up?"

"Definitely."

After the girls were settled in their sleeping bags and the lights turned out, Melina retreated to the main-floor family room, turned on the TV there, flipped channels.

Josh came in a few minutes later. "What are you watching?"

Melina muted the volume on a reality show. "Nothing. How's your homework going?"

"Bad."

"What is it?"

"An assignment to find history in our daily environment. The project proposal is due on Monday."

"Who's your teacher? Cruikshank?"

"Yeah."

"He assigned my class that project last year."

"What did you do for it?"

"Everybody else interviewed their grandparents, but I researched the old railroad tracks running through Oakdale. The highlight of my presentation was when I took the class on a field trip to follow the path of the tracks through town. Alice Maeda helped me — she knows all about that stuff. I got an A+."

"What railroad tracks?"

"You're kidding, right?"

"No."

"You know the yellow-brick building on Main Street that Alice has been working on? The old doughnut shop? It used to be the train station, back when there were railroad tracks."

"No shit."

"That's what you should do your project on — the new library. Interview Alice on some historical facts about when it was a train station for your written report, then arrange for your history class to have a tour of the building as your presentation. Get Alice to conduct the tour. She'll know what to say, and you'll get the good mark."

"It's going to be a library?"

"God, Josh, don't you pay attention to anything that's going on around you?"

All huffy, Josh said, "Of course I do."

And Melina regretted her words. Because if Josh was paying attention to what was going on in his own house, he would have figured out, as Melina had, that his parents were on the brink of divorce. "Sorry," she said. "I shouldn't have said that. But what do you think of the project idea?"

He smiled. "I like the part about Alice giving the lecture and me getting the mark."

"So go for it. You've got the connections. You might as well use them."

Jake's band wasn't onstage when the dinner club arrived at Chuck's, a gloomy dive that looked to Alice like it had a long history of being a gloomy dive, complete with the requisite single men in dirty truckers' hats seated at the bar nursing beers and watching televised sporting events.

In the dimly lit room, it took Alice a minute to see that a small stage platform was backed against the far, windowless wall. The worn parquet dance floor in front of it was ringed by round wooden tables peopled with pot-bellied men and blowsy women talking about either baseball or labour unrest — she heard the word "strike" bandied about. Maybe they were bowlers? In the farthest, darkest corner of the room, six or eight youngish people huddled over two pitchers of beer.

While the remnants of the dinner club, led by Mary Ann, wandered around in search of an unstained table that could seat eight, Alice caught the attention of the bartender and confirmed that Rhythm and Blues was playing that night, had played one set already, and was due to come back on in fifteen minutes, after which time she could only hope the jukebox would be turned off.

She joined the group at the table they'd picked out and counted heads. Mary Ann, seated with Drew on one side and

Sam on the other, was fully enacting her role as Veronica, complete with hair-flipping gestures; Kate and Tom were trying to look comfortable in the shabby back-roads setting; and Phoebe was talking brightly about god knows what with a tired-looking Sarah. The others had declined to attend, pleading lack of dance aptitude. The fewer people the better, in Alice's opinion. Maybe they could all leave now. "You okay?" Alice said to Sarah, aside. "You sure you're up to this?"

"I won't stay long. I thought I might see if the band would be suitable for the country-club dance, but I'm fading fast."

Alice looked around. Where were Jake and the band? In a back room, no doubt. Should she try to find them, say hello, let him know she was here? No. Better to act casual, cool. Loosen up a bit. Try to recall how to act cool. And get that persistent image of a cat's tongue lapping up milk right out of her head.

Danielle came in her front door, listened for household noise, heard the upstairs TV on low. She walked through the ground floor, turned off lights, checked door locks, stopped in the kitchen to wipe off the cutting board, wash the paring knife Benny had used to slice apples for the kids, and toss the apple cores into the compost bin.

Upstairs, she peeked in at the boys — how angelic and sweet they looked when asleep — and walked into the master bedroom, where Benny's sleeping form looked neither angelic nor sweet. His bedside lamp and the TV were both on, and he was propped up on three pillows, his head slumped down to one side, his chin doubled, snoring.

Danielle picked up the remote control lying next to him on the bed and switched the TV off. Benny woke up, raised his head, and looked around wild-eyed. "What time is it?"

"Ten-thirty."

He turned off his bedside lamp, rolled over so his back was to her, and said in a sleepy voice, "How was the dinner club?"

"Good. How were the kids?"

"They fought a bit. And Alex missed you."

Danielle took off her good clothes, hung them up, and put on the T-shirt she slept in. "I had this strange conversation with Sam Orenstein tonight," she said. "Not strange — interesting. He came up with a crazy idea." How much sincerity and how much wine had there been in Sam's proposal? She wasn't sure.

Benny's breathing rumbled in, then out. He was asleep again. Oh well. At least he wasn't out at a bar with someone else's wife. They could talk in the morning. Danielle prepared for bed, lay down, and spent the next half hour imagining a life without cooking.

21

Still November 20, 2013

Chuck's was emptier and tackier than Mary Ann would have wanted, but it was dark, there was a dance floor, and she'd hauled enough members of the dinner club along to make her presence look less like a direct attack on Sam and more like a group outing. What her mother was doing there she didn't know, or care.

She sipped her gin and tonic, and leaned over to Drew, on her right. "Are you almost drunk enough to dance?"

He gripped his glass. "Getting there."

Mary Ann leaned the other way, placed a hand on Sam's shoulder. "Sam, I'm counting on you to request 'I Heard it Through the Grapevine' now."

He nodded and laughed in an infectious way that made her laugh along. Why hadn't she ordered a shot of tequila instead of the gin? Because she would love to have licked some salt off her thumb bone right about then, and sucked a lemon, and lived large. Larger.

In a couple of minutes, she was going to get up and dance by herself, arms above her head. She reached down and adjusted the neckline of her top to reveal more than a bit of her black bra, and tapped her foot in time to the country song playing on the jukebox.

The evening reminded her of a school concert she'd sung in back in fifth grade, in Ann Arbor, before her family had moved to Oakdale.

She'd been chosen from her school to be in a multi-district choir giving a special performance in honour of a politician, on a now-forgotten civic occasion. The children, dressed in uniform tunics, were required to sit quietly on risers between songs while speeches were made — after the choir had sung the "Star-Spangled Banner" and before they stood up to offer "America the Beautiful."

At the several rehearsals beforehand, Mary Ann had behaved well, like the compliant child she was. On the day of, she'd suffered having Sarah pull her hair back into a tight and shiny ponytail, lined up with the other choristers at the appointed place and time, filed onto the risers, sat down, crossed her ankles, folded her hands in her lap.

And started talking. The choir mistress had made it very clear that there was to be no talking, no moving, and no fidgeting while they were up there behind the podium, on display in front of the large audience. The kids chosen to perform had been selected as much for their ability to comport themselves in a dignified fashion as for their talent in singing, so they all did what they were told, which made it more dramatic and noticeable when Mary Ann went off-script.

She talked to the girl next to her, the ones behind and in front, ignored their better-behaved shushing. She made faces behind the back of the politician. She ignored her mother frowning at her from the audience. She laughed at the pointed finger and angry face of the choir mistress.

Mary Ann shut them all out, slouched down in her seat, talked some more. She knew exactly how naughty she was being, knew she'd get into big trouble later, but she couldn't help it. She hadn't been able to stop being bad.

Same thing now.

Jake was wearing black. Nothing showbizzy. A black T-shirt, black jeans, black Converse sneakers. He looked tall and fit and unpretentious, Alice thought. He looked good.

He didn't appear to see Alice or notice the dinner club table. There were lights shining in his face, in his eyes. The band was tuning up. He adjusted a microphone.

Mary Ann leaned forward, bringing her exposed cleavage dangerously close to Sam's hand, and half shouted to Alice, three people down, "That can't be him. The bald one in black. Tell me it isn't him."

Alice put a finger to her lips, hoped Jake hadn't heard Mary Ann above the sound of the guitarist trying out a riff, the keyboard player playing a few chords. "It's him."

Mary Ann's mouth was agape. She took a second look. "I would never have recognized him. Never in a million years." Mary Ann turned to Drew and started talking to him, probably telling him how much Jake had changed, how good-looking he used to be.

On Alice's other side, Phoebe gasped. "Will you look at that?"

A young black man stood in front of the center microphone. He wore a tight white T-shirt, black pinstripe dress pants, polished wingtips. What Alice could see of his body — entire upper — was buff.

"That's the most beautiful man I've ever seen," Phoebe said.

"I think his name is Tristan," Alice said.

"Tristan," Phoebe repeated, dreamily. And Alice hoped Mary Ann had not done anything insane like spike the soup with an aphrodisiac. Before she could ask, the band played a familiar riff, and in a falsetto voice, Tristan began to sing a Temptations song — "The Way You Do the Things You Do."

Mary Ann was up dancing within the first eight bars, up and facing Sam, beckoning to him in a way that she must have meant to be sexy but that Alice found ridiculous. What on earth, Alice thought, even while she found herself gazing fondly at Sam. *At his finely shaped nose and his juicy, kissable lips —*

"Aaagh!" Alice clapped her hand over her mouth.

Beside her, Phoebe said, "What? What's wrong?"

Alice shook her head. "Nothing." Except that she hadn't been mistaken earlier — the damned telepathy was back. She stood up, sat down, moved her chair back, and tried to distance herself from Mary Ann, whose mind was clearly in overdrive, and taking over Alice's own.

Alice erected a mental barrier in an attempt to shut out Mary Ann's thoughts, and concentrated instead on Jake, watched him sing backup and adroitly perform some guy-group dance steps. He was enjoying himself.

Mary Ann, meanwhile, had enticed Sam onto the dance floor, and had dropped the Veronica role in favour of a new comic-book super heroine — Sultry Woman, who could bewitch grown men with her come-hither gaze and bend males to her will with a flick of her finger. Sultry Woman danced with Sam a while, got him going — please no, Alice prayed, not the Bump — and when Sam was well-launched into the sort of gyrations Alice had previously associated with recreational drug use, Mary Ann started working on Drew.

Alice read Mary Ann's thoughts, turned to Phoebe, said, "What's wrong with Drew? Why does Mary Ann think he needs cheering up?"

Without taking her eyes off Tristan, Phoebe said, "He was recently dumped by someone. And I'm in love."

Alice tore herself away from staring at Jake, from checking for signs that in the past few days she'd built up some huge sexual fairy tale that had no bearing on any attraction she might feel for the actual person, and spared a moment to study Tristan. Undeniably hot would be her objective assessment. One she might have expressed if her mind hadn't been seized by an image of a woman in black satin lingerie, table dancing before a group of slavering men.

"Aaagh!" she cried again. She received an irritated look from Phoebe in response, and jumped at the touch of Sarah's finger tapping her on the shoulder from behind. "I'm leaving, Alice. Goodbye. I'll see you tomorrow."

"Let me walk you out to the parking lot."

"Don't worry about me. Stay and watch the show."

"No, I'll come. If I were leaving alone, I'd want someone to walk me out. And I could use some air."

Sam loved the band, loved the song, loved dancing. He performed his best moves, steps he hadn't pulled out in years — okay, decades — and didn't look half-bad doing them. And Mary Ann was such a good dancer. Loose and rhythmic and coordinated and laughing and happy and sexy.

The song ended, he clapped, and Mary Ann hugged him. She wrapped her arms around his neck and pressed her body against his so that he felt the soft mass of her breasts against his chest and a jolt of arousal in his dick and he didn't care that he was sweaty.

One of the backup singers, a bald guy, said into the mic, "I'd like to dedicate this next tune to all the women in this room who remember when …"

Mary Ann said, "I need water," took his hand, led him to the bar, and asked the bartender for two glasses, with ice.

"… It's been more than a few years since high school …"

She grabbed a glass as soon as it was set down on the bar,

drank from it, and so did he, and it tasted like standing under a waterfall on a hot day.

"… We all remember some missed opportunities, some people we regret passing up, not getting to know better …"

Mary Ann turned to face Sam, and said, "You're so gorgeous. So, so gorgeous."

"… So, tonight, for one night, let's travel back to the past, back to the way things should have been …"

Sam put his arm around Mary Ann's shoulders and pulled her close and kissed her, and it was a goddamned movie kiss, with music swelling all around — or was that the band, finally starting the next song? — except more lustful and drunk and heady. He chewed on her neck, and kissed the curve of her breast — the curve he'd been salivating over for the last half hour — and tasted perfume on her skin, a spicy taste completely unlike the floral scent Hallie used. He stopped his gnawing to take a breath (he was feeling a little dizzy), repeated the Hallie thought in his mind, and waited a second to see if conscious acknowledgement of his first stab at infidelity would affect his desire at all.

Nope. Before the betrayal idea could make its way through his sodden brain from the morality quadrant to the penis-control zone, Mary Ann took advantage of the break in the proceedings to climb onto his lap, fan out her skirt around her, and ride his bucking bronco. His fucking bucking bronco, which bounced right along. No qualms there.

The tremors started again in Alice's head when Jake was introducing his song and — could it be? — speaking directly to her. Though he wasn't looking at her, because the lights were still in his eyes, and she was moving around the room, trying to find a lead-lined pillar or bulletproof room divider to take refuge behind, to shield herself from Mary Ann's thoughts.

She settled on a chest-high, vinyl-covered booth back, and from behind it she listened to Jake, at the mic, talk about high school, about regrets and lost opportunities. He had a good speaking voice — soft and deep. The sound of it touched Alice, suffused her with a spreading lightness, *a thrill she could feel right down to the rosy tips of her —*

NO. That soft-porn thought had not originated in Alice's mind. That sex yodelling could only be coming from Mary Ann.

Alice turned and looked around the room. Where were they? From the sound of the fevered mind noises Alice was hearing, Mary Ann and Sam must be necking by now, if not all-out fucking. Though not in this room, Alice hoped.

She spotted them, bodies melded together, jammed against the bar. Mary Ann's top was half-off, and one leg was wrapped around Sam's ass. She was riffling his hair, while Sam administered a lovebite that Mary Ann seemed especially responsive to, if the escalation in the pace of the panting in Alice's mind was any indication.

Alice set off toward them, tried to obliterate the mental image of waves crashing on surf that Mary Ann was projecting — how cliché — noticed that Mary Ann still had on at least one shoe, and hoped that underneath Mary Ann's skirt, everyone's underwear was still on.

Alice reached the entangled pair, tapped Mary Ann on the shoulder, and said, "You have to stop."

Between kisses and sighs, Mary Ann said, "Can't stop. Feels too good."

Over the music, Alice yelled, "Don't stop making out. Just stop broadcasting it!"

Mary Ann broke free, said, "What did you say?" and let go of Sam, who slumped over and rested his head on her shoulder.

Alice took hold of Mary Ann's face with both hands and looked into her dilated pupils. "I'm reading your mind. All of it. In detail. AND I DON'T WANT TO!"

Mary Ann licked her swollen lips. "Are you kidding? The telepathy's back?"

"Yes. And you've got to stop sending out signals. I don't want to see your crashing waves."

Mary Ann's smile was smudged. "They're pretty spectacular waves, aren't they?"

Alice elbowed Sam. "Get up, Sam. Grab your purse, Mary Ann. I'm taking you two someplace private. And hurry. I've got my own party to attend."

Kate and Tom danced, arm in arm, to the Four Tops tune the bald singer had introduced. "This whole scene is incredible," Kate said. "Like a party out of the eighties. Any minute now, someone's going to lay down lines of coke on the tabletop and hand us a rolled-up hundred dollar bill. What's come over these people?"

"I don't know what's possessed Mary Ann. And Sam. Perhaps it was something they ate."

"Not just them. That young woman Phoebe is enthralled by the lead singer in the band. See how she's dancing near him, trying to catch his eye?"

"At least Alice seems unaffected. Look, she's at the bar with Mary Ann and Sam. Let's hope she's trying to talk sense into them."

"Don't be so sure. She's a part of this, too. Check out the guy who's singing now. Aren't we here because her friend plays in the band? Did you hear what he said before, about reconnecting? Now we know what kind of friend. You're looking at public foreplay, all around us."

Tom snuck a glance back at Sam and Mary Ann, on their way out the door with Alice. "Do you think it's still considered infidelity if your spouse is likewise engaged?"

Kate felt something like frustration, or irritation, or anger, or all three, boil up inside her. Something that made her reach down and grab Tom by the balls.

He stepped back. "What are you doing?"

"Just checking to see if you're as aroused as everyone else in the room."

"I'm not, thank you very much."

"And why not?"

"So how do I do it again?" Mary Ann said.

Alice was patient. "You construct walls around your thoughts, and I won't be able to read them. Remember?"

They were in Alice's car. Alice was driving. Mary Ann and Sam were in the backseat. Sam was humming — too far gone, Alice hoped, to follow the conversation.

Alice said, "I think it's the sender who has to block off transmission, not the receiver. And having physical distance between us should help. If we do both these things, I might be able to survive the rest of the evening without experiencing your rapture in living colour."

"To 96 Maple, if you please," Sam said from the back seat. "And step on it."

Mary Ann twirled a strand of hair with her finger. "Okay. I'm going to think about what I'd like to do to Sam when we get to his house, then I'll construct walls around my thoughts. Brick walls, right?"

"Brick, stone, concrete, whatever. Just stay away from the sticks and hay."

"I'll huff," Sam said, "and I'll puff."

"Brick walls, then."

"Make them thick. I don't want to see that thought. Now, go."

Alice opened her mind a crack, saw Mary Ann throw together a brick tower that could have belonged to Rapunzel. "Cute," Alice said, "but you forgot the rose bush."

Mary Ann dabbed in a rose bush, leaned out the window and waved at Alice, blew a kiss, then bricked up the window behind her, disappeared from view.

"Good so far."

"And I'll blow your house down," Sam said.

"Here goes," Mary Ann said. "I'm going to get dirty now."

Alice cringed, waited, still saw only the tower, the rose bush. "Very good. I can't see anything of what's going on inside. Unless you're not actually thinking your lascivious thoughts. Are you?"

"Should I let the walls down so you can see?"

"No, don't."

"The only thing is: that takes a lot of concentration. What if my mind gets distracted by what my body's doing?"

Alice sighed. "You may as well go ahead and test it. Kiss him or something, and I'll see if the tower stays up."

"Come here, bubba," Mary Ann said, and beckoned to Sam. Sam leaned in, and off they went.

Alice averted her eyes from the rearview mirror, listened with distaste to their lip smacking and slurping and vocalized heavy breathing, and watched the tower in her mind's eye. It shook and it swayed, but it did not fall down.

"Very good," Alice said, "keep it up." She pulled into Sam's driveway.

"Yo ho ho and a bottle of rum," Sam sang.

"Have fun," Alice said, and watched them walk up the driveway, arm in arm.

At the front door, Mary Ann turned back for a second, clutched her forehead, and sent Alice a picture of Jake, singing on stage. *You, too*, said her voice in Alice's ear.

Tom opened the driver side door of his car and got in.

"Is Drew okay?" Kate said.

"Other than sobbing quietly and repeating Hallie's name, yes."

"He'll thank us tomorrow for driving him and his car home."

"I'm sure."

"But can you speed it up? I want to get away from here."

Tom drove faster. "I'm having trouble understanding you this evening. One minute you complain about debauchery, the next you appear disappointed that I'm not among the debauched."

Kate gave him the silent treatment for a few minutes, until they were clipping along on the main road. She said, "You're just not very passionate anymore."

Tom said, "I'm not twenty-two anymore, either."

"That's bullshit and you know it. You could still be passionate at fifty-two if you had something to get excited about. If real estate development and extra-marital sex don't do it for you, find something that does."

"What about you? What excites you?"

"Me? I'm not the passionate type. I'm more down-to-earth and practical. You're the one who's supposed to have dreams."

Alice parked her car and ran to the door of Chuck's, fought down the fear she'd taken too long driving Mary Ann and Sam back to Oakdale, had left it too late, and Jake would be gone. Though it was only 11:15. Bands didn't stop playing at eleven o'clock, did they? That's what she'd told herself all the way back. There was lots of time still to make this her night. There had to be.

She swung open the heavy door and heard no loud live music, only the muted tones of the jukebox. The band's instruments still seemed to be up onstage, on their stands. The table that the dinner club had occupied was empty, littered with dirty glasses and beer bottles. And there were maybe fifteen customers in the room.

She asked the bartender if Rhythm and Blues were finished for the night. "I think they're coming back for one more set," he said, with the face of someone who wished they weren't.

Alice asked for a ginger ale as thanks for this information, and because her mouth felt dry. A ginger ale with lots of ice. The bartender slid the glass over to her, took her money, and said, "They're sitting in the booth around the corner there."

"Who are?"

"The band."

Alice spotted the tops of heads over the edge of the booth in question, heard a gust of male laughter, could think of no good reason to walk over and interrupt the party.

They stood up and became recognizable as the drummer, the bass player, the keyboard guy, and Tristan, with a woman attached to his side who looked an awful lot like Phoebe. And there was Jake, at the back of the group.

"Hey, Alice!" Phoebe called. She turned to Jake. "I told you she'd come back."

The others wandered off. Jake ducked his head — embarrassed? — and came over to Alice. "I wondered what had happened to you," he said.

Alice sat on the edge of a bar stool. She was exhausted. "I had to drive someone home, and it took longer than I thought. I'm sorry I missed part of your song, but I liked what I heard.

You have a lovely voice." Shit. Was she coming on too strong? Did it matter anymore?

Jake said, "Wanna dance?"

"Now? To this?" *This* being early Rolling Stones.

"We'll pick another song."

He went to the jukebox and leaned over it. She leaned with him, and they read the list of selections while she worried about having sweaty armpits and dry mouth, and little prickles of excitement ran up and down her arms at the mere thought of touching him, being held by him.

Or were they going to fast dance?

"Pretty slim pickings," Jake said, and she pointed shyly to a Bad Boys song, the group's biggest hit. A ballad called "My Baby Tonight," which Alice had a feeling had been composed expressly for middle school slow dances.

Jake said, "At least a few of those guys can sing." He dropped in some quarters, selected the song, and took Alice's hand, led her onto the deserted dance floor.

They stood still, facing each other in dancing position, waiting for the song to start. Jake said, "What happened to your friends?"

Alice released Jake's hand for a second to cover her yawning mouth. "They're not exactly night owls. Except Phoebe."

Jake chuckled. "Tristan scores again. And here comes your song."

The syrupy string-heavy arrangement began, and they started to dance, a simple step and sway kind of slow dance that incorporated a gradual turn. Jake knew how to lead, but his touch was too light on her back, his hands too cool. Their bodies were nowhere near close enough together.

Time to take control, do a Mary Ann. Alice tightened her grip on Jake's shoulder, pulled herself closer, and started to sing — a small-voiced, mild kind of singing.

The lyrics of the song were so bland they were almost meaningless, full of rhymes like blue and you, and me and see, and sprinkled liberally with the word *baby*.

Alice could drop every baby and darlin' into its rightful spot in the song, but she'd laugh in the face of anyone who tried to address her that way in real life. She wasn't laughing now, though. Now that Jake had started to sing the chorus, had moved his mouth close to her ear, had picked up the lines that belonged to the Voice, was harmonizing with the Voice's raspy delivery, was crooning to her with a gentle affection that made her close her eyes and press her forehead into his shoulder, that slowed her pulse to the tempo of the music, that aroused every nerve ending on every inch of her skin, that made her want the song to never end.

22

November 21, 2010

Sam woke up first, coughing. He stopped coughing to breathe, looked at the clock, saw it was three a.m., and realized with a shudder that the naked woman sleeping beside him was not Hallie, but Mary Ann Gray, with whom, if he was recalling the events of the last few hours with any accuracy, he had recently engaged in a bout of rip-roaring sex. Holy fuck.

He crept out of bed, careful not to wake her, ducked into the ensuite bathroom, closed the door behind him, turned on the dimmer switch very low, peed for about an hour, flushed, and checked his reflection in the mirror.

He looked terrible. His hair looked like someone had sat on his head (understandable — someone had). His eyes were bloodshot and sunken, his skin — even in the dim light — had a greenish tinge. And he could smell the booze coming out of his pores. Not surprising considering how much he'd had to drink. Sparkling wine before dinner, several glasses of red with a couple of shots of whiskey at the bar. Enough alcohol to screw up his digestive system. To send him over to the toilet in a hurry, so he could kneel down and throw up all the rich food he'd eaten, throw up like some underage punk who gets wasted and can't hold his liquor.

If only his daughters could see him now.

When he was finished retasting everything he'd eaten — he wouldn't be going anywhere near that butter-soaked pommes Anna dish for years — he washed his face, brushed his teeth, swished with mouthwash three times, showered, put on a bathrobe, went downstairs, drank a gallon of water, poured himself a tall glass of orange juice, and collapsed into a chair in his study.

He visualized his marriage kaput, the house sold, his daughters no longer his daily companions. He saw his family circle turned into some complicated custody arrangement, the girls polite and distant with him, the way they acted with strangers.

What had he done?

Or to put it another way, what hadn't he done? Without allowing the weight of the guilt bearing down on his chest to lessen by even an ounce, he thought back to the sex with Mary Ann. It had been wrong and immoral and not the kind of activity he'd want to indulge in on a daily basis, but man, they'd had a good time. Mary Ann had been so enthusiastic. And responsive. Unbelievably so. Plus she kept telling him he was gorgeous. And sounding like she not only meant it, she found this alleged gorgeousness of his to be exciting.

No one had ever called him gorgeous before.

Cute, maybe.

Hallie used to think he was cute.

Hallie, his wife, the mother of his children, the woman he loved and had no desire to leave, opportunities for rip-roaring sex with Mary Ann notwithstanding.

What had he done?

Mary Ann woke face down on the mattress. She felt around on the bed beside her — no one was there. She sat up, looked for a bedside clock, found one glowing on a night table. 4:14

a.m. She reached for a pillow and grabbed hold of a big down-filled square covered with a damask case. Hallie's pillow probably, which was kind of weird if you thought about it. Mary Ann didn't feel like thinking about it. She stuck the pillow behind her head, leaned back, and checked her vital signs.

Head was foggy and fuzzy, clear thinking a strain. Still half cut, then. Upper body was naked under the sheet, skin a little chafed, rubbed — a not unpleasant sensation. Like after a mud wrap at a spa.

Her stomach was sending out signals of instability. Could they be hunger pangs? They could. She hadn't eaten much dinner, except for a few spoonfuls of soup. She'd been too excited to eat, too raring.

Her lower body was also naked and ached internally — ouch. The insides of her thighs were slick with bodily fluids — yuck. And gross — her hands smelled like latex.

She shivered. At the thought she'd had sex at all, after nine months without. And with someone not only new but married. In Hallie's bed. Not such a horrible thing, when you considered what Hallie had been up to with Drew, right?

She got up, turned on a light, found and put on her bra, opened dresser drawers until she located Sam's T-shirts, put on a not-brand-new not-too-old one that was long enough to cover her ass, wandered into the hallway, found a linen closet and took out a towel, went to the bathroom and washed up, wiped away with a tissue the more obvious mascara smears on her face, brushed her teeth (she'd brought a toothbrush in her tote bag), attempted to sort out her hair, slipped on the clean underwear and the knee-length nightshirt she'd packed, went downstairs and found Sam in his study. He was wearing a bathrobe and writing on a pad. A glass of orange juice sat on the desk.

"Hi, doll," he said. "You couldn't sleep either?"

Mary Ann smiled at the doll part. "I woke up from this wild dream about you and me having incredible sex. Together. Isn't that weird?"

"Oh, Mary Ann. What am I going to do with you?"

"How about sharing your orange juice?"

He passed her the glass, and she took a sip, but stopped herself from drinking it all. She was so thirsty. And hungry. She gestured to his writing pad. "What are you doing?"

"Other than feeling guilty as sin, and worrying what will happen to my marriage when Hallie finds out what we did? The marriage that I have no desire to break up?"

"Your marriage can survive a one-night stand. But what were you writing?"

He looked down at the pad, as if he'd forgotten. "I was making a to-do list."

"For your novel?"

"No. I'm thinking of embarking on a new enterprise — a prepared food shop, right here in Oakdale. Did I mention it to you last night?"

"No, you didn't. And I'd like to hear about it, but I don't think I can talk about food unless I'm eating some. Would you think I was rude if I scrambled some eggs?"

"Go ahead. There's challah for toast, too, if you like."

"You want some?"

"No thanks. Juice is about all I can handle right now."

They moved into the kitchen, she made herself eggs and toast, and Sam sat on a stool at the counter and told her about his and Danielle's idea for turning the Oakdale Dinner Club into a shop.

"It sounds promising," Mary Ann said when he'd done talking. "And I'm sure you can make it work. But I have one question."

"What's that?"

"Any way we could have sex again before I have to leave?"

Alice couldn't sleep with Jake in her bed, with Jake in her apartment. She was too used to having the whole mattress to herself, or to at least being the only adult in the bed. So at five a.m. she sat on her enclosed porch, dressed in her sweats, wrapped in a blanket, and exhaled frosty breath. Sat there alone and felt fatigue tug at her face and pull it down and to the sides. She knew sleep wouldn't come until Jake was gone.

She reviewed the evening, the night. The dinner club part had gone well, hadn't it? She'd supplied enough food and chairs and forks, and her oven hadn't blown up, no fire had started. Everyone seemed to get along, and it didn't matter anymore that her efforts to prevent Tom from seeing Mary Ann seduce Sam were unsuccessful. Not after the performance they'd put on at the bar.

But there was something Tom had said when she'd talked to him earlier that had sparked an idea. Something — was it about the apartment? — she'd made a mental note to file away and think about later. She exercised her tired mind, tried to find the note, couldn't.

She saw the sex with Jake, the sex that had been so sensuously quiet and slow. She rocked a bit in her chair at the thought of the slow dance at Chuck's — the spinning room, her twirling head. She laughed about Mary Ann and her crazy telepathy. Where had that come from, and after how many years? Twenty? Twenty-four?

Jake called Alice's name softly from the living room. She turned around, saw his shadowy figure. He was fully dressed.

He stepped onto the porch, sat down in a chair beside her. "You okay?" His voice was modulated to the hour, to the stillness.

"Yeah. Tired. You?"

He produced a crumpled pack of cigarettes from his shirt pocket, offered her one.

"No thanks."

He lit one, and she watched the lazy white smoke drift out of his mouth.

He touched her cheek. "I feel bad about leaving so early."

"Don't feel bad." Any minute now, she'd be able to run to her room and jump into her bed. Alone. "I understand."

"I'll call you as soon as I'm back from the trip."

"You'd better."

"And I'll email you from Thailand."

"Will not."

"Will too."

"Wanna bet?"

He set his cigarette down in the ashtray and reached out a hand to shake hers. "Winner of the bet pays for our next dinner out."

"Done." Alice stood up, pulled him up with her, and hugged him — a long, deep one.

The phone rang in Alice's dream, and even after she answered it, it kept on ringing. At the same time, Mary Ann knocked on the door and yelled, "Alice! Alice, are you there?"

Alice wanted to scream, it was so annoying. She woke herself up instead, heard the real phone ring, lifted the receiver, mumbled hello.

"Finally!" said Mary Ann's voice. "I didn't want to call, but when I tried contacting you on the telepathic line and it didn't work, I figured I had no alternative."

Alice groaned, rolled over onto her back, and held onto her head with her free hand.

"Say something, Alice."

"I feel like shit."

"Tell me about it. I got four hours of sleep last night. My body's currently running on the fat stored in my inner thighs."

"Nice image. What time is it?"

"Nine o'clock. Time to return to the world of parenting. Sam has to go pick up his girls from my house. And you have to drive me home and help maintain the fiction I slept at your place last night."

"Oh god."

"I know. Is Jake still there?"

"No."

"Didn't he stay over?"

"Yeah, but he left."

"Then get up and come over here real quick."

Alice groaned again. "Will there be coffee?"

"I'll see what I can do." Mary Ann lowered her voice. "So how was it?"

"I'll only hurry if there's coffee with real cream. Not milk."

"All right, all right. Bring a mug."

Mary Ann said to Sam, "Your turn," and went to deal with the coffee while Sam called Mary Ann's house.

He talked to Melina, asked if Mary Ann was back from Alice's yet, and how were his girls doing. "They just woke up?" he said. "How about I come by around ten to get them, then? Okay, good. Thanks."

Mary Ann said, "So we're all set. Our tracks are covered."

"I hope so. It would be terrible if Hallie found out about this from someone other than me."

"You could just not tell her."

"And add insult to injury?"

"How do you know she hasn't cheated on you somewhere along the line?" His face fell, and she said, "It's possible, that's all I'm saying."

"Hallie? Hallie wouldn't — shit. I didn't think she would."

"I'm sorry. I wasn't trying to sully her name." Yes, she was, but she'd stop now. "I just don't want you to feel too bad about what's happened."

"I know."

Gorgeous but tormented, that's what Sam was. Mary Ann rubbed his back, soothed him the way she would one of her children, then tapped him lightly, twice — the signal for hug's over. "Do you have cream for Alice's coffee?"

Alice rang the doorbell at Sam's house, walked past him without speaking when he admitted her with a cheery good morning, found the kitchen, poured coffee into a large plastic travel mug, added cream. Stood there, bleary-eyed and silent, sipping it, and didn't ask where Mary Ann was.

Sam said, "So, Alice, if there was a food shop on Main Street that served Mary Ann's soups and Danielle Pringle's salads and mains and Sarah MacAllister's desserts, would you buy your meals there?"

Alice turned toward him. "What?"

Mary Ann came into the kitchen. "Okay. Let's go."

Alice grunted.

"Mornings aren't Alice's best time," Mary Ann said to Sam, and pushed Alice out the door.

In the car, Mary Ann said, "There are so many things to say about last night, I don't know where to start."

"That's okay. I'm not up to talking."

"You know what I don't understand? Why did the telepathy came back?"

"Beats me."

"And how come we can't do it today when it was coming in so clear last night?"

"We can. I saw you knocking at my mental door. Heard you, too. In my sleep."

"You did? Then what am I thinking of right now?"

Alice lifted a corner of the curtain that covered her mind and glimpsed Mary Ann's thought picture. "An orange cat sitting on an elephant's back. Why, I don't know. I can't do this right now."

"Okay. We'll try again later."

They covered a block in silence. Only a few more to Mary Ann's house.

Mary Ann said, "Aren't you curious about how it went with me and Sam?"

Alice tried to make her voice rise above a monotone. "How'd it go with you and Sam?"

"Amazingly. Aside from him getting a bad case of the guilts. But I think I could make a habit of this."

"Of Sam?"

"Of sleeping around."

Melina was tidying up the girls' breakfast dishes when Mary Ann and Alice arrived. "Good morning," she called out, and saw that while Mary Ann seemed her usual upbeat self, Alice looked dead.

"How are you doing?" Melina said to Alice.

"I didn't sleep much," Alice said, Mary Ann coughed, and Alice added, "With Lavinia not home, I mean. How is she?"

"Fine," Melina said. Sheesh. If Alice and Mary Ann expected people to believe they'd spent the night in the same place, they should have organized themselves better. But hey, no judgment.

While the girls watched TV in the family room, Melina recounted the highlights of her babysitting stint — Annabelle's toothbrush crisis, Kayla's nocturnal wandering, Lavinia's early waking. Mary Ann listened attentively to all of this while Alice stared into space. "And what about Josh?" Mary Ann said. "Did he behave himself?"

"Yes, he did. He was good company for me."

Josh had entered the room dressed in a T-shirt and jeans and was standing in front of the open fridge. He looked more awake than Alice, but not much. "I'd still be asleep if everybody wasn't making so much noise down here," he said.

Mary Ann handed Melina a cash-stuffed envelope, thanked her profusely, and said, "I'll run you home on the way to pick up Griffin from his sleepover. Alice, can you watch the kids a minute? I won't be long."

When Mary Ann and Melina had left, Alice sat down at the kitchen table and closed her eyes.

Josh rattled some cutlery in the drawer. "Hey, Alice, can I ask you a favour?"

Alice opened her eyes. "Are you talking to me?"

"Yeah. There's no one else here."

"Oh. Right."

"I'm thinking of doing a history project on the old train station. Could I interview you about it, and arrange to have my class come visit? And you could maybe give the class a tour?"

Alice closed her eyes again. "Sure."

"Thanks. I'll email you about it, okay?"

"Fine."

"Like later today, I'll email you."

"Uh-huh."

The doorbell rang, making Alice jump and say *fuck*, loudly.

Josh said, "You sure swear a lot."

"Just answer the goddamned door, Josh."

He did, to admit Sam, who greeted Alice and asked her how she was as if he hadn't seen her fifteen minutes earlier. After he'd collected his girls and left, Lavinia said she wanted to go home, Mary Ann returned with Griffin, and Kayla asked her mother what they were doing for the day.

"We might go bowling later," Mary Ann said. "You up for that, Alice?"

"I hate bowling," Josh said.

"Can I bring a friend?" Griffin said.

Alice made her escape with Lavinia. "I'll call you later, Mary Ann. Much later."

23

Later the same day

"Yay, Kayla!" Mary Ann yelled, right in Alice's ear. "A strike! That's great, honey. Now help Lavinia lift the ball." Mary Ann leaned back in the hard plastic chair and said to Alice, "You look much better than you did this morning. Much less likely to pass out within the next ten minutes."

"Your mom rescued me. She took Lavinia for a few hours and made paintbox cookies with her while I napped. But what's your secret? Where did you get those bright eyes and rosy cheeks? Did you get a nap in too, or are you on some banned substance you ought to be sharing with me?"

"Griffin!" Mary Ann yelled. "It's your turn. And stop wrestling!" She turned back to Alice. "If I'm bright-eyed, it's because I've spent the day mentally reliving the sex I had last night."

"Stop right there. I've already heard enough."

"Meanwhile, you've told me next to nothing about your night. Was Jake's penis python-like or not?"

"You're incorrigible."

"You know what was great about Sam?"

"I beg you — no anatomical descriptions."

"He smelled so clean. Everywhere. Bob sometimes had this musty kind of smell —"

"Stop! If I tell you about Jake, will you spare me any more details?"

"Okay, go."

From the foot of her lane, Kayla called out, "The game's over. Should we play another one?"

"Yes."

"But we want to get candy from the machines. Can we, please?"

"Please?" Lavinia said.

"Here are some quarters," Mary Ann said. "Get candy, then come back and bowl some more. And Kayla, keep a close eye on Lavinia." She turned back to Alice. "Start at the beginning and leave nothing out."

Alice searched for the right words. "The sex was good. It was intense. And powerful." Alice's mouth opened and closed. There was nothing more to add.

"That's it? That's all you're going to say? What a rip-off."

"Okay, if you must know, there was something weird about the whole exchange."

"Tell me anything. I won't be shocked."

"Get this, then: when it was all over, I couldn't wait for him to leave."

"Gee, not me. All I could think about when Sam and I finished each round of sex was — how long till the next one?"

"It gets worse. When he told me he was going away for three weeks on some tours he's doing in Thailand and India, I was relieved."

"There were gross smells, weren't there?"

"NO. My attitude had nothing to do with smells. I was relieved because as much as I liked being with him, I don't want him hanging around, disrupting my life."

The girls came back then, hands full of little pink-and-yellow candy pacifiers, which they gloated over in front of

Griffin and his friend until they asked for their own quarters.

When the boys had departed for the candy machines and the girls had resumed bowling, Mary Ann said, "You're not saying you regret sleeping with Jake, are you?"

"Not at all. The sex was great. Intense and —"

"Yeah, I know, powerful. And would you do it again? With him?"

"Sure." Alice smiled. "As long as he doesn't stay over."

"I thought that was supposed to be the guy's line."

"I think I'm just a loner by nature."

"You were inclined that way even as a teenager," Mary Ann said, and into Alice's mind popped a picture that she gathered was meant to be of her younger self — bracelets clattering, hair swinging — the day they'd been summoned to the principal's office.

Alice said, "You make me look so arrogant. Was I that bad?"

Mary Ann sent another picture that made Alice's bearing less aloof. "How about this? Not arrogant, but confident. And totally different from anyone else."

Alice snapped her fingers. "That's it, Mary Ann. That's why the telepathy came back. High school."

"Huh?"

"Don't you see? The reason we could talk with our minds last night is because we were acting like juveniles — harbouring crushes, dancing, getting drunk, making out in public. You especially."

Mary Ann patted her hair. "I liked being Veronica."

Alice was still thinking. "But why is it still with us now, when we're acting more like our responsible adult selves?"

Mary Ann gave a thumbs-up sign to Griffin, who was calling her attention to the big slash on the overhead monitor signaling his latest spare. She turned to Alice. "Do you think it might have something to do with Bob?"

"Bob, who's not in the country?"

"Yeah, that one. Maybe he acted as some kind of inhibitor. And now that I'm free of him, we can mind-read again."

"You're free of him because you slept with someone else?"

"No, because I've decided to divorce him."

"What? When did that happen? When Sam went down on you?"

"Now who's being indelicate? And within earshot of the kids, too." Mary Ann leaned closer. "Two days ago I had an epiphany about the subject in the park, when I was out walking the dog. And this morning, I emailed him in Singapore and asked for a divorce."

"You asked for a divorce by email?"

"It's fitting, don't you think, given how I found out about him and his girlfriend?"

"I'd forgotten about that, but I guess using email to break your news does make a kind of twisted sense. How do you think he'll take it?"

"I doubt he'll be happy, but he can't be surprised. If he wants to stay married, he shouldn't travel seven months out of twelve or have fallen in love with some young floozy, now should he?"

Alice knew better than to take any side other than Mary Ann's on this subject. And one thing Alice *hadn't* forgotten was how quick she'd been to call Bob a shit, an asshole, and a cocksucker when Mary Ann had told her about his cheating nine months before. "Should I congratulate you?"

"You should. I'm thrilled about the idea, and can't wait to start over. I'm going to ask Tom if he'll hire me to work free-lance for his company after the Main Street project winds up."

"This is all too much to take in." Alice stood up, stretched, and sat down again. "But if your theory is correct that we're only telepathic when we're both uncommitted to a romantic relationship, what will happen to our powers when you and Sam become a couple? How do you know it was Bob the individual who was the inhibitor? Maybe it was Bob, the husband."

"You don't understand," Mary Ann said. "I don't want to pair up with Sam."

"You don't? What, then? You're going to be single?"

"I think I'll become a femme fatale, embark upon a series of brief but satisfying love affairs. Sow the wild oats I missed out on in my youth."

Alice smiled at the image Mary Ann was transmitting, an image of Mary Ann costumed in a sexy, slit-skirt black suit, accessorized with black stilettos, a bouffant hairdo, dark sunglasses, and red lipstick. She climbed out of a limo, the flashbulbs popped, and a crowd of good-looking young men — were they strippers? *No*, Mary Ann corrected her, *they're models!* — danced attendance on her. "It's a look," Alice said.

"The new me."

"In that case, you're really going to have to work on your wall-building."

24

November 22, 2010

As soon as Mary Ann walked into the office on Monday morning, Phoebe said, "So how'd *your* night go?"

Mary Ann shook her head. "You first."

"Okay. Tristan was unbelievable. Un-fucking-believable. I can't even begin to tell you. I'm a woman transformed."

"That good, huh?"

"Better. What about you? How'd you make out? Pun intended."

"Let me put it this way: I didn't get much sleep Saturday night."

"At your age?"

"Nice talk."

"Sorry. I just meant — I don't know what I meant. Considering how hot and heavy you two were in the bar, I shouldn't be surprised you did a marathon."

Mary Ann held up a hand. "I know that making out in public was not a discreet thing to do, and I apologize. I slipped into teen mode there for a while."

"Hey, I didn't mind. It was entertaining. I think that bar should ask you guys to come back, and include a live sex show as part of the talent line-up. It could bring in a whole new batch of customers."

Mary Ann made to swing at Phoebe, and Drew walked in, with bags under his eyes. "Well, if it isn't the two wild women."

Phoebe said, "Mary Ann was just apologizing for her public display of affection at Chuck's, and I was telling her not to. We've all done crazy things when gripped by wild sexual urges. Haven't we, Drew?"

Drew sat in one of the waiting room chairs. "Yeah, but some of us regret those things."

Mary Ann said, "You shouldn't. You should allot yourself a number of no-strings, just-for-fun flings in your lifetime and enjoy them for what they are. Before you get married and settle down."

"I'm never getting married," Drew said.

Mary Ann said, "Does that mean you're single and available?"

Drew was still glum. "Depends if I decide to take a vow of celibacy."

"You seem awfully sorry for yourself," Phoebe said. "I suggest you dive into your work and forget your personal life for a day."

"Good idea," Drew said, and tramped upstairs.

When he'd gone, Phoebe said, "Poor guy seems pretty down."

Mary Ann was listening to Drew's footsteps overhead. "Do you think he's ready for a rebound fling yet?"

Phoebe's eyes widened. "You're joking, right?"

"Of course I am." Not.

Sam was on the phone, in his study, in the middle of the afternoon, when he thought he heard the front door open and close. Chutney heard it, too. He lifted his head from where he lay sleeping under Sam's desk, got up, and trotted downstairs to investigate.

Sam didn't hear anything else, and he wasn't expecting anyone — the cleaning woman had left an hour before, the girls were at school, Hallie wasn't due home from London for two more days. So he wrapped up the conversation with one of his old suppliers, a meat man, hung up the phone, went exploring, and almost shit his pants when he found Hallie in the kitchen, filling the dog dish with water.

She knew about him and Mary Ann. Someone must have told her. And she'd come home early to confront him about it. Good thing he'd laundered the sheets and put them back on the bed. He said, "Hallie, what a surprise. How come you're home early?"

She set Chutney's dish on the floor. "I got fired."

Pulse still pounding in his ears. "What?"

"That prick Andrew Bathgate fired me. Can you fucking well believe it? And in London, too."

She didn't know about him and Mary Ann. "What do you mean? Why?"

"He put it down to a difference in personal style. A euphemism for fuck off. So aggravating. Is there any mail?"

Sam ducked into the dining room and picked up Hallie's mail from the table, happy for an excuse to remove himself from her steely glare, even if the steel had been meant for Andrew Bathgate.

He handed her the pile of envelopes and tried to think straight, come up with a normal reaction to her news. "Why didn't you call me when this happened?" Yes. That's what an innocent person would ask.

"I don't know. I was embarrassed. And pissed off. And I needed time to process it." She pulled a butter knife out of the cutlery drawer, started slitting open the mail. "How're the girls? I missed them."

"They're good. Except Jessica still has a bit of a cold. They missed you, too. Annabelle's been marking the days off on the calendar on the fridge until your arrival date. See?" He pointed to the calendar and Hallie smiled.

She turned back to him, seemed to be checking his face over. Looking for love bites, maybe. "And how are you doing? You need a haircut."

"I'm good. I've been doing a lot of thinking while you've been away. In the last few days especially."

"So have I, and you know what? To hell with Morris Communications. Who needs them? It's time to start fresh, move on to the next stage of our lives. Don't you agree?"

"You weren't thinking of that suggestion I made a while back that we go around the world on a boat, were you? Because I don't think —"

"No. No boat. Let's wipe away all the shit that's been going on lately, forget it ever happened, and concentrate on our future. On the kids, your book, a new job for me — whatever that might be. That's where we should be directing our energies."

"About the book —"

"I haven't been very supportive about it, and I'm sorry. From now on I will be. Let's get that sucker published."

"I've put the book aside for a little while, but I've got another idea. If you want to hear it."

"I hope it's an idea for a new business."

"Yeah, it is. I'm thinking of opening up a prepared food shop on Main Street. In one of the old houses Tom fixed up. I'd take all the best recipes from the women around here and build up a boutique operation. The Oakdale Dinner Club, I'd call it."

Hallie didn't respond at first, which Sam was sure meant that she hated the idea. Until she said, "I like it."

"You do?"

"It builds on your strengths, it fits with market trends on convenience foods, it's a quick start-up, it doesn't require too much capital."

"A woman named Danielle Pringle has a farm nearby, and she grows some amazing heirloom vegetables and fancy greens —"

"Even better, it's a franchisable concept. In a few years, we could be seeing The Oakdale Dinner Club brand of frozen entrees in every supermarket freezer."

"I was thinking more of a small, local, part-time type of operation."

"Naturally, it would have to start out that way. Start out small and humble, build word of mouth, create cachet, get New Yorkers out here just so they can eat Oakdale food. You could develop a reputation, then look to do a cooking show on TV, and write cookbooks, and develop a line of branded foods."

She was going way overboard. But she wasn't trashing the idea. "I can't believe you like it."

"Why not? This is what we've wanted for a while, isn't it? For you to start another small business that can be built into something bigger?"

"It is?"

"Sure. And now that I'm unemployed, I could look after some of the administrative and financial details."

They hadn't come close to dealing with the infidelity issue, and yet Sam felt they'd turned a corner somewhere in there. A corner they hadn't been anywhere near for ages.

"When do the girls get picked up from school?" Hallie said. "Maybe I'll drive over. Surprise them."

Two weeks ago it might have bothered Sam that Hallie didn't know the afternoon dismissal time. Not today. "School ends at three-thirty. And I'm sure they'd love to see you."

The Orensteins spent a quiet evening at home. Sam made pancakes for dinner, Hallie spent time with each of the girls in turn, and late in the evening the whole family was tucked up in their beds.

Hallie rested her head on Sam's chest and said, quietly, "He thinks I have a drinking problem."

Sam's head came up off the pillow. "Who does?"

"Andrew Bathgate."

His head dropped back down and spun around a few times. "Do *you* think you have a drinking problem?"

"Maybe. A little. Though if I've been drinking more than I should, it's because I've had to endure the hell that was working for that asshole, in that thankless job."

"I didn't know you hated the job that much." And he should have known. The same way he shouldn't have turned a blind eye to her wine consumption. Or overconsumption.

"Well, I did. And I'm going to cut down on the drinking. I didn't drink anything tonight."

Sam stroked Hallie's hair. Now that she was being open about her failings, he should man up and make his confession too. "Hallie, there's something I have to tell you about, something I've done."

She sat up and pulled the sheet around her body. She was so beautiful.

"No," she said. "Don't say anything. We've both made mistakes, but I want to forget about them, put them behind us. I want to go to sleep tonight and make a fresh start tomorrow like it's our first morning in Oakdale. Like we've just moved in. Okay?"

It might have made Sam feel better to unburden his guilt

about Mary Ann. But a confession wouldn't help Hallie any, he could see that. So for now, he'd bury the guilt, put it away. He reached for her, brought her back to lie with her head on his chest, and put his arm around her shoulders.

"The neighbours seem friendly enough," he said, "but do you think there's any decent food to be had around here?"

25

Six weeks later — January 2011

On a dreary Wednesday, Alice called Tom at his office. She said, "I was ready to leave a message, and you're there. I thought you'd be out developing your next project."

"Why do that when I could sit here reflecting on my misspent life instead?"

"What do you mean, misspent? Has something bad happened?"

"No, all is well. My apologies. That was a poor attempt at joke making."

"Good, because I want to ask you a favour. In a moment of stupor, I agreed to give a class from the local high school a tour of the station building, complete with architectural history. It's Josh Gray's history class. Mary Ann's son? And it's all set up for next Monday at one o'clock, only someone's called a departmental meeting here for that morning, and it'll be tight for me to get back up to Oakdale from the city in time. So I wondered if you might be in the neighbourhood and able to fill in, to get started anyway, then I'll run in late and finish up. What do you say?"

"I'm happy to help, but I wouldn't know how to begin addressing young people."

"Oh, come on. If anyone can talk, it's you. And the whole thing's supposed to be an hour-long visit, at the most, including walking through the building and a question period, so there'll be a minimum of lecturing. And I'll be there as soon as possible after my meeting."

"Very well. I shall be there. At the station, one o'clock Monday."

"Thanks, Tom. You're a peach. Coffee and brownies on me afterwards at the new bakery."

Alice's meeting ended late. She made good time out of the city, though, and might have reached Oakdale by one o'clock anyway if road work on the highway hadn't backed up traffic, and added a half hour to her driving time.

She pulled up at the station building — the new library — at one-twenty. The empty school bus that had transported Josh's class was parked in front. She walked up to the library door, opened it, and heard, in the echoey space, the sound of Tom's voice.

"Imagine, if you would, that this building is in the center of a bustling town, filled with grand edifices. Healy's Hotel, a fine four-storey establishment that features a wraparound veranda, stands across the street. The town hall, an imposing brick building fronted by a columned colonnade that was inspired by no less a monument than the Parthenon in Athens, can be seen at the end of Main Street. Imagine yourself to be one of the Scottish and Irish immigrants arriving here in the late eighteen hundreds, come across the ocean to take a domestic job in the large houses of the prosperous tradesmen who live here, tradesmen who were immigrants themselves only twenty years before."

Alice slipped inside the door, unnoticed by the group of teenagers standing with their faces turned to Tom. He stood on the second-floor gallery, cutting a dramatic figure in a navy blue suit, blue shirt, blue-green tie. Tara Peterson, the new librarian, stood off to the side. Alice tiptoed over, whispered hi, and asked how Tom was doing.

Tara whispered back. "I'm going to ask Mr. Gagliardi to give tours more often. He's so articulate, he's a natural storyteller."

Alice stepped back, listened some more, and saw how Tom's gift of the gab had grabbed his audience's attention, how his theatricality suited the occasion. A born teacher, that's what he was. Unlike Alice. "I'll be back," she said. Tara nodded without taking her eyes off Tom, and Alice went down the hall to the community room.

She spent a blissfully quiet half hour there, reading an archeological journal she'd carried around for a week in her briefcase, and re-entered the main space just before two, in time to catch a teacher announcing that the student who organized the field trip had something to say to Mr. Gagliardi.

"On behalf of the class," Josh said, "I'd like to thank you for giving us a tour of the building, and for telling us so many interesting things about it." A few people clapped and whistled. "And I'd like to thank Alice — Ms. Maeda — for arranging the tour, even though she isn't here right now."

"Here I am," Alice called out. Everyone turned and looked at her and she said, "Thank you all for coming," and the round of thanks continued until the kids had filed out through the front door.

In the quiet that followed, Alice said to Tom, "I hear you were mesmerizing. Sorry I was late, I got stuck in traffic. Did you miss me?"

"Yes, I did," Tom said. He pulled out a handkerchief and mopped his brow. "But this was an edifying experience. Most edifying."

"Ready for that brownie and coffee?"

* * *

Tom and Alice sat in the wrought-iron café chairs that furnished the new bakery and sipped their coffees. "Pinch hitting for me today is not the only thing I have to thank you for," Alice said.

"What else could there be?"

"Remember your idea that I take an au pair to Italy?"

"You said you didn't have one."

"I don't, but I've arranged to take along my sometimes babysitter, a girl named Melina Pappas. I'm not the only person on the team who has a young child, so Melina's going to run a small combination day camp and daycare over there, the parents will pitch in to pay her, and that way she gets to see the world and earn money, and I get to go on a dream dig without leaving Lavinia."

"How fortuitous."

"Try to sound like you care when you say that."

"I'm sorry. I envision you happy and fulfilled in Tuscany, while I, the stooped middle-aged man, trudge from meeting to construction site."

"That's crazy. You have excellent posture."

"I'll be the upright middle-aged man trudging around construction sites, then."

"What's all this about trudging? You're going to make a mid-life career change and become a teacher."

"What makes you think that?"

"Didn't you know? I'm psychic."

Mary Ann ran into Sam at the park in the middle of the afternoon. Not her usual dog-walking time, but she'd taken a day off work to deal with her increasingly complicated personal life, and had missed the morning stroll, making divorce-related calls.

She waved at Sam from the park entrance, and walked across the baseball field to meet him. "Hi there. Have you been avoiding me?"

Sam reached down to pat Honey. "Maybe. I don't know what to say to you. I'm afraid I was relieved when I got your email saying the dinner club was disbanded."

"Don't worry. I won't bite. You made your position clear about your marriage, and I respect that."

"Thank you." A half smile. "I still feel awkward."

"I've seen Hallie picking the girls up at school a few times, and she hasn't avoided me. You didn't tell her?"

"No."

"Good. I didn't tell Bob, either. Though we *are* getting a divorce."

Sam paled. "You are?"

"Nothing to do with you — it's been coming for a while. Though you know what was odd?"

"What?"

"That no one seems to have blabbed around town that you and I were pawing each other at Chuck's that night."

"I've worried about that, too. About the news getting back to Hallie."

"I guess, when you think about it, the only people there who knew us were not from Oakdale, they were outsiders. Except Alice. And she wouldn't talk."

Sam said, "I wanted to ask you something about Alice. I was pretty drunk that night —"

"Though functioning quite well for someone under the influence."

"— and I don't necessarily remember everything that happened —"

"I do."

"Mary Ann."

"Sorry."

"I was going to say that I had a vague recollection of you and Alice talking about reading each other's minds. About real telepathy, I mean. Did that happen, or did I hallucinate it?"

Mary Ann whistled for Honey. "The only thing I can think of that we might have said was 'great minds think alike' — it's kind of the motto of our friendship."

"*Do* you two think alike?"

"Sometimes."

"Maybe that was it." He didn't sound too sure.

Mary Ann produced a ball from her pocket, showed it to an excited Honey, used her tennis arm to throw it far and high across the field. "So what's happening with that food shop idea you had?"

26

Four months later — May 2011

Alice gave Lavinia a snack of dried apricots and almonds at the kitchen table and called Mary Ann. "Is it still okay for me to bring Lavinia over to be babysat during the shop opening?"

"Sure. Melina will be here at six. What about Jake? Is he coming?"

"He doesn't know many people in Oakdale aside from Phoebe, so no."

"Some people wouldn't dream of going to a social function alone when they have a perfectly good fuck buddy to wear on their arm."

"Who are you taking?"

"I may go alone, too. Or drag Josh along."

"What happened to your new guy? Greg, is it? Or is that over already?"

"It's Grégoire, and I don't know, he's been clingy lately."

"Can't have that."

"Plus it didn't seem like a great idea to bring him to a party at which two of my former beaus will be present."

"But you and Drew and Sam are so sophisticated about it all."

"Aren't we, though?"

"See you there."

"I'll save you a samosa."

Alice hung up and turned to Lavinia. "What should we take over to Mary Ann's house? Do you want to bring one of your games or books? Or will you play with Kayla's things?"

Lavinia crunched on an almond. "Kayla said to bring my bead kit. So we can make bracelets."

"Kayla said that? When?"

"I don't know."

"Did you see her at school today?" Alice didn't think the sixth graders saw much of the daycare kids in a typical day.

"She told me. I heard her."

"Whatever. Do you know where the kit is? Are all the pieces still in it?"

"It's in my room." Lavinia opened her mouth and showed Alice its contents — a chewed-up apricot sprinkled with almond fragments.

"Very nice," Alice said. "Now close your mouth, finish chewing that, and swallow it. I'll get your bead kit and we'll go."

Melina said, "Pizza again for the kids tonight?"

Mary Ann checked her reflection in the door of the microwave. "I do feed them properly on nights when you're not here. I give them vegetables. Organic ones, sometimes."

"I know you do."

"It'll be rough on us when you're in Europe. The kids will miss you, and my social life will be greatly curtailed."

"There's always Josh," Melina said. "He could babysit."

"He won't be around much either. Haven't you heard? He's going on a summer study program. To Rome, of all places. He's developed a new interest in European culture. His father's paying for it."

Versus Melina's working vacation to Europe. "Josh is lucky."

Mary Ann said, "Frankly, I think a summer away will do him good. He's getting too big to be hanging around here. Literally too big. Have you noticed how he's grown in the last few months?" She called up the back stairs. "Josh! Come on! We'll be late."

Josh came into the kitchen, and Melina saw that he *had* grown. He'd developed a manly looking jaw and shoulders as well. And was that stubble on his chin?

"Mom," Josh said. "Promise you won't kill me?"

"You're not going out dressed like that, I hope."

"I'm not going at all, if that's okay."

"Why not?"

"My stomach's kind of upset. I don't feel like being around all that fancy food."

Mary Ann placed a hand on his forehead. "Are you sick?"

He moved her hand away. "I don't have a fever. Just an upset stomach. It was probably the lunch they served in the cafeteria at school today. The ham in the quiche tasted off."

"Take it easy, then. And don't bug Melina."

"Why would you say that? Do I ever bug Melina?"

Melina said, "He doesn't."

"Good. Off I go. I won't be long."

Danielle opened the door of the shop, causing the bell above the door to ring, and saw Sarah, in a navy canvas apron over her clothes, laying out a platter of food on a round, skirted table in the middle of the space. "Hi, Sarah. Am I early? The place looks fabulous."

"You're right on time," Sarah said. "And it does look good, doesn't it?"

"Aren't you worried that no one will come? What if only

five people show up, and Sam is stuck with food for fifty? It would be so embarrassing."

"People will come," Sarah said. "People always come for free food. And don't we know everyone in Oakdale, anyway?"

"Maybe *you* do."

"The original dinner club members are guaranteed to attend — that's ten. More, if they bring dates. And the rest will follow. Don't worry. The place will be packed in thirty minutes."

Sam came out of the kitchen with a tray full of glasses of champagne. "Hi, Danielle. Thanks for sending the flowers over. They're beautiful."

"You're welcome. Now tell me what I can do to help out."

"Nothing. This whole enterprise is about you not doing anything. And we're totally under control, anyway. The waiters are pouring drinks in the kitchen, the cold platters are starting to come out, the hot food's in the warming oven. So, I'd like to propose a toast." He handed them each a glass. "To the Oakdale Dinner Club."

They all swallowed a mouthful of the wine.

"To Sam having a bright idea," Sarah said, "and making it happen, and hiring me to help run it!"

"To hardly ever cooking again," Danielle said.

The bell over the shop door rang again and Hallie came in, greeting everyone. Sam went over, kissed her, and told her how good she looked. The bit of weight she'd put on in the last few months suited her. "How'd it go with the kids?"

"They were a little reluctant to stay with the new babysitter, but she pulled her iPhone out of her purse and opened up a game, and that cheered them up. How're things here?"

A waiter emerged from the kitchen with another tray of glasses. "Champagne, madam?" he said to Hallie.

"No thanks. But I'd love some mineral water when you have a chance."

The waiter set down his tray and headed back to the kitchen. "I'll get you that right away."

Sam said, "So this is it. Here we go."

"It's going to be a big success, Sam, I know it is."

"I think so, too. And you know what's the strangest thing? In the middle of all the frantic preparations this afternoon, I had an idea for my novel."

"Today?"

"I know. It was when the cooks were making the new samosas. They have a reddish cast to them because of the beets in the filling, and when I saw the first cooked one, it hit me. The secret of the ashram, the linchpin of the whole mystery just has to be —"

The bells on the door rang and a loud voice called out, "Danielle, *mon petit chou*." The voice came from a large woman wearing a hat. "What a darling little shop. I wouldn't have expected such charm in this backwater."

"Holy crap," Sam said. "It's Adele Beauchamp." And he went over to suck up.

Melina was in the kitchen when she heard someone come in the back door. "Josh? Is that you?"

Honey ran in from the mudroom, with Josh behind her. "Who else would it be?"

"You're right. Who else? I'm making hot chocolate for the kids. Want some?"

"Sure, thanks. But were you thinking I might be my dad?"

"I guess I was. Sometimes I forget he's moved out. Sorry."

"Don't be. He's living it up in the city. He doesn't miss Oakdale at all."

Melina poured hot milk into a mug. "And does that bother you?"

"It's better this way — Mom and Dad living their own lives instead of pretending they got along, when it was so obvious they didn't."

Melina stirred the milk. Who was this new clear-eyed, realistic Josh? "So you're not going to Europe this summer to avoid your mom dating?"

"It's more like I'm going there so I can meet people and party without her watching over me. This could be my big summer, I'm hoping."

"Your coming of age."

"And I won't be that far from where you'll be."

"Really?"

"Maybe I'll come visit you guys one weekend, see what's doing."

"How old are you now?"

"Seventeen."

Seventeen, mature, shoulders, jaw, tall. "Yeah, we should get together. After babysitting four kids all day, I'm going to need a break. Give me your email address and I'll send you our contact info."

The party was in full swing when Alice walked into The Oakdale Dinner Club, which was filled with wall-to-wall Oakdalians, and some city folk who'd driven up specially.

Alice fought her way to the drinks table set up in the middle of the store, and congratulated a happy-looking Sam on the way. She stopped to say hello to Sarah and Danielle, and to be introduced to Danielle's husband, Benny, who was sampling a morsel of sauced chicken from a paper cone. Benny said to Danielle, "You made this. It's your chicken korma. I'd know it anywhere."

"I'm telling you, I didn't cook anything here."

Benny took another bite, shook his head. "I don't believe you. This is exactly how you make it."

Danielle grinned. "Alice, have you met my mother? She's in from the city. Alice Maeda, Adele Beauchamp."

Alice shook Adele's hand and said, "So are you going to write about this place in the *Times*? Start some word of mouth?"

Adele dabbed at her lips with a napkin. "I couldn't do that, dear. It would be unethical, considering Danielle's involvement in the enterprise."

"Of course not," Danielle said.

"I'm sorry," Alice said. "I didn't mean to suggest —"

Adele nudged Alice. "I did, however, bring one of my colleagues from the Dining section with me. And I can't see why one of them shouldn't write about it."

Alice gave her a thumbs up. "Good thinking."

"I'm sure they'll rave. The food is delicious, and well presented, and that samosa man is delightful, he'd make good copy. Did you know he's writing a culinary mystery? You never told me that, Danielle."

Mary Ann's voice cut into Alice's mind. *Tear yourself away from that weirdo in the hat and check this out. I think I've found my summer fling. Am I dreaming, or has Carl the construction foreman been working out?*

Alice laughed at the sight of the big pink neon arrow Mary Ann had painted in her thought picture, the one that was pointing to Carl, and was inscribed with the words, "Hot stuff." *He's okay*, she thought back, *if you like them with a head of hair*.

Alice excused herself from Danielle's gang and set off toward Tom, whose head she could see towering above the fray over to one side. She squeezed past Lisa and Amy, who each held a glass of wine in one hand and one of Sarah's cream puffs in the other, and emerged victorious at Tom's side. Though she had to grab on to Kate's arm to keep from tripping over a table leg on her final approach.

She apologized for the arm gripping, the three greeted each other, and Tom said, "How go the preparations for Tuscany?"

"Everything's organized. We leave in two weeks."

Kate said, "We?"

"Me, Lavinia, and Melina — our babysitter." And Jake would be leading bike tours for most of the summer in the south of France, just around the corner.

Drew came along and introduced them to his new friend Jane. "We met at an IT seminar," Drew said. And Kate, Tom, and Alice all nodded and said, "Isn't that nice."

Drew and Jane moved on and Tom snagged three stuffed endives from a passing waiter's tray and handed them around. Kate said, "This joint sure is jumping."

Alice tasted a hit of brie and pancetta. "Sam seems like a real go-getter. And his last business was a big success, wasn't it?"

"It was," Tom said, "but he didn't find his true calling until he came to Oakdale. Similar to my experience with discovering my teaching vocation."

Kate linked her arm in Tom's. "Help me set him straight, Alice," she said. "Tom has decided that Oakdale is imbued with some kind of supernatural quality. And I keep saying that Oakdale's just a town. A pretty town, but just a town."

"What do you think, Alice?" Tom said. "Is Oakdale magical?"

Alice looked around the room, at Mary Ann baring her throat for Carl over by the pastry case, at Hallie speaking earnestly with three guys in suits who might be investors, at Sam wiping the sweat off his forehead with his sleeve and sharing a laugh with Sarah, at Danielle facing Benny with one hand on her chest and the other raised in oath-swearing position, at Drew and Jane, their heads bent together over one of the store's computer terminals.

"Is Oakdale magical?" Alice said. "Oh, definitely."

Josh and Griffin were upstairs and Melina was helping Kayla and Lavinia make beaded ID bracelets at the kitchen table when she got a text from her friend Jen. Melina picked up her phone, got drawn into a chat, and didn't look up until she heard Lavinia giggle madly next to her.

"Make Honey dance!" Lavinia cried. "Higher! Faster! Make her chase her tail!" Now both girls laughed. While the dog slept on the floor under the table.

Her attention still on her phone, Melina said, "What are you guys doing?"

Lavinia said, "Kayla showed me a movie of Honey dancing. It's so funny!" And giggled some more.

Movie? What movie? Jen texted she had to go, and Melina turned her phone screen-down on the table. "Sorry, guys. What's going on?"

Kayla gazed at Melina with her big, blue, twelve-going-on-thirteen-year-old eyes. "Nothing."

"What movie are you talking about? Did you make a video of Honey?"

"No."

"So what, then?" Next to Melina, Lavinia hummed and picked out all the orange beads from the pile.

Kayla said, "We imagined that Honey was dancing."

"You were pretending, you mean?"

"Sort of like pretending. And sort of like we're talking to each other, but without talking. Do you know what I mean?"

Author's note

I'd like to thank my first readers Louise Moritsugu and Ehoud Farine, and my literary agent Margaret Hart of the Humber Literary Agency, for their suggestions, encouragement, and support. And I am grateful to Diane Young, Shannon Whibbs, and Cheryl Hawley for their editorial guidance, and to everyone else at Dundurn who helped produce, sell, and promote the book.

Recipes follow for three of the dishes discussed, served, and consumed in the course of the novel. For more recipes please visit my website, which can be found online at *http://kimmoritsugu.com*.

Sarah MacAllister's Stilton Shortbread

1/2 cup butter, softened
1 cup Stilton or other blue cheese, crumbled
1 1/2 cups all-purpose flour
1/4 cup pecans, ground
1 tbsp sugar
1/2 tsp salt
30–35 pecan halves, preferably toasted

1. In a stand mixer, or using a handheld electric beater, cream butter with sugar and salt.
2. Beat in flour on low speed until well incorporated and mixture looks like small peas.
3. Mix crumbled blue cheese in bowl or mini food processor with ground pecans, then beat into flour mixture quickly, until evenly distributed.
4. Using hands, remove dough to floured cutting board and form into a ball. Cut ball in half and form each half into a cylinder about 1 1/2 inches wide and 8–9 inches long. Wrap in plastic wrap and chill in fridge for an hour or more.
5. At bake time, line a large baking sheet with parchment paper and preheat oven to 325°F.
6. Slice dough into 1/3–inch rounds and place on baking sheet. They will not spread, so they need not be placed too far apart, but they should not be touching.
7. Press a pecan half into the top of each round.
8. Bake for 15–20 minutes until lightly browned on the edges and bottoms.
9. Let cool before serving.

Makes 30–35 small cookies.

Sam Orenstein's Aloo Gobi

2 cups cauliflower florets (about half a cauliflower), chopped
    into 2-inch chunks
2 cups red-skinned potatoes (about 4 smallish ones), chopped
    into 2-inch chunks
2–3 tbsp canola oil
2 tsp cumin seeds
2 tbsp minced fresh ginger
1/2 tsp ground turmeric
1/2 tsp ground coriander
1/2 tsp ground cardamom
1/2 tsp salt

1. Preheat oven to 400°F.
2. Mix cauliflower florets and potato chunks with oil and
   spices in large bowl. Toss to coat evenly.
3. Spray a baking sheet with cooking spray. Arrange cauliflower and potato mixture on baking sheet in one layer.
   Use a second baking sheet if necessary.
4. Roast for 30 minutes at 400°F, turning vegetables after
   15 minutes.
5. Serve garnished with chopped hard-boiled eggs and
   chopped parsley.

Makes 4 side-dish servings.

Tom Gagliardi's Squash, Goat Cheese, & Toasted Pistachio Crostini

1 pound butternut squash, cut in 1–2 inch cubes
3–4 stalks fresh thyme
2–3 tbsp extra-virgin olive oil
1/4 tsp cayenne pepper
1/4 cup maple syrup or honey
1 cup goat cheese, crumbled
1/2 cup pistachios, shelled and chopped, toasted 5–10 minutes on a baking sheet in a 325°F oven, cooled
6 slices (2 inches by 4 inches each, approximately) of focaccia or other rustic, rough-textured bread

1. Toss squash cubes with 1–2 tbsp oil, thyme stalks, and cayenne pepper, and roast on baking sheet in 400°F oven for 20–25 minutes, turning once halfway through, until lightly browned on edges.
2. Turn squash into bowl and mash roughly, the texture should still be chunky.
3. Strip thyme leaves from stalks, add to squash. Discard stalks.
4. Combine squash with maple syrup or honey, and season with salt and pepper to taste.
5. Toast bread slices in oven or toaster, brush with olive oil.
6. To assemble crostini, spread a slice of toasted bread with squash mixture, top with a spoonful of goat cheese, and garnish with chopped, toasted pistachios.

Makes 6 slices of crostini.